Elsie's Motherhood

Elsie's Motherhood

✤

Book Five of
The Original Elsie Classics

Martha Finley

Elsie's Motherhood
by Martha Finley

Any unique characteristics of this edition:
Copyright © 2000 by Cumberland House Publishing, Inc.

Published by Cumberland House Publishing, Inc.,
431 Harding Industrial Drive, Nashville, Tennessee 37211.

Cover design by Bruce Gore, Gore Studios, Inc.
Photography by Dean Dixon Photography
Hair and Makeup by Calene Radar
Text design by Heather Armstrong

Printed in the United States of America
1 2 3 4 5 6 7 8 -- 04 03 02 01 00

PREFACE

IN COMPLIANCE WITH THE expressed desire of many of Elsie's friends and admirers, the story of her life is continued in this, the fifth volume of the series. When about to undertake its preparation, the suggestion was made to the author that to bring in the doings of the Ku Klux would add interest to the story. At the same time it would give a truer picture of life in the South during the years 1867–68 in which its events take place. I have relied upon the published reports of the Congressional Committee of Investigation as the source of information and marked these sections with an *. They were diligently examined and care was taken not to go beyond the facts there given with regard to the proceedings of the Klan, the clemency and paternal acts of the Government, or the kindly, fraternal feelings and deeds of the people of the North toward their impoverished and suffering brethren of the South.

These things have become matters of history; vice and crime should be condemned wherever found. Naught has been set down in malice, for the author has a warm love for the South as part and parcel of the dear land of her birth.

May this child of her brain give pain to none, but prove pleasant and profitable to all who peruse its pages, and especially helpful to young parents

—M.F.

CHAPTER FIRST

Meantime, a smiling offspring rises round,
And mingles both their graces. By degrees
The human blossom blows, and every day,
Soft as it rolls along, shows some new charm,
The father's lustre, and the mother's bloom.

—THOMSON'S SEASONS

"MAMMA! PAPA, TOO!" It was a glad shout of a chorus of young voices as four pairs of little feet came pattering up the avenue and onto the veranda; then as many ruby lips were held up for the morning kiss from the children's dearly loved father.

They had already had their half-hour with mamma, which made so sweet a beginning of each day; yet she, too, must have a liberal share of the eagerly bestowed caresses. And Bruno, a great Newfoundland, the pet, playfellow, and guardian of the little flock, testified his delight in the scene by leaping about among them, fawning upon one another, wagging his tail, and uttering again and again a short, joyous bark.

Then followed a merry romp, cut short by the ringing of the breakfast bell, when all trooped into the house. Harold was riding on papa's shoulder, mamma following with Elsie, Eddie, and Vi, while Dinah, with baby Herbert in her arms, brought up the rear.

The children had been very happy, full of laughter and sweet innocent prattle; but a sudden hush fell upon them when seated about the table in the bright, cheerful breakfast parlor. Little hands were meekly folded and each young head bent reverently over the plate, while in a few simple words that all could understand, their father gave God thanks for the food and asked His blessing upon it.

The Ion children were never rude even in their play, and their table manners were almost perfect. They were made the constant companions of cultivated, refined parents whose politeness sprang from genuine unselfishness that was never laid aside. It was shown on all occasions, to rich and poor, old and young alike. They were governed with a wise mixture of indulgence and restraint, mildness and firmness; they imitated the copies set before them and were seldom other than gentile and amiable in their deportment, not only toward their superiors, but to equals and inferiors also.

They were never told that "children should be seen and not heard," but when no guests were present, were allowed to talk in moderation; a gentle word or look of reproof from papa or mamma being quite sufficient to check any tendency to boisterousness or undue loquacity.

"I think we should celebrate this anniversary, Elsie," remarked Mr. Travilla, stirring his coffee, and gazing with fond admiration into the sweet face at the opposite end of the table.

"Yes, sir, though we are rather late in thinking of it," she answered smilingly, the rose deepening slightly on her cheek as delicately rounded and tinted as it had been ten years ago.

Little Elsie looked up inquiringly. "What is it, papa? I do not remember."

"Do you not? Ten years ago today there was a grand wedding at the Oaks and your mamma and I were there."

"I, too?" asked Eddie.

"Yes, course, Eddie," spoke up five-year-old Violet. "Grandpa would 'vite you and all of us; and I b'lieve I 'member a little about it."

"Me, too," piped the baby voice of Harold. "Me sat on papa's knee."

There was a general laugh, the two little prattlers joining in right merrily.

"I really don't remember that as part of it, Harold," said papa. Meanwhile wee Elsie — as she was often called by way of distinguishing her from mamma, for whom she was named — shook her curly head at him with a merry "Oh, you dear little rogue, you don't know what you are talking about." And mamma remarked, "Vi has perhaps a slight recollection of May Allison's wedding."

"But this one at the Oaks must have been before I was born," said Elsie, "because you said it was ten years ago, and I'm only nine. Oh, mamma, was it your wedding?"

"Yes, daughter. Shall we invite our friends for this evening, Edward?"

"Yes, my dear wife, suppose we make it a family party, inviting only relatives, connections, and very intimate friends."

After a little more discussion it was decided they would do so. It was also decided that the children should have a full holiday. While their mother was giving orders and overseeing all of the necessary preparations for the entertainment, papa should take them all into the roomy family carriage and drive over to the Oaks, Roselands, Ashlands, and Pinelands to give the invitations. Besides these near friends only the minister and his wife were to be asked. But, as Adelaide and her family were at this time paying a visit to Roselands, and Lucy Ross was doing the same at her old home, and all the younger generation except the mere babies were to be included in the invitation, should all accept it would be by no means a small assemblage.

Early hours were named for the sake of the little ones — guests to come at six, refreshments to be served at eight, and the Ion children, if each would take a nap in the afternoon, to be allowed to stay up till nine.

How delighted they were. How the little eyes danced and sparkled, and how eagerly they engaged to fulfill the conditions — not to fret or look cross when summoned at nine to leave the drawing room and be put to bed.

"Oh, mamma, won't you wear your wedding dress?" cried little Elsie. "Do, dear mamma, so that we may see just how you looked when you were married to Papa."

Elsie smiled, "You forget, daughter, that I am ten years older now, and the face cannot be quite the same as it was that night."

"The years have robbed it of none of its beauty," said Mr. Travilla.

"Ah, love is blind," she returned with a blush and smile as charming as those of her girlhood days. "And the dress is quite out of date."

"No matter for that. It would gratify me as well as the children to see you in it."

"Then it shall be worn, if it fits or can be altered in time."

"Veil and all, mamma," pleaded Elsie, "it is so beautiful. Mammy showed it to me only the other day and told me you looked so, so lovely; and she will put the orange blossoms in your hair and on your dress just as they were that night, for she remembers all about it."

The children, ready dressed for their drive, were gathered in a merry group on the veranda, Eddie astride Bruno, waiting for papa and the carriage, when a horse came cantering up the avenue, and Mr. Horace Dinsmore alighted and stepped into their midst.

"Oh, grandpa, what you tum for?" cried Harold in a tone of disappointment. "We was dus doin' to 'vite you!"

"Indeed!"

"Yes, grandpa, it's a 'versary today," explained Vi.

"And mamma's going to be married over again," said Eddie.

"No; only to have a party and wear her wedding dress," corrected Elsie.

"Papa, good morning," cried their mother, coming swiftly through the hall. "I'm so glad, always so glad to see you."

"I know it," he said, pressing a fatherly kiss on the sweet lips, then holding her off for an instant to gaze fondly into the fair face. "And it is ten years today since I gave Travilla a share in my treasure. I was thinking of it as I rode over and that you should celebrate this anniversary at your father's house."

"No, no, Dinsmore, you must be our guest," said Travilla, coming out and shaking hands cordially with his old friend. "We have it all arranged—a family gathering—and Elsie to gratify us by wearing her bridal clothes. Do you not agree with me that she would make as lovely a bride today as she did ten years ago?"

"Quite. I relinquish my plan for yours; and don't let me detain you and these eager children."

"I thank you; I will go then, as the invitations will be late enough with all the haste we can make."

The carriage was at the door and in a moment grandpa and papa had helped the little ones. Not even baby Herbert was left behind, but seated on his mammy's lap cooed and laughed as merrily as the rest.

"Ah, mamma, you come, too!" pleaded the little voices, as their father took his place beside them. "Can't mammy and Aunt Dicey and the rest know what to do without you to tell them?"

"Not this time, dears; and you know I must make haste to try on the dress, to see if it fits."

"Oh, yes, mamma!" and throwing a shower of kisses, they drove off.

"A carriage load of precious jewels," Elsie said, looking after it as it rolled away. "How the ten years have added to my wealth, papa."

She stood by his side, her hand soft on his arm, and the soft sweet eyes lifted to his were full of a content and gladness beyond the power of words to express.

"I thank God every day for my little darling's happiness," he said low and tenderly, softly smoothing her shining hair.

"Ah, it is very great, and my father's dear love forms no small part of it. But come in, papa, I want to consult you about one or two little matters; you know that Edward and I rely very much upon your taste and judgment."

"To Roselands first," was Mr. Travilla's order to the coachman.

The old house of the Dinsmores, though shorn of the glory of its grand trees, was again in a beautiful place. The new house was in every respect a finer one than its predecessor. It was of a higher style of architecture, more conveniently arranged, more tastefully and handsomely furnished; lawns, gardens and fields had become neat and trim as in the days before the war, and a double row of young, thrifty trees bordered the avenue.

Old Mr. Dinsmore now resided there and gave a home to his two widowed and impoverished daughters—Mrs. Louise Conly and Mrs. Enna Johnson—and their families.

These two aunts loved Elsie no better than in earlier years—it was gall and wormwood to them to know that they owed all these comforts to her generosity; nor could they forgive her that she was more wealthy, beautiful, lovely and beloved than themselves. Enna was the more bitter and outspoken of the two, but even Louise seldom treated her niece to anything better than the most distant and frigid politeness.

In a truly Christian spirit, Elsie returned them pity and compassion because of their widowhood and straitened circumstances, invited them to her house, and when they came, received them with kindness and cordiality.

Her grandfather had grown very fond of her and her children, was often at Ion, and for his sake she occasionally visited Roselands. Adelaide's presence had drawn her there more frequently as of late. The invitation Mr. Travilla carried was to the grandfather, three aunts, and all their children.

Adelaide and Enna were in the drawing room when the Ion carriage drew up at the door.

"There's Travilla, the old scalawag. How I hate him! Elsie, too, I presume," exclaimed the latter, glancing from the window. "I'll leave you to entertain them," and she hastily left the room.

Adelaide flashed an indignant look after her, and hurried out to meet and welcome the callers. Mr. Travilla had alighted and was coming up the steps of the veranda.

"How d'ye do. I'm very glad to see you," cried Adelaide, extending her hand. "But where is Elsie?"

"We left her at home for once," he answered merrily, "but I come this morning merely as her ladyship's messenger."

"But won't you come in, you and the children?"

"Thanks, no, if you will permit me just to deliver my message and go, for I am in haste."

Mrs. Allison accepted the invitation for herself and children with evident pleasure, engaged that her sisters would do the same, then went to the carriage window for a moment's chat with the little ones, each of whom held a large place in her warm heart. "Aunt Addie," said Elsie in an undertone, "mamma's going to wear her wedding dress tonight, veil and all."

"Is she? Why that's an excellent idea. But don't tell it anywhere else you go; it will be such a nice surprise to the rest if we can keep it a secret."

"That was a good suggestion of Aunt Addie's." Mr. Travilla remarked as they drove down the avenue. "Suppose we carry it out. How many of you can refrain from telling what mamma is to wear tonight? How many can I trust to keep it a secret?"

"All of us papa!" "Me, papa, me!" "I won't tell," cried the little voices in chorus.

"Yes, I believe I can trust you all," he answered in his cheery way. "Now on to the Oaks, Solon, then to Pinegrove, Springbrook, and the Ashlands. That will be the last place, children, and as our hurry will then be over, you shall get out of the carriage and have a little time to rest before we start for home."

Reentering the house, Mrs. Allison went to the family sitting room, where she found both her sisters and several of the younger members of the household. "So they have asked for us?" exclaimed Louise in a tone of vexation, "and at such an unreasonable hour, too. Well," with a sigh of resignation, "I suppose we must show ourselves or papa will be displeased—so wonderfully fond of Elsie he has grown as of late."

"As well he may," returned Adelaide pointedly, "but Elsie is not here nor has anyone inquired for any of you."

"No, I presume not," interrupted Enna with a sneer. "We are not worth inquiring for."

Indignation kept Adelaide silent for a moment; she was sorely tempted to administer a severe and cutting rebuke. But Enna was no longer a child, and controlling herself she calmly delivered Mr. Travilla's message.

"Oh, delightful! Cousin Elsie always does give such splendid parties, such elegant refreshments!"

cried Virginia and Isadore Conly, girls of ten and twelve. "Mamma, you'll never think of declining?"

"No, your grandfather wouldn't like it," said Louise, as anxious as her daughters to enjoy the entertainment, yet glad to save her pride, by putting her acceptance on the score of pleasing her father.

"And you'll go, too, and take us, mamma, won't you?" anxiously queried Molly Percival, who was between her cousins in age.

"Of course, I'll go; we all want our share of the good things, and the pleasure of seeing and being seen," answered Enna, scorning Louise's subterfuge, "and if you and Dick will promise to make me no trouble, I'll take you along. But Bob and Betty may stay at home; I'm not going to be bothered with them—babies of five and three. But what shall we wear, Lu? I do say it's real mean of them to give so short a notice. But, of course, Elsie enjoys making me feel my changed circumstances. I've no such stock of jewels, silks, and laces as she, nor the full purse that makes it an easy matter for her to order a fresh supply at a moment's warning."

"You have all, and more than the occasion calls for," remarked Adelaide quietly. "It is to be only a family gathering."

CHAPTER SECOND

Though fools spurn Hymen's gentle powers,
We, who improve his golden hours,
By sweet experience know
That marriage, rightly understood,
Gives to the tender and the good
A paradise below.

—COTTON

MR. ALLISON HAD FULLY KEPT his promise to his daughter, Sophy, and Ashlands was again the fine old place it had been prior to the war. The family, consisting of the elder Mrs. Carrington, a young man named George Boyd—a nephew of hers who had taken charge of the plantation—Sophy, and her four children, had now been in possession for over a year.

Sophy, still an almost inconsolable mourner for the husband of her youth, lived a very retired life, devoting herself to his mother and his orphaned little ones.

Mrs. Ross, expecting to spend the fall and winter with them, had brought all her children and a governess, Miss Fisk—who undertook the tutelage of the little Carringtons also during her stay at Ashlands, thus leaving the mothers more at liberty for the enjoyment of each other's society.

It was in the midst of school hours that the Ion carriage came driving up the avenue. Philip Ross, lifting his head from the slate over which he had been bending for the last half-hour, rose hastily, threw down his pencil, and hurried from the room. He paid no attention to Miss Fisk's query, "Where are you going, Philip?" or her command, "Come back instantly: it is quite contrary to rules for pupils to leave the schoolroom during the hours of recitation, without permission." Indeed, he had reached the foot of the staircase before the last word had left her lips—she being very slow and precise in speech and action, while his movements were of the quickest.

"What now is to be done in this emergency?" soliloquized the governess, unconsciously thinking aloud. "Miss Gertrude Ross," turning to a girl of nine whose merry blue eyes were twinkling with fun, "follow your brother at once and inform him that I cannot permit any such act of insubordination; he must return instantly to the performance of his duties."

"Yes ma'am," and Gertrude vanished, glad enough of the opportunity to see for herself who were the new arrivals. "Phil," she said, entering the drawing room where the guests were already seated, "Miss Fisk says you're an insubordination and must come back instantly."

"Gertrude," said her mother, laughing, "come and speak to Mr. Travilla and your little friends. Yes, Phil, to be sure; how came you here when you ought to be at your lessons?"

"Because I wanted to see Elsie Travilla," he answered nonchalantly.

"Yes, but you should have asked for permission. I ought to send you back."

"But you won't, ma, you know that as well as I do. I'll not go back a step while Elsie stays."

"Well, well, it seems you are bound to have your own way, as usual," Lucy answered, half-laughing, half sighing, then resumed her talk with Mr. Travilla.

Seeing that the little Travillas had listened to this colloquy in blank amazement, she felt much mortified at Phil's behavior, and on receiving the invitation threatened to leave him at home as a punishment. But this only made matters worse. He insisted that go he would, and if she refused permission he should never, never love her again as long as he lived. And she weakly yielded.

"Lucy," said her mother, when the guests were gone, and the children had left the room, "you are ruining that boy."

"Well, I don't see how I can help it, mamma! How could I bear to lose his affection?"

"You are taking the very course to bring that about. It is the weakly indulged, not the wisely controlled, children who lose—first respect and then affection for their parents. Look at Elsie's little family for instance; where can you find children ruled with a firmer hand, or more devotedly attached to their parents?"

Eddie was at that moment saying to his father as they drove away in the carriage, "Papa, isn't Phil Ross a very, *very* naughty boy, to be so saucy and disobedient to his mamma?"

"My son," answered Mr. Travilla with gentle gravity, "when you have corrected all Eddie Travilla's faults it will be time enough to attend to those of others." And the child hung his head and blushed for shame.

It was Mr. and Mrs. Horace Dinsmore who did the honors at Ion early in the evening, receiving and welcoming each bevy of guests, and replying to the oft repeated inquiry for the master and mistress of the establishment, that they would make their appearance shortly.

Elsie's children, most sweetly and becomingly dressed, had gathered about "Aunt Rosie," in a corner of the drawing room, and seemed to be waiting with a sort of intense but quiet eagerness for the coming of some expected event.

At length every invited guest had arrived. All being so thoroughly acquainted, nearly all related, there was an entire absence of stiffness and constraint, and much lively chat had been carried on; but a sudden hush fell upon them, and every eye turned toward the doors opening into the hall, expecting they knew not what.

There were soft footfalls, a slight rustle of silk, and Adelaide entered, followed by Mr. Travilla with Elsie on his arm, in bridal attire. The shimmering satin, rich, soft lace, and orange blossoms became her well; and never, even on that memorable night ten years ago, had she looked lovelier or more bride-like; never had her husband bent a prouder, fonder look upon her fair face than now as he led her to the center of the room, where they passed in front of their pastor.

A low murmur of surprise and delight ran round the room, but suddenly was stilled, as the venerable man rose and began to speak.

"Ten years ago tonight, dear friends, I united you in marriage. Edward Travilla, you then vowed to love, honor, and cherish till life's end the woman whom you now hold by the hand. Have you repented of that vow? And would you now desire to be released?"

"Not for worlds: there has been no repentance, but my love has only grown deeper and stronger day by day."

"And you, Elsie Dinsmore Travilla, also vowed to love, honor, and obey the man you hold by the hand. Have you repented?"

"Never, sir; never for one moment." The accents were low, sweet, clear, and full of pleasure.

"I pronounce you a faithful man and wife; and may God, in His good providence, grant you many returns of this happy anniversary."

Old Mr. Dinsmore stepped up, kissed the bride, and shook hands with the groom. "Blessings on you for making her so happy," he said in quivering and quiet tones.

His son followed, then the others in their turn, and a merry scene ensued.

"Mamma, it was so pretty, *so* pretty," little Elsie said, clasping her arms about her mother's neck, "and now I just feel as if I'd been to your wedding. Thank you, dear mamma and papa."

"Mama, you are so beautiful, I'll just marry you myself, when I'm a man," remarked Eddie, giving her a hearty kiss, then gazing into her face with his great dark eyes full of love and admiration.

"I, too," chimed in Violet. "No, no, I forget. I shall be a lady myself, so I'll have to marry papa."

"No, Vi, oo tan't have my papa; he's dus' my papa, always," objected Harold, climbing his father's knee.

"What a splendid idea, Elsie," Lucy Ross was saying to her friend. "You have made me regret, for the first time, not having kept my wedding dress; for I believe my Phil and I could go through that catechism quite as well as you and Mr. Travilla. The whole thing, I suppose, was quite original?"

"Among us, my namesake daughter proposed the wearing of the dress—and the ceremony," turning to the minister, "was your idea, Mr. Wood, was it not?"

"Partly my idea, Mrs. Travilla—your father, Mrs. Dinsmore, and I planned it together."

"Your dress is as perfect a fit as when made, but I presume you had it altered," observed Lucy, making a critical examination of her friend's dress."

"No, not in the least," answered Elsie, smiling.

The banquet to which the guests were presently summoned, though gotten up so hastily, more than fulfilled the expectation of the Misses Conly, who as well as their mother and Aunt Enna did it ample justice. There was a good deal of gormandizing done by the spoiled children present, in spite of feeble protests from their parents. But Elsie's well trained little ones ate contentedly what was given them, nor even asked for the rich dainties on which the others were feasting; knowing that papa and mamma loved them too dearly to deny them any real good.

"Holloa, Neddie and Vi, why you have certainly been overlooked!" said Philip Ross, coming toward the two little ones with a plate heaped up with rich viands. "You've taken nothing but ice cream and plain sugar biscuit; here, take some of this pound cake and these bonbons. They are delicious, I do mean to tell you!"

"No, thank you. Mamma says pound cake is much too rich for us, and would make us sick," said Eddie.

"Specially at night," added Vi, "and we're to have some bonbons tomorrow."

"Goodest little tots ever I saw," returned Philip laughing. "Ma wanted me to let 'em alone, but I told her I'd risk the getting sick," he added with a pompous grownup air.

"Phil, you certainly are an insubordination, as Miss Fisk said," remarked his sister Gertrude, standing near, "I believe you think you're 'most a man, but it's a great mistake."

"Pooh, Ger! People that live in glass houses shouldn't throw stones. I heard you telling ma you wouldn't wear the dress she laid out for you. Elsie Travilla, please allow me the pleasure of refilling your saucer."

"No, thank you, Phil. I've had all mamma thinks good for me."

"Time to go to bed, chillens," said mammy, approaching the little group. "De clock jes gwine strike nine. Here, Uncle Joe, take dese empty saucers from dese little uns."

Promptly and without a murmur the four little folks prepared to obey the summons, but cast wistful longing glances toward mamma, who was merrily chatting with her guests on the other side of the room. Just then the clock on the mantel struck, and excusing herself she came quickly toward them. "That is right, dears. Come and say goodnight to papa and friends; then go with mammy and mamma will follow in a few moments."

"What dear sweet creatures they are! Perfect little ladies and gentlemen," remarked Mrs. Wood, as, after a courteous goodnight, they went cheerfully away with their mammy.

"I wish mine were half as good," said Mrs. Ross.

"Now, ma, don't expose us." cried Phil. "I've often heard you say Mrs. Travilla was a far better little girl than you; so of course her children ought to be better than yours."

"Some children keep their good behavior for company," sneered Enna, "and I have no doubt these little paragons have their naughty fits as well as ours."

"It is quite true that they are not always good," Elsie said with patient sweetness. "And now I beg you will all excuse me for a few moments, as they never feel quite comfortable going to bed without a last word or two with mamma."

"I would never be such a slave to my children!" muttered Enna, looking after her as she glided from the room. "If they couldn't be content to be put to bed by their mammies, they might stay up all night."

"I think Mrs. Travilla is right," observed the pastor. "The responsibilities of parents are very great. God says to each one, 'Take this child and nurse it for me, and I will give thee thy wages.'"

❦❦❦❦❦❦❦

CHAPTER THIRD

Delightful task! To rear the tender thought,
To teach the young idea how to shoot,
To pour the fresh instruction o'er the mind,
To breathe the enlivening spirit and to fix
The generous purpose in the glowing breast!

—THOMSON'S SEASONS

THE ION LITTLE FOLKS WERE ALLOWED an extra nap the next morning, their parents wisely considering plenty of sleep necessary to the healthful development of their mental and physical powers. They themselves, however, felt no necessity for a like indulgence—their guests having departed in time to allow their retiring at the usual hour. They were early in the saddle, keenly enjoying a brisk canter of several miles before breakfast.

On their return, Elsie went to the nursery, Mr. Travilla to the field where his men were at work. Half an hour later they and their children met at the breakfast table.

Solon came in for orders.

"You may have Beppo saddled, Solon," said Mr. Travilla, "and have Prince and Princess at the door also, immediately after prayers."

The last named were a pair of pretty little gray ponies belonging respectively to Eddie and his sister

Elsie. They were gentle and well trained for both saddle and harness.

Nearly every day the children rode them, one on each side of their father, mounted on Beppo, his beautiful bay. Occasionally they drove behind them in the phaeton with their mother or some older person. One or the other of the children would often be allowed to hold the reins on a straight and level road, for their father wished them to learn to both ride and drive with ease and skill.

Little Elsie's great ambition was "to be like mamma" in the ease and grace with which she sat her horse, as well as in everything else, while Eddie was equally anxious to copy his father.

Violet and Harold ran out to the veranda to watch them mount and ride away.

"Papa," said Vi, "shall we, too, have ponies of our own and ride with you, when we're as big as Elsie and Eddie?"

"I intend you shall, little daughter, and if you and Harold will be here with your hats on, all ready to start at once when we come back, I will give you each a short ride before the ponies are put away."

"Oh, thank you, papa! We'll be sure to be ready," they answered, and ran in to their mother to tell her of papa's kind promise and to have their hats put on.

Elsie, who was in the sitting room with Herbert on her lap, rejoiced in their joy, and bade Dinah prepare them at once for their ride.

"Bress dere little hearts! Dey grows hansomer ebery day," exclaimed an elderly Negress, who had just come in with a basket on her arm.

"Don't say such things before them, Aunt Sally," said her mistress in a tone of gentle reproof. "Their young hearts are only too ready to be puffed up with vanity and pride. Now what is your report from the quarter?"

"Well, missus, dere's lots ob miseries down dere dis mornin'—ole Lize, she's took wid a misery in her side; an' Uncle Jack, he got um in his head; ole Aunt Delia's got de misery in de joints wid de rheumatiz; an 'ole Uncle Mose, he's 'plainin' ob de misery in his back, can't stan' up straight no how; an' Hannah's baby got a mighty bad cold, can't hardly draw his breff, 'twas took dat way in de night; an' Silvy's boy tore his foot on a nail."

"Quite a list," said Elsie. And giving her babe to Aunt Chloe, she selected a key from a bright bunch lying in a little basket held by a small maid at her side, unlocked a closet door, and looked over her medical store. "Here's a plaster for Uncle Moss to put on his back, and one for Lize's side," she said, handing each article in turn to Aunt Sally, who bestowed it in her basket. "This small bottle has some drops that will do Uncle Jack's head good; and this larger one is for Aunt Delia. Tell her to rub her joints with it. There is medicine for the baby, and Hannah must give him a warm bath. If he is not better directly we must send for the doctor. Now, here is a box of salve, excellent for cuts, burns, and bruises; spread some on a bit of rag and tie it on Silvy's boy's foot. There, I think that is all. I'll be down after a while, to see how they are all doing," and with some added directions concerning the use of each remedy, Aunt Sally was dismissed.

Then Aunt Dicey, the housekeeper, came for her orders for the day ahead and such supplies from pantry and storehouse as were needed in carrying them out.

In the meantime, the riding party had returned. Harold and Violet had been treated to a ride about the grounds, the one in his father's arms, Beppo stepping carefully as if he knew he carried a tender babe, the other on one of the ponies close at papa's side and under his watchful eye.

It was a rosy, merry group mamma found upon the veranda, chatting to each other and laughing merrily as they watched their father cantering down the avenue on his way to the fields to oversee the work going on there.

They did not hear their mother's step till she was close at hand asking in her own sweet, gentle tones, "My darlings, had you a pleasant time?"

"Oh, yes, mamma, so nice!" and they gathered about her, eager to claim her ever-ready sympathy, interested in their joys no less than their sorrows.

They had been taught to notice the beauties of nature — the changing clouds, the bright autumn foliage, plants and flowers, insects, birds, stones — all the handiwork of God; and the elder ones now never returned from walk or ride without something to tell of what they had seen and enjoyed.

It was surprising how much they learned in this easy pleasant way, how much they gained almost imperceptibly in manners, correctness of speech, and general information, by this habit of their parents of keeping them always with themselves and patiently answering every proper question. They were encouraged not only to observe, but also to think, to reason, and to repeat what they had learned; thus fixing it more firmly in their minds. They were not burdened with long tasks or many studies, but required to learn thoroughly such as were set before them, and trained to a love for wholesome mental food—the books put into their hands being carefully chosen by their parents.

Though abundantly able to afford a governess, Elsie preferred teaching her darlings herself. There was a large, airy room set apart for that purpose. It was furnished with every suitable appliance—books, maps, globes, pictures, an orrery (after the Earl of Orrery, which is a model of the planets), and a piano. There were pretty rosewood desks and chairs. The floor was a mosaic of beautifully grained and polished woods. The walls, adorned with a few rare engravings, were of a delicate neutral tint, and tasteful curtains were hung at each window.

Thither mother and children now repaired, and spent the following two happy hours giving and receiving instruction.

Harold had not yet quite mastered the alphabet. His task was, of course, soon done, and he was permitted to take himself to the nursery or elsewhere, with his mammy to take care of him. If he chose to submit to the restraint of the schoolroom rather than leave mamma and the others, he might do so.

Violet could already read fluently, in any book suited to her years, and was learning to spell, write, and sew.

Eddie was somewhat further advanced, and Elsie had begun arithmetic, history, and geography; music, also, and drawing, for both of which she had already shown talent.

School over, she had a half-hour of rest, then went to the piano for an hour's practice, her mamma sitting by to aid and encourage her.

Mr. Travilla came in, asking, "Where is Eddie?"

"Here, papa," and the boy came running in with face all aglow with delight. "Oh, are you going to teach me how to shoot? I saw you coming with that pistol in your hand and I'm so glad."

"Yes," his father answered, smiling at the eager face. "You will not be anxious, little wife?" turning to her with a tender loving look.

"No, my husband; surely I can trust him with you, his own wise, careful, loving father," she answered with a confident smile.

"Oh papa, mayn't I go along with you? And won't you teach me, too?" cried Violet, who was always ready for any excitement.

"Not today, daughter. Only Eddie and I are going now; but sometime I will teach you all. It is well enough for even ladies to handle a pistol on occasion, and your mamma is quite a good shot."

Vi looked disappointed but did not fret, pout, or ask a second time, for such things were not allowed in the family by either parent.

"Mamma's good little girl," the mother said drawing her caressingly to her side, as Mr. Travilla and Eddie left the room. "I am going to walk down to the quarter this afternoon and will take you and your brother and sister with me, if you care to go."

"Oh, mamma, thank you! Yes, indeed, I do want to go," cried the little one, her face growing bright as usual. "May we be there when the bell rings? 'Cause I do like to see the dogs." And she clapped her tiny hands like the chiming of the silver bells.

Her sister laughed, saying, "Oh, yes, mamma, do let us."

The Ion Negroes were paid liberal wages, and yet as kind and generously cared for as in the old days of slavery; even more so, for now Elsie might lawfully carry out her desire to educate and elevate them to a higher standard of intelligence and morality.

To this end Mr. Travilla had added to the quarter a neat schoolhouse, where the children received instruction in the rudiments during the day, the adults in the evening, from one of their own race whose advantages had been such as to qualify him for the work. There, too, the master and mistress of Ion held a Sunday school class themselves on Sunday afternoons.

Aunt Sally, the nurse, also instructed the women in housewifery ways, and Dinah taught them sewing; Elsie encouraging and stimulating them to effort by bestowing prizes on the most diligent and proficient.

Eddie came in from his first lesson in the use of firearms, flushed and excited.

"Mamma, I did shoot," he cried exultingly. "I shooted many times, and papa says I'll make a good shot some day if I keep on trying."

"Ah! Did you hit the mark?"

"Not quite this time, mamma," and the bright face clouded slightly.

"Not quite," laughed Mr. Travilla, drawing his boy caressingly toward him. "If you please, mamma, do not question us too closely; we expect to do better another time. He really did fairly well considering his age and that it was his first lesson.

"Papa," asked Vi, climbing his knee, "were you 'fraid Eddie would shoot us if we went along?"

"I thought it safer to leave you at home."

"Papa, mamma's going to take us walking this afternoon; we're to be there when the bell rings, so we can see those funny dogs."

"Ah, then I think I shall meet you there and walk home with you."

This announcement was received with a chorus of exclamations of delight; his loved companionship would double their enjoyment; it always did.

'Twas a pleasant, shady walk, not too long for the older children, and Harold's mammy would carry him when he grew weary. They called at the schoolroom and witnessed the closing exercises. Then they visited all the aged and ailing ones, Elsie inquiring tenderly concerning their "miseries," speaking words of sympathy and consolation and giving additional advice—remedies, too—and some little delicacies to whet the sickly appetites.

As they left the last cabin, in the near vicinity of the post where hung the bell that summoned the men to their meals and gave notice of the hour for quitting work, they saw the ringer hurrying toward it.

"Oh, mamma, we're just in time!" cried Vi. "How very nice!"

"Yes," said her sister, "mamma always knows how to make things come out right."

Every Negro family owned a cur, and at the first tap of the bell they always, with a united yelp, rushed for the spot, where they formed a ring around the post, each seated on his haunches and brushing the ground with his tail, with a rapid motion, from side to side, nose in the air, eyes fixed upon the bell, and the throat sending out a prolonged howl so long as the ringing continued. The din was deafening, and far from musical, but it was a comical sight, vastly enjoyed by the young Travillas, who saw it only occasionally.

Mr. and Mrs. Travilla were walking slowly homeward, the children and Bruno frolicking, jumping, dancing, and running on before. After a while the two little girls grew somewhat weary, and subsided into a slower pace.

"Vi," said Elsie, "don't you believe Aunt Delia might get better of those 'miseries' in her bones, if she had some nice new red flannel things to wear?"

"Yes, let's buy her some," and a pretty dimpled hand went into her pocket, and out came a dainty, silken purse, mamma's gift on her last birthday, when she began to have a weekly allowance, like Elsie and Eddie.

"Yes, if mamma approves."

"Course we'll 'sult mamma 'bout it first, and she'll say yes; she always likes us to be kind and — char — char — "

"Charitable? Yes, 'specially to Jesus' people, and I know Aunt Delia's one of His. How much money have you, Vi?"

"I don't know; mamma or papa will count when we get home."

"I have two dollars and fifty cents; maybe Eddie will give some if we haven't enough."

"Enough of what?" queried Eddie, overhearing the last words as he and Bruno neared the others in their gambols.

Elsie explained, asking, "Would you like to help us, Eddie?"

"Yes, and I'm going to buy some 'baccy,' as he calls it, for old Uncle Jack."

Mamma was duly consulted, approved of their plans, took them the next day to the nearest village, let them select the goods themselves, then helped them to cut out and make the garments. Eddie assisted by treading needles and sewing on buttons, saying "that would do for a boy because he had heard papa say that he had sometimes sewed on a button for himself when he was away at college."

To be sure the work might have been given to the seamstress, but it was the desire of these parents to train their little ones to give time as well as money.

CHAPTER FOURTH

O, what a state is guilt!
How wild! How wretched!

—HAVARD

THE WAR HAD BROUGHT MANY changes in the neighborhood where the Travillas resided. Some who had been reared in the lap of luxury were now in absolute want, having sacrificed almost their last dollar in the cause of secession—to which, in numerous instances, the husbands, sons, and brothers had also fallen victim.

Though through the clemency of the government there had been no executions for treason, no confiscation of property, many plantations had changed hands because of the inability of the original owners to work them, for the lack of means to pay the laborers.

Elsie's tender sympathies were strongly enlisted for these old friends and acquaintances. And their necessities often relieved by her bounty when they little guessed from whence help had come. Her favors were doubled by the delicate manner of their bestowal.

The ability to give largely was the greatest pleasure her wealth afforded her, and one in which she indulged to the extent of disposing yearly in that way, of the whole surplus of her ample income. She did not wait to be importuned, but constantly sought out worthy objects upon whom to bestow that of which she truly considered herself but a steward who must one day render a strict account unto her Lord.

It was she who had repaired the ravages of war in Springbrook, the residence of Mr. Wood, her pastor. It was she who, when the Fosters of Fairview, a plantation adjoining Ion, had been compelled to sell it, had bought a neat cottage in the vicinity and had given them the use of it at a merely nominal rent. And many other like deeds had she done—always with the entire approval of her husband, who was scarcely less generous than herself.

The purchaser of Fairview was a Mr. Leland, a northern man who had been an officer in the Union army. Pleased with the southern climate and the appearance of country, he felt inclined to settle there and assist in the development of its resources. He therefore returned sometime after the conclusion of peace, bought this place, and moved his family thither.

They were people of refinement and culture, quiet and peaceful, steady attendants upon Mr. Wood's ministry, and in every way conducted themselves as good citizens.

Yet they were not popular. The Foster family, particularly Wilkins, the only son, hated them as their supplanters, and saw with bitter envy the rapid improvement of Fairview under Mr. Leland's careful cultivation. It was no fault of his that they had been compelled to part with it, and he had paid a fair price; but envy and jealousy are ever unreasonable. Their mildest term of reproach in speaking of him was "carpetbagger."

Others found fault with Mr. Leland as paying too liberal wages to the Negroes (including Mr. Horace Dinsmore and Mr. Travilla in the same charge), and hated him for his outspoken loyalty to the government. For though he showed no disposition to seek office or meddle in any way with the politics of others, he made no secret of his views when occasion seemed to call for their expression. It was not a prudent course under existing circumstances, but accorded well with the frank and fearless nature of the man.

Messrs. Dinsmore and Travilla, themselves strong Unionists, though the latter was more discreet in the utterance of his sentiments, found in him a kindred spirit. Rose and Elsie were equally pleased with Mrs. Leland, and pitying her loneliness, called frequently, inviting a return of their visits, until now the three families had become tolerably intimate.

This state of things was extremely displeasing to Louise and Enna, scarcely less so to their father. But the others, convinced that they were in the path of duty in thus extending kindness and sympathy to deserving strangers, who were also "of the household of *faith*," were not to be deterred by remonstrance or vituperation. "Scalawags"—a term of reproach applied by the Democrats of the South to the Republicans, who were natives of that section—was what Enna called her brother, his son-in-law and daughter, when out of hearing of her father. Although vexed at their notice of the Lelands, he was too strongly attached to his only remaining son, and too sensible of the kindness he had received at the hands of Mr. Travilla and Elsie, to permit anything of that sort.

The Lelands had several young children, well bred and of good principals, and it angered Louise and Enna that Elsie evidently preferred them to their own rude, deceitful, spoiled offspring as companions and playmates for her little ones.

Elsie and her husband were very desirous to live on good terms with these near relatives, but not to the extent of sacrificing their children's morals. Therefore they did not encourage a close intimacy with their Roselands cousins; yet ever treated them politely and kindly, and made a valuable present to each on every return of his or her birthday, and on Christmas; always managing to select something specially desired by the recipient of the favor.

Mr. and Mrs. Dinsmore pursued a similar course. Rosie was allowed to be as intimate as she chose at Ion, and with her Aunt Sophy's children, but never visited Roselands except with her parents or sister; nor were the Roseland cousins ever invited to make a lengthy stay at the Oaks.

One afternoon, several weeks later, Mary and Archie Leland came over to Ion to spend an hour with their young friends.

The weather was delightful, and the children preferred playing out of doors; the girls took their dolls to the summer-house in the garden, while with kite, ball, and marbles, the boys repaired to the avenue.

"Who are they?" asked Archie, as looking up at the sound of approaching footsteps, he saw two boys, a good deal older than themselves, coming leisurely toward them.

"My cousins, Wal Conly and Dick Percival," answered Eddie. "I wish they hadn't come; they always tease me so."

"Hilloa!" cried Dick. "Why, Ed Travilla, you play with carpetbaggers, eh? Fie on you! I wouldn't be seen with one."

"That's not polite, Dick. Archie's a good boy; mamma and papa say so. And I like him very much for a playfellow."

"You do? Ah, that's because you're a scalawag."

"What's that?"

"What your father is and your grandfather, too."

"I don't care; I want to be just like my papa."

"But it isn't nice," put in Walter, laughing. "Scalawag's the meanest thing alive."

"Then you shall not call papa that, nor Grandpa!" and the child's great dark eyes flashed with anger.

"Whew! I'd like to see you hinder me. Look here, Ed," and Dick pulled out a pistol. "What d'ye think o' that? Don't you wish you had one? Don't you wish you could shoot?"

"I can," returned Eddie, proudly. "Papa's been teaching me, and he's given me a better pistol than that one."

"Hey! A likely story!" cried the two tormentors, with an incredulous laugh. "Let's see it now."

"It's in the house, but papa said I should never touch it 'cept when he gives it to me; not till I grow to be a big boy."

"Nonsense!" cried Dick. "If 'twas there, you'd bring it out fast enough. I sha'n't believe a word of the story until I see the pistol."

"I'll show you if I'm not telling the truth," exclaimed Eddie, flushing hotly, and turning about as if to go in the house.

But Archie laid a hand on his arm, and speaking for the first time since the others had joined them, "Don't, Eddie," he said persuasively, "do not disobey your father. I know you will be sorry for it afterward."

"Hold your tongue, you young carpetbagger," said Dick. "Run and get it, Ed."

"No, never mind about the pistol; he can't shoot," said Walter, mockingly. "If he can, let him take yours and prove it."

Eddie remembered well that his father had also forbidden him to touch firearms at all, except when with him. But the boy was naturally proud and willful, and in spite of all the careful training of his parents, these human faults would occasionally show themselves.

He did not like to have his word doubted. He was eager to prove his skill, which he conceived to be far greater than it was; and as his cousins continued to twit and tease him, daring him to show what he could do, he was sorely tempted to disobey.

They were slowly walking on farther from the house as they talked. Finally, when Dick said, "Why, Ed, you couldn't hit that big tree yonder. I dare you to try it," and at the same time offered him the pistol, the little fellow's sense of duty finally gave way and, snatching the weapon from Dick's hand, he fired, not allowing himself time, in his haste and passion, to take proper aim.

In their excitement and preoccupation, none of the boys noticed Mr. Travilla riding into the avenue a moment before, closely followed by his body servant Ben. Almost simultaneously with the report of the pistol the former tumbled from the saddle and fell heavily to the ground.

With a cry, "Oh, Massa Ed'ard's killed!" Ben sprang from his horse and bent over the prostrate form, wringing his hands in fright and grief. He was his master's foster brother and devoutly attached to him.

The fall, the cry, the snorting and running of the frightened horses, instantly told the boys what had happened, and Eddie threw himself on the ground screaming in agony of grief and remorse, "Oh, I've killed my father, my dear, dear father! Oh, papa, papa! What shall I do? What shall I do?"

Mr. Leland, coming in search of his children, the men passing the gate returning from their work, all heard and rushed to the spot. The blacks crowded about the scene of the accident, sobbing like children at the sight of their loved master and friend lying there apparently lifeless.

Mr. Leland, his features working with emotion, at once assumed the direction of affairs. "Catch the horses," he said, "and you, Ben, mount the fleetest and fly for the doctor. And you," turning to another, "take the other and hurry to the Oaks for Mr. Dinsmore. Now, the rest of you, help me to carry your master to the house. I will lift his head; there gently, gently, my good fellows, I think he still breathes. But Mrs. Travilla!" he added, looking toward the dwelling. "All seems quiet there; they have not heard, I think, and she should be warned. I wish—"

"I will go. I will tell my mamma," interrupted a quivering child voice at his side.

Little Elsie had pushed her way through the crowd and dropping on her knees on the grass was raining kisses and tears upon the pale, unconscious face.

"You? Poor child!" Mr. Leland began in piteous tones; but she had already sprung to her feet and was flying toward the house with the fleetness of the wind.

One moment she paused in the spacious entrance hall, to recover her breath, calm her features, and remove the traces of her tears. "Mamma, mamma," she called. Meanwhile she was saying to herself, "Oh, Lord Jesus, give me the right words to speak to her."

She hardly knew to which apartment to direct her steps, but, Hark! There was the sound of the piano and mamma's sweet voice singing a song papa had brought home only the other day, and that he liked. Ah, would she ever sing again now that he—

But no, not even in thought could she say that dreadful word. But she knew now that mamma was in the music room, and earnestly repeating her silent petition for help, she hurried thither.

The door was open; with swift, noiseless steps she gained her mother's side. Passing an arm about her neck, and half averting her own pale, agitated face, "Mamma," she said in low, tremulous tones, 'God is our refuge and strength, a very present help in trouble!' Mamma, Jesus loves you, Jesus loves you! He will help you to bear—"

"My daughter, what is it?" asked the mother in a tone of forced calmness. A terrible pang shot through her heart. "Your father? Eddie? Vi?"—then starting up at a sound as of the feet of those who bore some heavy burden, she ran into the hall.

For a moment she stood as one transfixed with grief and horror.

"He breathes, he lives still," Mr. Leland hastened to say.

Her lips moved but no words came from them. Silently motioning them to follow her, she led the way to his room and pointed to the bed. They laid him on it and at that instant consciousness returned to Mr. Travilla.

"Dear wife, it is nothing," he faintly murmured, lifting his eyes to her face as she bent over him in speechless anguish.

She softly pressed her lips to his brow, her heart too full for utterance.

The words sent a thrill of gladness to the heart of little Elsie, who had crept in behind the men, and stood near the bed silently weeping. Her father lived. Now Eddie's frantic screams seemed to ring in her ears (in her fear for her father she had scarcely noticed them before) and she must go and tell him the glad news. She was not needed here. Mamma was not conscious of her presence, and she could do nothing for the dear injured father. She stole quietly from the room.

On the veranda she saw Violet crying bitterly, while Mary Leland vainly tried to comfort her.

"Don't cry so, little sister," Elsie said, going to her and taking her in her arms in a tender motherly fashion. "Our dear papa is not killed. I saw him open his eyes, and heard him say to mamma, 'Dear wife, it is nothing.'"

Vi clung to her sister with a fresh burst of tears, but this time they were tears of joy. "Oh, I'm so glad! I thought I had no papa anymore."

A few more soothing words and caresses and Elsie said, "Now I must go and tell poor Eddie. Do you know where he is?"

"Don't you hear him crying off in the grounds?" said Mary. "I think he's just where he was."

"Oh, yes!" and Elsie hastened off in the direction of the sounds.

She found him lying on the grass still crying in heartbroken accents, "Oh, I've killed my father, my dear, dear father! What shall I do? What shall I do?"

Dick and Walter were gone. Like the guilty wretches they were, they fled as soon as they saw what mischief they had caused. But Archie, too kindhearted and noble to forsake a friend in distress, was still there.

"You didn't mean to do it, Eddie," he was saying, as Elsie came within hearing.

"No, no," burst out the half-distracted child. "I wouldn't hurt my dear papa one bit for all the world! But it was 'cause I disobeyed him. He told me never to touch firearms when he wasn't by to help me do it right. Oh, oh, oh, I didn't think I'd ever be such a wicked boy! I've killed my father! Oh! Oh!"

"No, Eddie, no, you have not killed him; papa opened his eyes and spoke to mamma," said his older sister, hurrying to his side.

"Did he? Oh, Elsie, is he alive? Isn't he hurt much?" asked the child, ceasing his cries for the moment, and lifting his tear-swollen face to hers.

"I don't know, Eddie dear, but I hope not," she said low and tremulously, the tears rolling fast down her cheeks, while she took out her handkerchief and gently wiped them away from his.

He dropped his head again, with a bitter, wailing cry. "Oh, I'm afraid he is, and I— I— shooted him!"

Fortunately Dr. Burton's residence was not far distant, and Ben, urging Beppo to his utmost speed and finding the doctor at home, had him at Mr. Travilla's bedside in a wonderfully short space of time.

The doctor found the injury not nearly so great as he had feared. The ball had struck the side of the head and bounced off, making a mere scalp-wound, which, though causing insensibility for a time, would have no very serious or lasting consequences. The blood had already been sponged away, and the wound closed with sticking plaster.

But the fall had jarred the whole system and caused some bruises, so that altogether the patient was likely to have to keep to his bed for some days. And the doctor said he must be kept quiet and as free from excitement as possible.

Elsie, leaving Aunt Chloe at the bedside, followed the physician from the room.

"You need give yourself no anxiety, my dear Mrs. Travilla," he said cheerily, taking her hand in his for just a moment, in his kind fatherly way—for he was an old man now, and had known her from her early childhood. "The injuries are not at all serious, and there is no reason why your husband should not be about again in a week or so. But how did it happen? What hand fired the shot?"

"Indeed I do not know, have not asked," she answered, with an emotion of surprise at herself for the omission. "It seems strange I should not, but I was so taken up with grief and fear for him, and anxiety to relieve his suffering, that I had no room for other thought. Can you tell us, sir?" turning to Mr. Leland, who was standing near.

"I— I—did not see the shot," he replied with some hesitation.

"But you know. Tell me, I beg of you."

"It was an accident, madam, entirely an accident. There can be no question about that."

"But tell me all that you know," she entreated, growing very pale. "I see you fear to wound me, but it were far better I should know the whole truth about the whole affair."

I suppose your little son must have been playing with a pistol," he answered, with evident reluctance. "I heard him screaming, 'Oh, I've killed my father, my dear, dear father!'"

"Eddie!" she groaned, staggering back against the wall, and putting her hands over her eyes.

"My dear madam!" "My dear Mrs. Travilla," the gentlemen exclaimed simultaneously, "do not let it distress you so, since it must have been the merest accident, and the consequences are not so serious as they might have been."

"But he was disobeying his father, and has nearly taken his life," she moaned low and tremulously, the big tears coursing down her cheeks. "Oh, my son, my son!"

The gentlemen looked uneasily at each other, scarcely knowing what consolation to offer; but a well-known step approached, hastily, yet, with caution, and the next instant Elsie was clasped in her father's arms.

"My darling, my poor darling!" he said with emotion, as she laid her head on his chest, with a burst of almost hysterical weeping.

He caressed her silently. How could he ask the question trembling on his lips? What meant this bitter weeping? His eye sought that of the physician, who promptly answered the unspoken query with the same cheery report he had just given her.

Mr. Dinsmore was intensely relieved. "Thank God that it is no worse!" he said in low, reverent tones. "Elsie, daughter, cheer up, he will soon be well again."

Mr. Leland, taking leave, offered to return and watch by the sick bed that night; but Mr. Dinsmore, while joining Elsie in cordial thanks, claimed it as his privilege.

"Ah, well, don't hesitate to call upon me whenever I can be of use," said Mr. Leland, and with a kindly "Good evening" he and the doctor retired, Mr. Dinsmore seeing them to the door.

Returning, he found Elsie still in the parlor where he had left her.

She was speaking to a servant, "Go, Prilla, look for the children, and bring them in. It is getting late for them to be out."

The girl went, and Elsie saying to her father that Prilla had brought word that Mr. Travilla was now sleeping, begged him to sit down and talk with her for a moment. The tears fell fast as she spoke. It was long since he had seen her so moved.

"Dear daughter, why distress yourself thus?" he said, folding her in his arms, and drawing her head to a resting-place upon his chest. "Your husband's injuries are not very serious. Dr. Burton is not one to deceive us with false hopes."

"No, papa. Oh, how thankful I am to know he is not in danger, but—oh papa, papa! To think that Eddie did it! That my own son should have so nearly taken his father's life! I grow sick with horror at the very thought!"

"Yet it must have been the merest accident—the child idolizes his father."

"I had thought so, but he must have been disobeying that father's positive command else this could not have happened. I could never have believed my son could be this disobedient, and it breaks my heart to think of it all."

"The best of us do not always resist temptation successfully, and doubtless in this case it has been very strong. And he is bitterly repenting. I heard him crying somewhere in the grounds as I rode up the avenue, but could not then take time to go to him, not knowing how much you and Travilla might be needing my assistance."

"My poor boy; he does love his father," she said, wiping her eyes.

"There can be no question about that, and this will be a life-long lesson to him."

"Papa, you always bring me comfort," she said gratefully. "And you will stay with us tonight?"

"Yes, I could not leave you at such a time. I shall send a note to Rose, to relieve her anxiety in regard to Edward's accident, and let her know that she need not expect me home until morning. Well, Prilla," as the girl reappeared, "what is it? Why have you not brought the children?"

"Please, sah, Massa Dinsmore, Mars Eddie won't come, he jis' lie on de ground an' scream an' cry, 'Oh, I've killed my fader, my dear, dear fader,' an Miss Elsie she confortin' an' coaxin', an' pleadin', but he won't pay no pretention to anybody."

Elsie wept anew. "My poor child! My poor little son! What am I to do with him?"

"I will go to him; trust him to me," Mr. Dinsmore said, leaving the room with a quick, firm step.

CHAPTER FIFTH

If hearty sorrow
Be a sufficient ransom for offence,
I tender it here;
I do as truly suffer,
As e'er I did commit.

—SHAKESPEARE

"OH, EDDIE, DEAR, DO GET UP and come into the house!" entreated his sister. "I must leave you if you don't, for Prilla said mamma had sent for us; and you know we must obey."

"Oh I can't, I can't go in! I can't see mamma! She will never love me anymore!"

"Yes, she will, Eddie; nothing will ever make her stop loving us; and if you're really sorry for having disobeyed poor, dear papa, you'll not go on and disobey her now."

"But, I've been such a wicked, wicked boy. Oh, Elsie, what shall I do? Jesus won't love me now, nor mamma, nor anybody."

"Oh, Eddie," sobbed his sister, "don't talk so. Jesus does love you and will forgive you, if you ask Him; and so will mamma and papa; for they both love you and I love you dearly, dearly."

The two were alone, Archie having gone home with his father.

A step drew nearer, and Mr. Dinsmore's voice spoke close at hand in tones sterner and more peremptory than he really meant them to be.

"Edward, get up from that damp grass and come into the house immediately. Do you intend to add to your poor mother's troubles by your disobedience, and by making yourself sick?"

The child arose instantly. He was accustomed to yielding to his grandfather's authority quite as to that of his parents.

"Oh grandpa, please don't be hard on him! His heart's almost broken, and he wouldn't have hurt papa on purpose for all the world," pleaded little Elsie, hastening to Mr. Dinsmore's side, taking his hand in both of hers, and lifting her tear-dimmed eyes beseechingly to his face.

"Yes, grandpa ought," sobbed Eddie, "I've been such a wicked, wicked boy; I deserve the dreadfullest whipping there ever was. And papa can't do it now!" he cried with a fresh burst of grief and remorse, "and mamma won't like to. Grandpa, it'll have to be you. Please do it quick, 'cause I want it over."

"And has all this distress been only for fear of punishment?" asked Mr. Dinsmore, taking the child's hand and bending down to look searchingly into his face.

"Oh no, no, no, grandpa! I'd rather be whipped any day than to know I've hurt my papa so. Grandpa, won't you do it quick?"

"No, my son, I am not fond of such business and shall not punish you unless requested to do so by your father or mother. The doctor hopes your father will be about again in a week or two, and he can attend to your case himself."

"Oh, then he won't die! He won't die, our dear, dear papa!" cried both children in a breath.

"No, God has been very good to us all in causing the ball to strike where it could do but little injury. And Edward, I hope this will be such a lesson to you all your life as will keep you from ever disobeying again."

They were passing up the avenue, Eddie moving submissively along by his grandfather's side, but with tottering steps, for the dreadful excitement of the last hour had exhausted him greatly. Perceiving this, Mr. Dinsmore took him in his arms and carried him in the house.

Low, pitiful sobs and sighs were the only sounds the little fellow made till set down on the veranda; but then clinging to his grandfather's hand, he burst out afresh, "Oh, grandpa, I can't go in! I can't, I can't see mamma, for she can't love me anymore."

The mother heard and came quickly out. The tears were coursing down her cheeks, her mother heart yearned over her guilty, miserable child. Stooping down and stretching out her arms, "Eddie, my little son," she said in tender, tremulous accents, "come to mother. If my boy is truly sorry for his sin, mamma has no reproaches for him — nothing but forgiveness and love."

He threw himself upon her bosom, "Mamma, mamma, I am sorry, oh, so sorry! I will never, never disobey papa or you again."

"God helping you, my son; if you trust in your own strength, you will be sure to fall."

"Yes, mamma! Oh, my dear mamma, I've been the wickedest boy! I've disobeyed my father and shooted him; and oughtn't I to have a dreadful whipping? Shall grandpa do it?"

Mrs. Travilla lifted her full eyes inquiringly to her father's face.

"It is all his own idea," said Mr. Dinsmore with obvious emotion, "and I do think he has already had a far worse punishment by far in his grief and remorse."

Elsie heaved a sigh of relief. "I think his father would say so, too; it shall be decided by him when he is able. Eddie, my son, papa is too ill now to say what should be done with you. I think he does not even know of your disobedience. You will have to wait some days. The suspense will be hard to bear, I know. But my little boy must try to be patient, remembering that he has brought all this suffering on himself. And in the meantime, he has mamma's forgiveness and love," she added folding him to her heart with a tender caress.

Sorely the children missed their precious half-hour with mamma that night, and every night and morning of their papa's illness. She could leave him only long enough each time to give them a few loving words and a kiss all around, and they scarcely saw her through the day as they were not admitted to their father's room at all.

But they were very good; lessons went on nearly as usual, little Elsie keeping order in the school-room, even willful Eddie quietly submitting to her gentle way, and grandpa kindly attending to the recitations. He rode out with them, too, and he, Aunt Rosie, or their mammies, took them for a pleasant walk every fine day.

Friends and neighbors both were very kind and attentive, none more so than the Lelands. Archie told his father how, and by whom, poor Eddie had been teased, provoked, and dared into firing the pistol. Mr. Leland told Mr. Dinsmore the story, and he repeated it to his father and sisters.

The old gentleman was sufficiently incensed against the two culprits to administer a severe castigation to each, while Elsie was thankful to learn that her son had not yielded readily to the temptation to disobedience. She pitied him deeply. She noted how weary to him were those days of waiting, how his happy spirits had forsaken him, how anxious he was for his father's recovery, and how he longed for the time when he should be permitted to go to him with his confession and petition for pardon.

At length that time came. Mr. Travilla was so much better that Dr. Burton said it would do him no harm to see his children, and to hear all the details of his accident.

The others were brought in first and allowed to spend a few minutes in giving and receiving caresses, their little tongues running very fast in their exuberant joy over their restored father.

"Elsie, Vi, Harold, baby — but where is Eddie?" he asked, looking a little anxiously at his wife, "Not sick, I hope?"

"No, my dear, he will be in presently," she answered, the tears starting to her eyes. "No one of them has found it harder to be kept away from you than he. But there is something he has begged me to tell you before he comes."

"Ah!" he said with a troubled look in his eyes, a suspicion of the truth dawning upon him. "Well, darlings, you may go now, and mamma will let you come in again before your bedtime."

The children withdrew and Elsie told Edward the entire story, dwelling more particularly upon the strength of the temptation and the child's agony of grief and remorse.

"Bring him in here, wife," Mr. Travilla said, his eyes full, his voice husky with emotion.

There was a sound of sobs in the hall without as she opened the door. "Come, son," she said, taking his hand in hers, "papa knows it all now."

Half eagerly, half tremblingly he suffered her to lead him in.

"Papa," he burst out sobbingly, scarcely daring to lift his eyes from the floor, "I've been a very wicked, bad boy; I disobeyed you and — and —"

"Come here to me, my little son." How gentle and tender were the tones.

Eddie lifted his head and with one joyful bound was in his father's arms, clinging about his neck and sobbing out upon his shoulder his grief, his joy, his penitence. "Papa, papa, can you forgive such a naughty, disobedient boy? I'm so sorry I did it! I'm so glad you didn't die, dear, dear papa, so glad you love me yet."

"Love you, son? I think if you knew how much, you would never want to disobey again."

"I don't, papa, oh, I don't! I ask God earnestly every day to give me a new heart, and help me always to be good. But mustn't I be punished? Mamma said it was for you to say, and grandpa didn't whip me and he won't 'less you ask him."

"And I shall not ask him, my son. I fully and freely forgive you, because I am sure you are very sorry and do not mean to disobey again."

How happy the child was that at last his father knew and had forgiven all.

Mr. Travilla improved the occasion with a short but very serious talk with him on the sin and danger of disobedience; and his words, so tenderly spoken, made a deep and lasting impression.

But Eddie was not yet done with the pain and mortification consequent upon his wrongdoing. That afternoon the Ashland ladies called bringing with them the elder children of both families. While their mammas conversed in the drawing room the little people gathered on the veranda.

All was harmony and good will among them till Philip Ross, fixing his eyes on Eddie, said with a sneer, "So Master Ed, though you told me one day you'd never talk to your mamma the way I talk to mine, you've done a good deal worse. I don't set up for a pattern, good boy, but I'd die before I'd shoot my father."

Eddie's dark eyes sought the floor while his lips trembled and two great tears rolled down his burning cheeks.

"Phil Ross," cried Gertrude, "I'm ashamed of you! Of course, he didn't do it on purpose."

"Maybe not; he didn't disobey on purpose? Hadn't his father—"

But catching a reproachful, entreating look from Elsie's soft, hazel eyes, he stopped short and turning away, began to whistle carelessly. Meanwhile Vi, putting her small arms about Eddie's neck, said, "Phil Ross, you shouldn't 'sult my brother so, 'cause he wouldn't 'tend to hurt papa; no, not for all the world." Harold chimed in, "'Course my Eddie wouldn't!" and Bruno, whom he was petting and stroking with his chubby hands, gave a short, sharp bark, as if he too had a word to say in defense of his young master.

"Is that your welcome to visitors, Bruno?" queried a young man of eighteen or twenty, alighting from his horse and coming up the steps to the veranda.

"Oh, please, you must excuse him for being so ill-mannered, Cousin Cal," little Elsie said, coming forward and offering her hand with a graceful curtsey very like her mamma's. "Will you walk into the drawing room? Our mothers are there."

"Presently, thank you," he said, bending down to snatch a kiss from the sweet lips.

She shrank from the caress almost with aversion.

"What's the use of being so shy with a cousin?" he asked laughingly. "Why, Molly Percival likes to kiss me."

"I think Molly would not be pleased if she knew you said that," remarked the little girl, in a quiet tone, and moving farther from him as she spoke.

"Holding a reception, eh?" he said, glancing about the group. "How d'ye, young ladies and gentlemen? Holloa, Ed! So you're the brave fellow that shot his father? Hope your grandfather dealt out justice to you in the same fashion that Wal and Dick's did to them."

Eddie could bear no more, but burst into an agony of tears and sobs.

"Calhoun Conly, do you think it very manly for a big fellow like you to torment such a little one as our Eddie?" queried Elsie, with rising indignation.

"No, I don't," he said frankly. "Never mind, Eddie, I take it all back, and own that the other two deserve the lion's share of the blame and punishment, too. Come, shake hands and let's make up."

Eddie gave his hand, saying in broken tones, "I was a disobedient son, but papa has forgiven me, and I don't mean ever to disobey him ever again."

CHAPTER SIXTH

So false is faction, and so smooth a liar,
As that it never had a side entire.

—DANIEL

By the first of December Mr. Travilla had entirely recovered from the ill effects of his accident—which had occurred early in the month of November—and life at Ion resumed its usual quiet, regular, but pleasant routine, varied only by frequent exchange of visits with the other families of connection, and near neighbors, especially the Leland family.

Because of the presence among them of their northern relatives, this winter was made a happier one than either of the last two, which had seen little mirth or joviality among the older ones, subdued as they were by recent, repeated bereavements. Time had now somewhat assuaged their grief, and only the widowed ones still wore their garb of mourning.

A round of family parties for old and young filled up the holidays; and again just before the departure of the Rosses and Allisons in the early spring, they were all gathered at Ion for a farewell day together.

Some of the blacks in Mr. Leland's employ had been beaten and otherwise maltreated only the previous night by a band of armed and disguised men, and the conversation naturally turned upon that awful occurrence.

"So the Ku Klux outrages have begun in our neighborhood," remarked Mr. Horace Dinsmore, and went on to denounce their proceedings in unmeasured terms.

The faces of several of his auditors flushed angrily. Enna shot a fierce glance at him, muttering, "scalawag" half under her breath, while his older father said testily, "Horace, you speak too strongly. I haven't a doubt the rascals deserved all they got. I'm told one of them at least had insulted some lady, Mrs. Foster, I believe, and that others had been robbing henroosts and smokehouses."

"That perhaps may be so, but at all events every man has a right to a fair trial," replied his son. "And so long as there is no difficulty in bringing such matters in front of the civil courts, there is no excuse for lynch law, which is apt to visit its penalties upon the innocent as well as the guilty."

At this, George Boyd, who, as the nephew of the elder Mrs. Carrington and a member of the Ashlands household, had been invited with the others, spoke warmly in defense of the organization, asserting that its main object was to defend the helpless, particularly in guarding against the danger of the insurrection of the blacks.

"There is not the slightest fear of that," remarked Mr. Travilla. "There may be some turbulent feelings among them, but as a class they are quiet and, I assure you, inoffensive."

"Begging your pardon, sir," said Boyd, "I find them quite the reverse—demanding their wages as soon as they are due, and not satisfied with what one chooses to give. And that reminds me that you, sir, and Mr. Horace Dinsmore, and that carpetbagger of Fairview are entirely too liberal in the wages that you pay."

"That is altogether our own affair, sir," returned Mr. Dinsmore, haughtily. "No man or set of men shall dictate to me how I spend my money. What do you say, Travilla?"

"I take the same position, and I shall submit to no such infringement of my liberty to do as I will with my own."

Elsie's eyes sparkled—proud of her husband and father. Rose, too, smiled and approved.

"Sounds very fine," growled Boyd, "but I say you've no right to put up the price of labor."

"Papa," cried young Horace, straightening himself and casting a withering look upon Boyd, "I hope neither you nor Brother Edward will ever give in to them a single inch. Such insolence!"

"Let us change the subject," said old Mr. Dinsmore. "It is not an agreeable one."

It so happened that a few days after this the Messrs. Dinsmore, Travilla, and Leland were talking together just within the entrance to the avenue at Ion when Wilkins Foster, George Boyd, and Calhoun Conly came riding by.

They brought their horses to a walk as they neared the gate, and Foster called out sneeringly, "Two scalawags and a carpetbagger! Fit company for each other."

"So we think, sir," returned Mr. Travilla coolly, "though we do not accept the epithets you so generously bestow upon us."

"It is an easy thing to call names; any fool is equal to that," said Mr. Leland, in a tone of unruffled good nature.

"True, and the weapon of vituperation is generally used by those who lack brains for argument or are on the wrong side," observed Mr. Dinsmore.

"Is that remark intended to apply to me, sir?" asked Foster, drawing himself up with an air of hauteur and defiance.

"Not particularly, but if you wish to prove yourself skilled in the other and more manly weapon, we are ready to give you the opportunity."

"Yes, come in, gentlemen, and let us have a free and friendly discussion," said Mr. Travilla.

Boyd and Conly at once accepted the invitation, but Foster, reining in his horse in the shade of a tree at the gate, said, "No, thank you; I don't care to alight, can talk from the saddle as well as anywhere. I call you scalawags, Messrs. Dinsmore and Travilla, because though natives of the south, you have turned against her."

"Altogether a mistake," observed Travilla.

"I deny the charge and call upon you to prove it," said Mr. Dinsmore.

"Easy task, you kept away and took no part in our struggle for independence."

"That is we (I speak for Travilla and myself) had no share in the effort to overthrow the best government in the world, the hope of the down-trodden and oppressed in all the earth. It was a struggle that we foresaw would prove, as it has, the almost utter destruction of our beloved South. They who inaugurated secession were no true friends to her."

"Sir," cried Boyd, with angry excitement, "ours was as righteous a cause as that of our revolutionary forefathers."

Mr. Dinsmore shook his head. "They fought against unbearable tyranny, and that, after having exhausted every other means of obtaining a redress of their grievances; and we had suffered no oppression at the hands of the general government."

"Hadn't we?" interrupted Foster fiercely. "Were the provisions of the Fugitive Slave Law carried out by the North? Didn't some of the Northern States pass laws in direct opposition to it? And didn't Yankee abolitionists come down here interfering with our institutions and enticing our Negroes to run away, or something worse?"

"Those were the acts of private individual states, entirely unsanctioned by the general government, which really had always favored us more than otherwise."

"But uncle," said Conly, "there would have been no secession but for the election of Lincoln, an abolitionist candidate."

"And who elected him? Who but the Democrats of the South? They made a division in the Democratic Party, purposely to enable the Republicans to elect their man, that they might use their man as a pretext for secession."

A long and hot discussion followed, each one present taking more or less part in it. It was first the causes of the war, and then the war itself. After that it was the reconstruction policies of Congress, which were bitterly denounced by Foster and Boyd.

"Never was a conquered people treated so shamefully!" cried the former. "It is a thing hitherto unheard of in the history of the world, that gentlemen should be put under the hand of their former slaves."

"Softly, sir," said Leland. "Surely you forget that the terms proposed by the fourteenth amendment substantially left the power of the state governments in your hands, and enabled you to limit suffrage and office to the white race. But you rejected it, and refused to take part in the preliminary steps for reorganizing your state governments. So the blacks acquired the right to vote and hold office. They were, as a class, well meaning, but ignorant, and their old masters refused to accept office at their hands, or advise them in regards to their new duties, so they fell an easy prey to unscrupulous white men, whose only care was to enrich themselves by robbing the already impoverished states, through corrupt legislation.* Now, sir, who was it that really put you under the rile of your former slaves, if you are there?"

Foster attempted no reply, but merely reiterated his assertion that no conquered people had ever been so cruelly used. Messrs. Travilla, Dinsmore, and Leland replied with a statement of facts. Before the war was fairly over, the government began to feed, clothe, shelter, and care for the destitute of both colors, and millions were distributed in supplies. In 1865 a bureau was organized for this purpose, and expended in relief, education, and aid to the people of both colors, and all conditions, thirteen million, two hundred and thirty thousand, three hundred and twenty seven dollars, and forty cents. Millions more were given by charitable associations and citizens of the North. The Government sold thousands of farm animals in the South, at low rates, and large quantities of clothing and supplies at merely nominal prices. There had been no executions for treason, no confiscation of lands, but that some estates abandoned by the owners during the war, and taken possession of and cultivated by the

Government, had been returned in better condition than they would have been in if permitted to lie idle. The railroads of the South were worn out by the war, woodwork rotted, rails and machinery totally worn out. The Government forces as they advanced, captured the lines, repaired the tracks, rebuilt bridges, and renewed the rolling stock. At the close of the war the Government might have held all these lines, but instead turned them over to the stockholders, sold them the rolling stock at low rates, and on long time, and advanced millions of dollars to the southern railroads. There were debts estimated, when the war began, at three hundred millions of dollars due the merchants of the North, but they compounded with their southern debtors, abating more than half their dues and extending time for the remainder. A bankrupt act was passed enabling those hopelessly involved to begin business anew. Sound institutions took the place of the old broken banks, and United States currency that of Confederate notes.*

Foster attempted no denial of these facts, but spoke bitterly of the corruption among the state government officials, resulting in ruinous taxation.

His antagonists freely admitted that there had been frauds and great extravagance, yet claimed that neither party was responsible for these, but members of both and persons belonging to neither who cared only for their own gains.* "And, who," they asked, "are responsible for their success in obtaining the positions which enable them thus to rob the community?"

"They had no vote from me," said Foster. "But, I say it again, we have been shamefully treated; if they'd confiscated my property and cut off my head, I'd have suffered less than I have as things have gone."

"Why not petition Congress for those little favors? Possibly it may not yet be too late," returned Leland, laughing.

This ended the talk. Foster put spurs to his horse and rode off in a rage.

"Come, Conly, we've surely had enough of this Republican discourse. Let us go, also," said Boyd, and with a hurried wave of his hand to the others, he hurried into the road and remounted.

But Conly did not follow. Elsie joined the group at that moment and laying her hand on his arm, said with one of her sweetest smiles, "Don't go, Cal, you must stay and take tea with us; it is already on the table."

"Thank you, I will," he said with a pleased look.

He was one of his cousin's ardent admirers, thinking her the most beautiful, intelligent, and fascinating woman he had ever seen.

She extended her invitation to Leland, Mr. Travilla seconded it warmly, but it was courteously declined, and each went his way.

"Papa, you will not forsake us?" Elsie inquired, putting both hands into his and smiling up into his face, her sweet soft eyes, brimful of fond, filial affection. "But you know you are at home and need no invitation."

"Yes," he said returning the smile, and holding the hands fast for a moment, "I am at home and shall stay for an hour or so."

CHAPTER SEVENTH

Disguise, I see though art a wickedness,
Wherein the pregnant enemy does much.

—*SHAKESPEARE'S TWELFTH NIGHT*

"WILL YOU WALK INTO the library, gentlemen? I have just received a package of new books, which, perhaps, you would like to examine," said Mr. Travilla to his guests as they left the tea table.

"Presently, thank you," Mr. Dinsmore answered, catching Elsie's eye, and perceiving that she had something for his private ear.

She took his arm and drew him out to her flower garden, while her husband and Calhoun together sought the library.

"Papa, I want a word with you about Cal. I do not like Foster and Boyd. That is, they seem to me to be unprincipled men, of violent temper and altogether very bad associates for him. You must have noticed how intimate he is with them of late."

"Yes, I regret it, but have no authority to forbid the intimacy."

"I know; but, papa, you have great influence; he is proud to be known as your nephew; and don't you think you might be able to induce him to give them up for some better friend; my brother, for instance? Papa, he is twenty-one now, and are not his principles sufficiently fixed to enable him to lead Cal and Arthur, doing them good instead of being injured by association with them?"

"Yes, you are right; Horace is not one to be easily led, and Calhoun is. I am glad you have spoken and reminded me of my duty."

"My dear father, please do not think I was meaning to do that," she cried blushingly. "It would be stepping out of my place. But Edward and I have had several talks about Cal of late, and decided that we will make him very welcome here, and try to do him good. Edward suggested, too, what a good and helpful friend Horace might be to him, if you approved, and I said I would speak to you first, and perhaps to my brother afterward."

"Quite right, I think Horace will be very willing. I should be loath to have him drawn into intimacy with Boyd or Foster, but as he likes neither their conduct nor their principles, I have little fear of that."

They sauntered about the garden a few moments longer, then rejoined the others, who were still in the library.

The children were romping with each other and Bruno on the veranda without—the merry shouts, the silvery laughter coming pleasantly in through the open windows.

"How happy they seem, Cousin Elsie," remarked Calhoun, turning to her.

"Yes, they are," she answered, smiling. "You are fond of children, Cal?"

"Yes, suppose you let me join them."

"Suppose we all do," suggested Mr. Dinsmore, seeing Travilla lay aside his book and listen with a pleased smile to the glad young voices.

"With all my heart," said the latter as he rose and led the way. "I find nothing more refreshing after the day's duties are done, than a romp with my children."

For the next half hour they were all children together; then Aunt Chloe and Dinah came to take the little ones to bed, and Elsie, after seeing her guests depart, followed to the nursery.

Mr. Dinsmore rode over to the Roselands with his nephew, conversing all the way in a most entertaining manner, making no allusion to politics or to Boyd and Foster.

Calhoun was charmed. When his uncle urged him to visit the Oaks more frequently, observing that he had been there but once since Horace's return from college, and proposing that he should begin by coming to dinner the next day and staying as long as suited his convenience, the invitation was accepted with alacrity and delight.

On returning home Mr. Dinsmore explained his views and wishes, with regard to Calhoun, to his wife and son, who at once cordially fell in with them in doing all they could to make his visit more enjoyable. In fact, so agreeable did he find it that his stay was prolonged to several days.

The morning papers brought news of several fresh Ku Klux outrages—beatings, shootings, and even a hanging.

Mr. Dinsmore read the account aloud at the breakfast table, and again made some remarks against the organization.

Calhoun listened in silence, then as Mr. Horace Dinsmore laid the paper down, "Uncle," said he doubtfully, and with a downcast troubled look, "don't you think the reconstruction acts form some excuse for the starting up of such an organization as the Klu Klux?"

"Let the facts answer," returned Mr. Dinsmore. "The organization existed as early as 1866; the reconstruction acts were passed in March, 1867."*

"Ah, yes, sir, I had forgotten the dates; I've heard that reason given; and another excuse is the fear of conspiracy among the Negroes to rob and murder the whites; and I think you can't deny that they can be thievish."

"I don't deny, Cal, that some individuals among them have been guilty of lawless acts, particularly stealing articles of food. But they are poor and ignorant—have been kept in ignorance so long that we can not reasonably expect in them a very strong sense of rights of property and the duty of obedience to the law. Yet I have never been able to discover any indication of combined lawlessness among them. On the contrary they are themselves fearful of attack."

"Well, sir, then there were those organizations in the other—the Republican Party, the Union Leagues, and Redstrings. I've been told the Ku Klux Klan was gotten up in opposition to them."

"I presume so, but all the Union Leaguers and Redstrings do not go about in disguise—robbing, beating, and murdering."

"But then the carpetbaggers," said Calhoun, waxing warm, "putting mischief into the Negroes' heads, getting into office and robbing the state in the most shameless wholesale manner—they're excuse enough for the doings of the Ku Klux."

"Ah!" said his uncle, "but you forget that their organization was in existence before the robberies of the state began. Also that they do not trouble corruptionists. And why? Because they are men of both parties. Some of them are men who direct and control, and might easily suppress the Klan. No, no, Cal, judged out of their own mouths, by their words to their victims, with some of whom I have conversed—their ruling motives are hostility to the government, to the enjoyment of the Negro of the rights given him by the amendment to the Constitution, and by the laws they are organized to oppose.* Their real object is the overthrow of the state governments and the return of the Negro to bondage. And, tell me, Cal, do you look upon these midnight attacks of overpowering numbers of disguised men upon the weak and helpless, some of them women, as manly deeds? Is it a noble act for white men to steal from the poor ignorant black his mule, his arms, his crops—all the fruit of his hard labor?"

"No, sir," returned Calhoun half-reluctantly, his face flushing hotly.

"No, emphatically no, say I!" cried Horace, Jr. "What could be more base, mean, or cowardly?"

"You don't belong, do you, Cal?" asked Rosie, quite suddenly.

He dropped his knife and fork, his face fairly ablaze, "What—what could make you think that, Rosie? No, no, I—don't belong to any organization that acknowledges that name."

A suspicion for the first time flashed upon Mr. Dinsmore, a suspicion of the truth. Calhoun Conly was already a member of the White Brotherhood, the name by which the Klan was known among themselves, Ku Klux being the one given to the world at large; that thus they might avail themselves of the miserable, Jesuitical subterfuge Calhoun had just used.

He had been wheedled into joining by Foster and Boyd, who utterly deceived him in regard to its objects. He had never taken part in the outrages and was now fully determined that he never would; resolving that while keeping its secrets—the penalty of the exposure of which was death—he would quietly withdraw and attend no more of its meetings. He understood the language of the searching look Mr. Dinsmore gave him and seized the first opportunity for a word in private to vindicate himself.

"Uncle," he said with frank sincerity, "I am not free to tell you everything, as I could wish, but I hope you will believe me when I assure you that I never had any share in the violent doings of the Ku Klux, and never will."

Mr. Dinsmore bent upon him a second look of keen scrutiny. Conly bore it without flinching. Extending his hand, his uncle replied, "I think I understand the situation, and I will trust you, Cal, and not fear that in entertaining you here I am harboring a hypocrite and spy who may betray my family and myself into the hands of midnight assassins."

"Thank you, uncle, you shall never have cause to repent of your confidence," the lad answered with a flush of honest pride.

He returned to Roselands the next day, and went directly to the upper room, at some distance from those usually occupied by the family, from whence came the busy hum of a sewing machine.

The door was securely fastened on the inner side, but opened immediately in response to three quick, sharp taps of a pencil that Calhoun took from his coat pocket.

It was his mother's face that looked cautiously out upon him. "Oh, you have returned," she said in an undertone. "Well, come in. I'm glad to see you."

He stepped in, and she locked the door again, and sitting down, resumed the work, which it seemed had been laid aside to admit him. She was making odd rolls of cotton cloth; stuffing them with cotton wool.

Mrs. Johnson, the only other person present, was seated before the sewing machine, stitching a seam in a long garment of coarse, white linen.

"How d'ye do, Cal?" she said, looking up for an instant to give him a nod.

He returned the greeting, and taking a chair by Mrs. Conly's side, "All well, mother?" he asked.

"Quite. You're just in time to tell me if these are going to look right. You know we've never seen any, and have only your description to go by."

She held up a completed roll. It looked like a horn, tapering nearly to a point.

"I think so," he said, "but, mother, you needn't finish mine. I shall never use it."

"Calhoun Conly, what do you mean?" she cried, dropping the roll into her lap, and gazing at him with fire in her eyes.

"You're not going to back out of it now, are you?" exclaimed his aunt, leaving her machine, and approaching him in sudden and violent anger. "You'd better take care, coward. They'll kill you if you turn coward, and right they should."

"I'll not turn traitor," he said quietly, "but neither shall I go any farther than I have gone. I should never have joined, if Boyd and Foster hadn't deceived me as to the objects of the organization."

"But you have joined, Cal, and I'll not consent to your giving it up," said his mother.

"I don't like to vex you, mother," he answered, reddening, "but—"

"But you'll have your own way, whether it displeases me or not? A dutiful son, truly."

"This is Horace's work, and he's a scalawag, if he is my brother," cried Enna, with growing passion, "but if I were you, Cal Conly, I'd be man enough to have an opinion of my own, and stick to it."

"Exactly what I'm doing, Aunt Enna. I went into the thing blindfold; I have found out what it really is—a cruel, cowardly, lawless concern—and I wash my hands of it and it's doings."

Bowing ceremoniously, he unlocked the door and left the room.

Enna sprang to it and fastened it after him. "If he was my son, I'd turn him out of the house."

"Father would hardly consent," replied her sister, "and if he did, what good would it do? Horace or Travilla would take him in, of course."

"Well, thank heaven, Boyd and Foster are made of sterner stuff and our labor's not all lost," said Enna, returning to her machine.

The two ladies had been spending many hours every day in that room for a week past, no one but Calhoun being admitted to their secrets. For whether in the room or out of it, they kept the door always carefully locked.

The curiosity of servants and children was strongly excited, but vain had been all their questions and coaxing, futile every attempt to solve the mystery up to the present time.

But three or four days after Calhoun's return from the Oaks, the thought suggested itself to mischievous, prying Dick and his co-conspirator Walter, that the key of some other lock in the house might fit that door they so ardently desired to open. They only waited for a favorable opportunity to test the question in the absence of their mothers from that part of the building. To their great joy, they discovered that the key of the bedroom they shared together was a duplicate of the one that had so long kept their masculine curiosity at bay.

It turned readily in the lock and with a smothered exclamation of delight they rushed in and glanced eagerly about.

At first they saw nothing in any way remarkable — the familiar furniture, the sewing machine, the work table and baskets of their mothers, a few shreds of white cotton and linen, a scrap here and there of red braid littering the carpet near the machine, and the low rocking chair used by Mrs. Conly.

"Pooh, nothing here to be secret about;" cried Walter, but Dick, nodding his head wisely said, "let's look a little further. What's in that closet?"

They ran to it, opened the door, and started back in sudden momentary affright.

"'Tain't alive," said Dick, the bolder of the two, quickly recovering himself. "Horrid thing! I reckon I know what 'tis." And he whispered a few words in his companion's ear.

Walter gave a nod of acquiescence in the opinion.

"Here's another 'most finished," pursued Dick, dragging out and examining a bundle he found lying on the closet floor. (The one that had startled them hung on the wall.) "We'll have some fun out of 'em one of these times when it's ready, eh, Wal?"

"Yes, but let's put 'em back, and hurry off now, for fear somebody should come and catch us. I'm afraid those folks in the drawing room may go, and our mothers come up to their work again."

"So they might, to be sure," said Dick, rolling up the bundle and restoring it to its former resting place. "We must be on the watch, Wal, or we'll miss our chance; they'll be sending them out o' this about as soon as they're finished."

"Yes. Who do you think they're for?"

The boys scorned the rules of English grammar, and refused to be fettered by them. Was not theirs a land of free speech—for the aristocratic class to which they undoubtedly belonged?

"Cal and Art, of course."

"Don't you believe it. Art cares for nothing but his books and Silverheels. Wasn't that a jolly birthday present, Dick? I wish Travilla and Cousin Elsie would remember ours the same way."

"Reckon I do. There, everything's just as we found it. Now let's skedaddle."

CHAPTER EIGHTH

A horrid spectre rises to my sight,
Close by my side, and plain, and palpable
In all good seeming and close circumstance
As man meets man.

—JOANNA BAILLIE

IT WAS A SULTRY SUMMER NIGHT, silent and still, not a leaf stirring, hardly so much as the chirp of an insect to be heard. The moon looked down from a cloudless sky upon green lawns and meadows, fields and forests clothed in the richest verdure; gardens, where bloomed lovely flowers in the greatest variety and profusion, filling the air in their immediate vicinity with an almost overpowering sweetness; a river flowing silently to the sea; cabins where the laborer rested from his toil, and lordlier dwellings where, perchance, the rich man tossed restlessly on his more luxurious couch.

Mr. and Mrs. Travilla had spent the earlier part of the evening at the Oaks, and after their return, tempted by the beauty of the night, had sat conversing together on the veranda long after their usual hour of retiring, but now they were both sleeping soundly.

Perhaps the only creature awake about the house or on the plantation, was Bungy the great watch dog, who, released from the chain that bound him during the day, was going his rounds keeping guard over his master's property.

A tiny figure clothed in white stole noiselessly from the house, flitted down the avenue out into the road beyond, and on and on till lost to the view in the distance. So light was the tread of the little bare feet, that Bungy did not hear it, nor was Bruno, sleeping on the veranda, aroused.

On and on it glided, the little figure, now in the shadow of the trees that skirted the roadside, now out in the bright moonbeams where they fell unimpeded upon dew laden grass and dusty highway alike.

Ion had been left more than a mile behind, yet farther and farther the small feet were straying, farther from home and love and safety, when a grotesque, hideous form suddenly emerged from a wood on the opposite side of the road.

Seeming of gigantic stature, it wore a long, white garment, that, enveloping it from head to foot, trailed upon the ground, rattling as it had moved, and glistening in the moonlight. The head was adorned with three immense horns, white, striped with red, a nose of proportionate size, red eyes and eyebrows, and a wide, grinning red month, filled with horrible tusks, out of which rolled a long, red tongue.

Catching sight of the small white form gliding along on the other side of the road, the creature uttered a low exclamation of mingled wonder, awe, and superstitious dread.

But at that instant a distant sound was heard like the rumble of approaching wheels, and it stepped quickly behind a tree.

Another minute or so and a stage came rumbling down the road. The hideous monster stepped boldly out from the shadow of the tree, there was the sharp crack of a rifle, and the driver of the stage tumbled from his high seat into the road. The horses started madly forward, but someone caught the reins and presently brought them to a standstill.

"Ku Klux!" loudly exclaimed several voices, as the trailing, rattling white gown disappeared in the recesses of the wood.

The stage door was thrown open, three or four men alighted, and going to the body, stooped over it, touched it, spoke to it, asking, "Are you badly hurt, Jones?"

But there was no answer.

"Dead, quite dead," said one.

"Yes, what shall we do with him?"

"Lift him into the stage and take him on to the next town."

The last speaker took hold of the head of the corpse, the others assisted, and in a few moments the vehicle was on its way again with a load of the living and dead.

No one had noticed the tiny white figure that was now crouched behind a clump of bushes weeping bitterly and talking to herself, but in a subdued way as if fearful of being overheard.

"Where am I? Oh, mamma, papa, come and help your little Vi! I don't know how I got here. Oh, where are you, my own mamma?" A burst of sobs, then "Oh, I'm so 'fraid! And mamma can't hear me, nor papa. But Jesus can. I'll ask Him to take care of me, and He will."

The small white hands folded themselves together and the low sobbing cry went up, "Dear Jesus, take care of your little Vi, and don't let anysing hurt her; and please bring papa to take her home."

At Ion little Elsie woke and missed her sister. They slept together in a room opening into the nursery off one side, and the bedroom of their parents on the other. Doors and windows stood wide open and the moon gave sufficient light for the child to see that Vi was no longer by her side.

Quietly slipping out of bed, she went softly about searching for her, thinking to herself all the while, "She's walking in her sleep again, dear little one, and I'm afraid she may get hurt; perhaps fall down the stairs."

She had heard such fears expressed by her papa and mamma since of late Violet had several times risen and strayed about the house in a complete state of somnambulism.

Elsie passed from room to room growing more and more anxious and alarmed every moment at her continued failure too find any trace of the missing one. She must have help.

Dinah, who had care of the little ones, slept in the nursery. Going up to her bed, Elsie shook her gently.

"What's de matter, honey?" asked the girl, opening her eyes and raising herself to a sitting posture.

"Where's Violet? I can't find her."

"Miss Wi'let? Ain't she fas' aseep side o' you, Miss Elsie?"

"No, no, she isn't there, nor in any of mamma's rooms. I've looked through them all. Oh, Dinah, where is she? We must find her. Come with me, quick!"

Dinah was already out of bed and turning up the night lamp.

"I'll go all ober de house, honey," she said, "but 'spect you better wake yo' pa. He'll want to look for Miss Wi'let hisself."

Elsie nodded assent, and hastening to his side softly stroked his face with her hand, kissed him, and putting her lips close to his ear, whispered half sobbingly, "Papa. Papa, Vi's gone. We can't find her anywhere, papa."

He was wide awake instantly. "Run back to your own bed, darling," he said, "and don't cry. Papa will soon find her."

He succeeded in throwing on his clothes and leaving the room without rousing his wife. He felt some anxiety, but the idea that the child had left the house never entered his mind until a thorough search seemed to give convincing proof that she was not in it.

He went out upon the veranda. Bruno rose, stretched himself, and uttered a low whine.

"Bruno, where is our little Violet?" asked Mr. Travilla, stooping to pat the dog's head and showing him the child's slipper. "Lead the way, sir; we must find her." There was the slightest tremble in his tones.

"Dinah," he said, turning to the girl who stood sobbing in the doorway, "if your mistress wakes while I am gone, tell her not to be alarmed. No doubt, with Bruno's help, I shall very soon find the child and bring her safely back. See, he has the scent already," as the dog who had been sniffing about suddenly started off in a brisk trot down the avenue toward the gate.

Mr. Travilla hurried after Bruno, his fatherly heart beating with mingled hope and fear.

On and on they went together, closely following the footsteps of the little runaway. The dog presently left the road that passed directly in front of Ion, and turned into another, crossing it at the right angles, which was the stage route between the next town and the neighboring city.

It was now ten or fifteen minutes since the stage had passed this spot bearing the dead body of the driver who had met his tragic end some quarter of a mile beyond.

The loud rumble of the wheels had awakened Vi, and as in a flash she had seen the whole—the horrible apparition in its glistening, rattling robes, step out from behind a tree and fire, and the tumble of its victim into the dusty road. Then she had sunk down upon the ground overpowered with terror.

But the thought of the almighty Friend, who, she had been taught, was ever near and able to help, calmed her fears somewhat.

She was still on her knees sobbing out her little prayer over and over again, when a dark object bounded to her side, and Bruno's nose was thrust unceremoniously into her face.

"Ah, papa will do that, now he has found his lost darling," said a loving voice, as a strong arm put aside the bushes, and grasped her small form with a firm, but tender hold. "How came my little one here so far away from home?" he asked, drawing her to himself.

"I don't know, papa," she sobbed, nestling in his arms and clinging about his neck, her wet cheek laid close to his. "That carriage waked me, and I was way out here, and that dreadful thing was over there by a tree, and it shooted the man, and he tumbled off on the ground. Oh, papa, hurry, hurry fast, and let's go home; it might come back and shoot us, too."

"What thing, daughter?" he asked, soothing her with tender caresses, as still holding her to himself, he walked rapidly toward home.

"Great big white thing, with horns, papa."

"I think my dear has been dreaming!"

"No, no, papa, I did see it, and it fired, and the man tumbled off, and the horses snorted and ran so fast; then they stopped and the other mans came back, and I heard them say, 'He's killed; he's quite dead.' Oh, papa, I'm so frightened!" She clung to him with convulsive grasp, sobbing almost hysterically.

"There, there, darling, papa has you safe in his arms. Thank God for taking care of my little darling," he said, clasping her closer. And quickening his pace, while Bruno wagging his tail and barking joyously, gamboled about them, now leaping up to touch his tongue to the little dusty toes, now bounding on ahead, and anon returning to repeat his loving caress; and so at last they arrived at home.

Mr. Travilla had scarcely left the house, ere the babe waked his mother. She missed her husband at once, and hearing a half-smothered sob coming from the room occupied by her daughters, she rose and with the babe in her arms, hastened to ascertain the cause.

She found Elsie alone, crying on the bed with her face half-hidden in the pillows.

"My darling, what is it?" asked the mother's sweet voice. "But where is Vi?"

"Oh, mamma, I don't know; that is the reason I can't help crying," said the child, raising herself and putting her arms around her mother's neck, as the latter sat down on the side of the bed. "But don't be alarmed, mamma, for papa has gone to find her."

At this moment Dinah appeared and delivered her master's message.

To obey his injunction not to be alarmed was quite impossible to the loving mother heart, but she endeavored to conceal her anxiety and to overcome it by casting her care on the Lord. The babe had fallen asleep again, and laying him gently down, she took Elsie in her arms and comforted her with caresses and words of hope and cheer.

"Mamma," said the little girl, "I cannot go back to sleep again till papa comes back."

"No, I see you can't, nor can I, so we will go put on our dressing gowns and slippers, and sit together at the window to watch for him, and when we see him coming up the avenue with Vi in his arms, we will run to meet them."

So they did, and the little lost one, found again, was welcomed by mother and sister and afterward by nurse and mammy, with tender loving words, caresses and tears of joy.

Then Dinah carried her to the nursery, washed the soiled, tired little feet, changed the bedraggled night-gown for a clean new one, and with many a hug and honeyed word, carried her back to her bed, saying, as she laid her down in it, 'Now, darlin', don't you get out ob heyah no mo' till mornin'.'"

"No, I'll hold her fast; and papa has locked the doors so she can't get out of these rooms," said Elsie, throwing an arm over Vi.

"Yes, hold me tight, tight," murmured Vi, cuddling down close to her sister, and almost immediately falling asleep, for she was worn out with both fatigue and excitement.

Elsie lay awake some time longer, her young heart singing for joy over her recovered treasure, but at length fell sleep also, with the murmur of her parents' voices in her ears.

They were talking together of Violet, expressing their gratitude to God that no worse consequences had resulted from her escapade, and consulting together how to prevent a repetition of it.

Mr. Travilla repeated to his wife the child's story of her awakening and what she had seen and heard.

"Oh my poor darling, what a terrible fright for her!" Elsie exclaimed. "Do you not think it must all have been a dream?"

"That was my first thought; but on further consideration I fear it may have been another Ku Klux outrage. I dare say, the disguise worn by them may answer to her description of 'the horrible thing that "shooted" the man.' I judge so from what I have heard of it."

"But who could have been the victim?" she asked with a shudder.

"I do not know. But her carriage was probably the stage; it was about the hour for it to pass."

Day was already dawning and the parents did not sleep again.

Mr. Travilla had gone on his regular morning round over the plantation, and Elsie stole softly into the room of her little daughters.

Though past their usual hour for rising they still slept and she meant to let them do so as long as they would. They made a lovely picture lying there clasped in each other's arms. Her heart swelled with tender emotions, love, joy, and gratitude to Him who had given these treasures and preserved them thus far from all danger and evil. She bent over them, pressing a gentle kiss upon each round rosy cheek.

Little Elsie's hazel eyes opened wide, and putting her arm about her mother's neck, "Mamma," she whispered, with a sweet, glad smile, "was not God very good to give us back our sweet Vi?"

"Yes, dearest, oh, so much better than any of us deserve!"

Violet started up to a sitting posture. "Mamma, oh mamma, I did have a dreadful, dreadful dream!—that I was way off from you and papa, out in the night in the woods, and I saw—"

She ended suddenly with a burst of frightened sobs and tears, hiding her face on the bosom of her mother who already held her closely clasped to her beating heart.

"Don't think of it, darling, you are safe now in your own sweet home with papa and mamma and sisters and brothers." Tender, soothing caresses accompanied the loving words.

"Mamma, did I dream it?" asked the child, lifting her tearful face, and shuddering as she spoke.

The mother was too truthful to say yes, though she would have been glad her child should think it but a dream.

"Perhaps some of it was, my daughter," she said, "though my darling did walk out in her sleep; but papa is going to manage things so that she can never do it again. And God will take care of us, my little darling."

The sobs grew fainter and softly sighing, "Yes, mamma," she said, "I asked Him to send papa to bring me home, and He did."

"And papa came in here this morning and kissed both his girls before he went downstairs. Did you know that?"

"Did he? Oh, I wished I'd waked up to give him a big hug!"

"I, too," said Elsie. "Papa loves us very much, doesn't he, mamma?"

"Dearly, my child; you are all his little ones."

Vi's tears were dried and when her father came in she met him with a cheerful face, quite ready for the customary romp, but days passed ere she was her own bright, merry self, or seemed content unless clinging close to one or the other of her parents.

While the family was at the breakfast table, Uncle Joe came in with the mail, his face full of excitement and terror.

"Dem Ku Kluxes, dey's gettin' awful dangerous, Massa," he said, laying down the bag with a trembling hand. "Dey's gone an' shot the stage drivah an' killed un dead on the spot. Las' night, sah, jes ober yondah in de road todder side o' Mars Leland's place, and—"

Mr. Travilla stopped him in the midst of his story, with a warning gesture and an anxious glance from one to another of the wondering, half-frightened little faces about the table.

"Another time and place, Uncle Joe."

"Yes, sah, beg pardon, sah, Massa Ed'ard," and the old man, now growing quite infirm from age, hobbled away talking to himself. "Sure nuff, you ole fool, Joe, might a' knowed you shouldn't tole no such tings fo' de chillun."

"Was it 'bout my dream, papa?" Vi asked with quivering lips and fast filling eyes.

"Never mind, little daughter, we needn't trouble about our dreams," he said cheerily, and began talking of something else, in a lively strain that soon set them all to laughing.

It was not until after family worship was over and the children had left the room that he said to his wife, "The Ku Klux were abroad last night and I have no doubt Uncle Joe's story is quite true, and that our poor little Vi really saw the murder."

Elsie gave him a startled, inquiring look. "You have other proof?"

"Yes, Leland and I met in going our rounds this morning, and he told me he had found a threatening note, signed 'K. K. K,' tacked to his gate, and had torn it down immediately, hoping to conceal the matter from his wife, who, he says is growing nervously fearful for his safety."

"Oh, what a dreadful state of things! Do these madmen realize that they are ruining their country?"

"Little they care for that, if they can but gain their ends—the subversion of the government, and the return of the Negro to his former state of bondage."

She was standing by his side, her hand on his arm. "My husband," she said in trembling tones, looking up into his face with brimming eyes, "what may they not do next? I begin to fear for you and my father and brother."

"I think you need not, little wife," he said, drawing her head to a resting-place on his shoulder, and passing his hand caressingly over her hair. I think they will hardly meddle with us, natives of the place, and men of wealth and influence. And," he added low and reverently, "are we not all in the keeping of Him without whom not one hair of our heads can fall to the ground?"

"Yes, yes, I will trust and not be afraid," she answered, smiling sweetly through her tears. Then catching sight, through the open window, of a couple of horsemen coming up the avenue, "Ah, there are papa and Horace now!" she cried, running joyfully out to meet them.

"Have you heard of last night's doings of the Ku Klux?" were the first words of Horace, Jr. when the greetings had been exchanged.

"Run away, dears, run away to your play," Elsie said to her children, and at once they obeyed.

"Uncle Joe came in this morning with a story that Jones, the stage driver, had been shot by them last night in this vicinity," Mr. Travilla answered, "but I stopped him in the midst of it, as the children were present. Is it a fact?"

"Only too true," replied Mr. Dinsmore.

"Yes," said Horace, "I rode into the town before breakfast, and found it full of excitement. The story's on everybody's tongue, and there is quite a large crowd by the door of the house where the body of the murdered man lay."

"And is the murderer still at large?" asked Elsie.

"Yes; and the worst of it is that no one seems to have the least idea who he is."

"The disguise preventing recognition, of course," said Mr. Travilla.

Then the grandfather and uncle were surprised with an account of little Vi's escapade.

"If Violet were my child," said Mr. Dinsmore, "I should consult Dr. Burton about her at once. There must be undue excitement of the brain that might be remedied by proper treatment."

Elsie cast an anxious look at her husband.

"I shall send for the doctor immediately," he said, and summoning a servant, dispatched him at once upon the errand.

"Don't be alarmed, daughter," Mr. Dinsmore said. "Doubtless a little care will soon set matters right with the child."

'Yes, I do not apprehend anything serious, if the thing is attended to in time," Mr. Travilla added cheerfully; then went on to tell of the notice affixed to Fairview gate.

They were all of the opinion that these evildoers, should, if possible, be brought to justice; but the nature and extent of the organization rendered it no easy matter for the civil courts to deal with them. The order being secret, the members were known as such only among themselves—when strangers, recognizing each other by secret signs. They were sworn to aid and defend a brother member under all circumstances; were one justly accused of a crime, others would come forward and prove an alibi by false swearing; were they on the jury, they would acquit him though perfectly cognizant of his guilt. In some places the sheriff and his deputies were members, perhaps the judge also.* Thus it happened that though one or two persons who had been heard to talk threateningly about Jones, as "a carpetbagger and Republican, who should be gotten rid of, by fair means or foul," were arrested on suspicion, they were soon at liberty again, and his death remained unavenged.

CHAPTER NINTH

I feel my sinews blackened with fright,
And a cold sweat mills down o'er my limbs
As if I were dissolving into water.

—DRYDEN

EARLY ONE EVENING A FEW DAYS subsequent to the tragic death of Jones, the Ion family carriage, well freighted, was bowling along the road leading toward the Oaks.

A heavy shower had laid the dust and cooled the air, and the ride past blooming hedgerows, and fertile fields was very delightful. The parents were in cheerful mood, the children gay and full of life and fun.

"Oh, yonder is grandpa's carriage coming this way!" cried Eddie as they neared the crossroad that must be taken to reach Roselands in the one direction, and the Ashlands in the other.

"Yes, turn out here, Solon, and wait for them to come up," said Mr. Travilla.

"On your way to the Oaks?" Mr. Dinsmore queried as his carriage halted along side of the other. "Well, we will turn about and go with you."

"No, we were going to Roselands but will put off the call to another day, if you were coming to Ion," Mr. Travilla answered.

No, the Dinsmores had not set out for Ion, but to visit Sophy at Ashlands; Daisy, her youngest child was very ill.

"I wish you would go with us, Elsie," Rose said to Mrs. Travilla. "I know it would be a comfort to Sophy to see you."

"Yes, we have plenty of room here," added Mr. Dinsmore, "and your husband and children can certainly spare you for an hour or so."

Elsie looked inquiringly at her husband.

"Yes, go, wife, if feel inclined," he replied pleasantly. "The children shall not lose their ride. I will go on to Roselands with them, make a short call, as I have a little business with your grandfather, then take them home."

"And we will have their mother there probably shortly after," said Mr. Dinsmore.

So the exchange was made and the carriages drove on, taking opposite directions when they came to the crossroad.

Arrived at Roselands, Mr. Travilla found only the younger members of the family at home, the older gentleman having driven out with his daughters. Calhoun thought however that they would return shortly, and was hospitably urgent that the visitors should all come in and rest and refresh themselves.

The younger cousins joined in the entreaty, and, his own children seeming desirous to accept the invitation, Mr. Travilla permitted them to do so.

They, with Aunt Chloe and Dinah, were presently carried off to the nursery by Molly Percival and the Conly girls, while their father walked into the grounds with Calhoun and Arthur.

"Wal," whispered Dick to his cousin, drawing him aside unnoticed by the rest, who were wholly taken up with each other, "now's our time for those Ku Klux things. They must be near done, and I reckon be packed off out o' the house afore long.

Walter nodded assent. They stole unobserved from the room, flew up to their own for the key, and hurried to the sewing room of their mothers. And finding there two disguises nearly completed, sufficiently so far for their purpose, arrayed themselves in them, slipped unseen down a back staircase, and dashing open the nursery door, bounded with a loud whoop, into the midst of its occupants.

Children and nurses joined in one wild shriek of terror, and made a simultaneous rush for the doors, tumbling over each other in their haste and affright.

But fortunately for them, Mr. Travilla and Calhoun had come in from the grounds, were on their way to the nursery, and entered it from the hall but a moment later than the boys did by the opposite door.

Mr. Travilla instantly seized Dick—Calhoun doing the same by Walter—tore off his disguise, and picking up a riding whip, lying conveniently at hand, administered a castigation that made the offender yell and roar for mercy.

"You scoundrel!" replied the gentleman, still laying on his blows, "I have scant mercy for a great strong boy who amuses himself by frightening women and little children."

"But you're not my father, and have no right, oh, oh, oh!" blubbered Dick, trying to dodge the blows and wrench himself free. "I'll—I'll sue you for assault and battery."

"Very well, I'll give you plenty while I'm about it, and if you don't want a second dose, you'll refrain from frightening my children in the future."

It was an exciting scene. Walter was getting almost as severe a handling from Calhoun. The nurses and children were huddling together in the farthest corner of the room, Baby Herbert screaming at the top of his voice, and the others crying and sobbing while shrinking in nervous terror from the hideous disguises lying in a heap upon the floor.

"Oh, take them away! Take them away, the horrid things!" screamed Virginia Conly, shuddering and hiding her face. "Wal and Dick, you wicked wretches, I don't care if they half kill you."

"Papa, papa, please stop. Oh, Cal, don't whip him any more. I'm sure they'll never do it again," pleaded little Elsie amid her sobs and tears, holding Vi fast and trying to soothe and comfort her.

"There, go," said Calhoun, pushing Walter from the room, "and if ever I catch you at such a trick again, I'll give you twice as much."

Dick, released from his captor with a like threat, hastened after his fellow delinquent, blubbering and muttering angrily as he went.

Calhoun gathered up the awful disguises, threw them in a closet, locked the door and put the key in his pocket.

"There!" he said, "they're out of sight and couldn't come after us if they were alive. There's no life in them — little else but linen and cotton."

Baby Herbert ceased his cries and cuddled down on Aunt Chloe's shoulder; the other four ran to their father.

He encircled them all in his arms, soothing them with caresses and words of fatherly endearment. "There, there, my darlings, dry your tears. Papa will take care of you; nothing shall hurt you."

"Papa, they's like that horrid thing that shooted the man," sobbed Vi, clinging to him in almost frantic terror. "Oh don't let's ever come here any more!"

"I so frightened, papa, I so frightened; p'ease tate Harold home," sobbed the little fellow, the others joining in the entreaty.

"Yes, we will go at once," said Mr. Travilla rising, Vi in one arm, Harold in the other, and motioning to the servants to follow, he was about to leave the room when Calhoun spoke.

"Do not go yet, Mr. Travilla. I think Grandpa and the ladies will be here directly."

"Thanks, but I will see Mr. Dinsmore at another time. Now, my first duty is to these absolutely terrified little ones."

"I am exceedingly sorry for what has occurred; more mortified than I can express—"

"No need for apology, Conly; but you must see the necessity for our abrupt departure. Good evening to you all."

Calhoun followed to the carriage door, helped to put the children in. Then addressing Mr. Travilla, "I see you doubt me, sir," he said, "and not without reason, I own. Yet I assure you I have no property in these disguises, never have worn, and never will wear such a thing—much less take part in the violence they are meant to protect from punishment."

"I am glad to hear you say so, Cal. Good evening, sir," and the carriage whirled away down the avenue toward home.

The rapid motion, and the feeling that the objects of their affright were far behind, seemed to soothe and reassure the children, yet each sought to be as near as possible to their loved protector.

Harold and the babe soon fell asleep, and on reaching home were carried directly to bed; but the older ones begged so hard to be allowed to "stay with papa till mamma came home" that he could not find it in his heart to refuse them.

The Dinsmore party found Sophy devoting herself to her sick child. The attack had been sudden and severe. All the previous night the mother had watched by the couch of the little sufferer with an aching heart, fearing she was to be taken from her; but now the danger seemed nearly over, a favorable change having taken place during the day.

Daisy had fallen into a deep slumber, and leaving the nurse to watch at the bedside, the mother received and conversed with her friends in an adjoining room.

Though evidently glad to see them, she seemed, after the first few moments, so depressed and anxious, that at length her sister remarked it, and asked if there were any cause other than Daisy's illness.

"Yes, Rose," she said, "I must own that I am growing very timid in regard to these Ku Klux outrages. Since they have taken to beating and shooting whites as well as blacks, women as well as men, who shall say that we are safe? I, a Northern woman, too, and without a protector."

"I do not think they will molest a lady of your standing," said Mr. Dinsmore, "the widow, too, of a Confederate officer. But where is Boyd, that you say you are without a protector?"

A slight shudder ran over Sophy's frame. "Boyd?" she said, drawing her chair nearer and speaking in an undertone. "He is my great dread, and for fear of wounding mother's feelings I have had to keep my terrors to myself. I know that he is often out, away from the plantation all night. I have for weeks past suspected that he was Ku Klux, and last night, or rather early this morning, my suspicions were so fully confirmed that they now amount almost to certainty. I had been up all night with Daisy, and a little before sunrise happening to be at the window, I saw him stealing into the house with a bundle under his arm, a—something white rolled up in the careless sort of way a man would do it."

"I am not surprised," said Mr. Dinsmore. "He is just the sort of man one would expect to be at such work—headstrong, violent tempered, and utterly selfish and unscrupulous. Yet I think you may dismiss your fears of him, and feel it rather a safeguard than otherwise to have a member of the Klan in your family."

"It may be so," she said, musingly, the cloud of care partially lifting from her brow.

"And at all events you are not without a protector, dear sister," whispered Rose, as she bade adieu. "'A father of the fatherless, and a judge of the widows is God in His holy habitation.'"

Elsie, too, had a word of sympathy and hope for her childhood friend, and with warm invitations to both the Oaks and Ion as soon as Daisy could be moved with safety, they left her, greatly cheered and refreshed by their visit.

"My own heart aches for her;" Elsie remarked as they drove away, "what a sad, terribly sad thing to be a widow!"

"Yes," responded Rose, "and to have lost your husband so—fighting against the land of your birth and love."

There was a long pause broken by a sudden, half-frightened exclamation from Rosie. "Papa! What if we should meet the Ku Klux?"

"Not much danger, I think; they are not apt to be abroad so early. And we are nearing Ion."

"I presume Edward has reached home before us," remarked Elsie. "I wonder how my little ones enjoyed their first visit to Roselands without their mother nearby."

She soon learned; for she had scarcely set foot on the veranda ere they were clinging about her and pouring out the story of their terrible fright.

She pitied, soothed, and comforted them, trying to dispel their fears and lead them to forgive those who had so ill-used them, though it cost no small effort to do so herself.

CHAPTER TENTH

Forgive, and ye shall be forgiven.

—*L*UKE 6:27

CALHOUN CONLY WAS MUCH perturbed by the occurrences of the evening. He was fond of his cousin Elsie and her children, and very sorry, for both her sake and theirs, that they had suffered this fright. He greatly respected and liked Mr. Travilla, too, and would feign have stood well in his esteem. He had hoped that he did, and also with his cousin Horace. He had been so kindly treated, especially of late, at both Ion and the Oaks; but now this unfortunate episode had placed him in a false position, and he could hardly expect to be again trusted or believed in.

Such were his cogitations as he sat alone on the veranda after the Ion carriage had driven away. "What shall I do?" he asked himself. "What shall I do to recover their good opinion?"

Just then Walter appeared before him, looking crestfallen and angry.

"I say, Cal, it's bad enough for you to have thrashed me as you did, without bringing mother and Aunt Enna, and maybe grandfather, too, down on me about those wretched masks and things, so give 'em up and let Dick and me put 'em back before they get home."

"Of course, put them back as fast as you can; pity you hadn't let them alone," said Calhoun rising. With a quick step leading the way to the nursery he added, "We must see what we can do to keep the young ones from blabbing; else putting them back will help your case very little."

"Oh, we'll never be able to do that!" exclaimed Walter, despairingly. "One or another of 'em is sure to let it out directly. And there come the folks now," as the rolling of wheels was heard in the avenue. "It's of no use. They'll know all about it in five minutes."

"Yes, sir, you and Dick have got yourselves into a fine box, besides all the trouble you've made for other people," said Calhoun angrily. Then, laying his hand on Walter's arm, as he perceived that he was meditating flight, "No, sir, stay and face the music like a man. Don't add cowardice to all the rest of it."

They heard the clatter of little feet running through the house and out onto the veranda, the carriage draw up before the door, then the voices of children pouring out the story of their fright, and the punishment of its authors, and the answering tones of their grandfather and the ladies—Mr. Dinsmore's expressing surprise and indignation, Enna's full of passion, and Mrs. Conly's of cold displeasure.

"Let go o' me! They're coming this way," cried Walter, trying to wrench himself free.

But the inexorable Calhoun only tightened his grasp and dragged him on to the nursery.

Dick was there trying to pick the lock of the closet door with his pocket knife.

"What are you about, sir? No more mischief today, if you please," exclaimed Calhoun, seizing him with his free hand, the other having enough to do to hold Walter.

"Give me the key, then," cried Dick, vainly struggling to shake off his cousin's strong grip.

The words were hardly off the boy's tongue when the door was thrown open and Mr. Dinsmore and his daughters entered hastily, followed by the whole crowd of younger children.

"Give you the key, indeed! I'd like to know how you got hold of mine and how you dared to make use of it as you have, you young villain! There, take that, and that! Hold him fast, Cal, till I give him a little of what he deserves," cried Mrs. Johnson, rushing upon her son in a towering passion, and cuffing him right and left with all her strength.

"Let me alone!" he roared. "'Tain't fair—old Travilla's hand half-killed me already."

"I'm glad of it! You ought to be half-killed and you won't get any sympathy from me, I can tell you."

"And you had a share in it, too, Walter?" Mrs. Conly was saying in freezing tones. "If you think he deserves any more than you gave him, Cal, you have my full permission to repeat the dose."

"Where are they who have caused of all this unseemly disturbance?"demanded the elder Mr. Dinsmore severely. "Calhoun, if you have the key to that closet and those wretched disguises are there, produce them at once."

The young man obeyed, while Enna, holding Dick fast, turned a half-frightened look upon her sister, to which the latter, standing with her arms folded and her back braced against the wall, replied with one of cold, haughty indifference.

Calhoun drew out the obnoxious articles and held them up to view, a flush of mortification upon his face.

The children screamed and ran.

"Be quiet! They can't hurt you at all," said the grandfather, stamping his foot. Then, turning to Calhoun, "Ku Klux—your property and Arthur's I presume—you are members doubtless?" and he glanced from one to the other of his older grandsons in mingled anger and scorn, Arthur having just entered the room to ascertain the cause of the unusual commotion.

He flushed hotly at his grandsire's words and look. "I, sir! I a Ku Klux?" he exclaimed in a hurt, indignant tone. "I, a midnight assassin stealing upon my helpless victims under cover of darkness and a hideous disguise? No, sir! How could you think so ill of me? What have I done to deserve it?"

"Nothing, my boy. I take it all back," said the old gentleman, with a grim smile. "It is not like you—a quiet, bookish lad, with nothing of the coward or the bully about you. But you, Calhoun?"

"I have no property in these, sir; and I should scorn to wear one or to take part in the deeds you have spoken of."

"Right. I am no Republican and was as strong for secession as any man in the South, but I am for open, fair fight with my own enemies or those of my country—no underhanded dealings for me, no cowardly attacks in overwhelming numbers upon the weak and defenseless. But, if these disguises are not yours, whose are they? And how came they here?"

"I must beg leave to decline answering that question, sir," replied Calhoun respectfully.

His mother and aunt exchanged glances.

"Ah!" exclaimed their father, turning to Enna, as with a sudden recollection. "I think I heard you claiming some property in these scarecrows. Speak out. Are they yours?"

"No, sir, but I'm not ashamed to own that I helped make them and that if I were a man I would wear one."

"You? You helped make them? And who, pray, helped you? Louise—"

"Yes, sir, Louise it was," replied Mrs. Conly drawing herself up to her full height, "and she is no more ashamed to own it, than is her sister. And if Calhoun was a dutiful son he would be more than willing to wear one."

"If you were a dutiful daughter, you would never have engaged in such business in my house without my knowledge and consent," retorted her father, "and I'll have no more of it, let me tell you, Madams Conly and Johnson—no aiding or abetting these midnight riders."

Then, turning to a servant, he ordered her to "take the hideous things into the yard and make a bonfire of them."

"No!" cried Enna. "Do you understand that you are ordering the destruction of another's property?"

"It makes no difference," he answered coolly. "They are forfeit by having been brought surreptitiously into my house. Carry them out, Fanny, do you hear? Carry them out and burn them."

"And pray, sir, what am I to say to the owners when they claim their property?" asked Enna with flashing eyes.

"Refer them to me," replied her father, leaving the room to see that his orders were duly executed.

Calhoun and Arthur had already slipped away. Dick was about to follow, but his mother again seized him by the arm, this time shaking him violently. She must have someone on whom to vent the rage that was consuming her.

"You—you bad, troublesome, wicked boy! I could shake the very life out of you!" she hissed through her shut teeth, suiting the action to the word. "A pretty mess you've made of it, you and Walter. Your birthday coming next week, too. There'll be no presents from Ion for you, you may rest assured. I hoped Mr. Travilla would send you each a handsome suit, as he did last year; but, of course, you'll get nothing now."

"Well, I don't care," muttered Dick. "It's your fault for making the ugly things." And freeing himself by a sudden jerk, he darted from the room.

Children and servants had trooped after Mr. Dinsmore to witness the conflagration, and Dick's sudden exit left the ladies sole occupants of the apartment.

"I declare it's too bad—too provoking for endurance!" exclaimed Enna, bursting into a flood of angry tears.

"What's the use of taking it so hard?" returned her sister.

"You're a perfect iceberg," retorted Enna.

"Well, that would account for my not crying over our misfortune, I presume—my tears being all frozen up," returned Mrs. Conley with an exasperating smile. "Well, there is comfort in all things. We may now congratulate ourselves that Foster and Boyd did not wait for these but supplied themselves elsewhere."

There was a difference of two years in the ages of Dick Percival and Walter Conly, but they were born on the same day of the same month, and their birthdays would occur in less than a week.

"I say, Wal, what precious fools we've been," remarked Dick as the two were preparing to retire that night. "Why didn't we remember how near it was to our birthday? Of course, as mother says, there'll be no presents from Ion this time."

"No, and I wish I'd never seen the hateful things," grumbled Walter, "but there's no use crying over spilt milk."

"No, and we'll pretend we don't care a cent. Mother shan't have the satisfaction of knowing that I do, anyhow," and Dick whistled a lively tune as he pulled off his boots and tossed them into a corner.

At about the same time, Elsie and her husband, seated alone together on their veranda, were conversing on the same subject. Mr. Travilla introduced it. They had been regretting the effect of the fright of the evening upon their children—Vi especially as the one predisposed to undue excitement of the brain—yet hoping it might not prove lasting.

Elsie had just returned from seeing them to bed. "I left them much calmed and comforted," she said, "by our little talk together of God's constant watch over us, His all-powerful and protecting care and love, and by our prayer that He would have them in His keeping."

He pressed her hand in silence, then presently remarked, "The birthday of those boys is near at hand. They certainly deserve no remembrance from us, but how do you feel about it?"

"Just as my noble, generous husband does," she said, looking up into his face with a proud, fond, and sweet smile.

"Ah, and how is that?"

"Like giving them a costlier and more acceptable present than ever before; thus, 'heaping coals of fire upon their heads.'"

"And what shall it be?"

"Whatever you think they would prefer and would not that be a pony apiece?"

"No doubt of it; and I will try to procure two worth having before the day comes round."

Talking with her little ones the next morning, Elsie told them of the near approach of the birthday of Dick and Walter, spoke of the duty of forgiveness and the return of good for evil, and asked who of them would like to make their cousins some nice present.

"I should, mamma," said little Elsie.

Eddie looked up into his mother's face, dropped his head, and blushing deeply muttered, "I'd rather flog them like papa and Cal did."

"So would I; they're naughty boys!" cried Vi, the tears starting to her eyes at the remembrance of the panic of fear their conduct had cost her and her brothers and sisters.

Their mother explained that it was papa's duty to protect his children from injury, and that that was why he had flogged naughty Dick; but now he had forgiven him and was going to return good for evil, as the Bible bids us. "And you must forgive them, too, dears, if you want God to forgive you," she concluded, "for Jesus says, 'If you forgive not men their trespasses, neither will your Father forgive your trespasses.'"

"I simply can't, mamma. I can't love them," said Eddie stoutly.

"Ask God to help you, then, my son."

"But mamma, I can't ask Him with my heart, 'cause I don't want to love them or forgive them."

"Can my boy do without God's forgiveness — without Jesus' love?" she asked, drawing him to her side. "You feel very unhappy when papa or mamma is offended with you. Can you bear your heavenly Father's frown?"

"Don't look so sorry, dear mamma. I love you ever so much," he said, putting his arms about her neck and kissing her again and again.

"I cannot be happy while my own dear little son indulges in such sinful feelings," she said, softly smoothing his hair, while a tear rolled down her cheek.

"Mamma, how can I help it?"

"Try to think kind thoughts of your cousins, do them all the kindness you can, and ask God to bless them, and to help you to love them. I want my little Vi to do so, too," she added, turning to her.

"Mamma, I will. I don't 'tend to say cross things 'bout 'em any more," Violet answered impulsively. "And I'll give 'em the nicest present I can get with all my pocket money."

"Mamma, must I give them presents as well?" asked Eddie.

"No, son, I do not say you must. You shall decide for yourself whether you ought to, and whether you will."

"Mamma, they made me hurt my dear father."

"No, Eddie, no one can *make* us do wrong. We choose for ourselves whether or not we will resist temptation or yield to it."

"Mamma, what shall we give?" asked the little girls together.

"Talk it over between yourselves, daughters. Decide how much you are willing to spend on them and what your cousins would probably like best. I want my children to think and choose for themselves, where it is proper that they should."

"But mamma, you will 'vise us."

"Yes, Vi, you may consult me, and shall have the benefit of my opinion."

The little girls held several private consultations during the day and in the evening came with a report to their mother. Elsie was willing to appropriate five dollars to the purpose, Vi three, and the gifts were to be books, if mamma approved and would help them select suitable ones.

"I think you have decided wisely," she said, "and as it is too warm for us to drive to the city, we will ask papa to order a variety sent out here, and he and I will help you in making a choice."

Eddie was standing by. Nothing had been said to him on the subject since his morning talk with his mother, but all day he had been unusually quiet and thoughtful.

"Mamma," he now said, "I've been trying to forgive them, and I'm going to buy two riding whips, one for Dick and one for Wal, if you and papa would like me to."

Her smile was very sweet and tender as she commended his choice, and told him his resolve had made her very happy.

The birthday found Dick and Walter in sullen, discontented moods, in spite of their resolve not to care for the loss of all prospects of gifts in honor of their birthdays.

"What's the use of getting up?" growled Dick. "It's an awful bore, the way we've been sent to Coventry ever since we got into that scrape with the young ones. I've a mind to lie abed and pretend sick just to scare mother and pay her off for her crossness."

"Maybe you might get sick in earnest," suggested Walter. "I'm going to get up anyhow," and he tumbled out upon the floor, "for it's too hot to lie in bed. Hark! There's Pomp coming up the stairs to call us now. Why what's all that, Pomp?" as the servant rapped, then pushing open the door, handed in a number of brown paper parcels.

"Dunno, Mars Wal," replied the man grinning from ear to ear. "Somethin' from Ion, an de rest's down stairs—one for each ob you."

"One what?" queried Dick, starting up and with one bound placing himself at Walter's side.

"Birthday present, sahs. Wish you many happy returns, Mars Wal and Mars Dick, an' hope you'll neber wear no mo' Ku Klux doins."

But the lads were too busily engaged in opening the parcels and examining their contents to hear or heed his words.

"Two riding whips—splendid ones—and four books!" exclaimed Walter. "And here's a note."

"Here, let me read it," said Dick. "I declare, Wal, I'm positively ashamed to have them send me anything after the way I've behaved."

"I, too. But what do they say?"

"It's from Travilla and Cousin Elsie," said Dick turning to the signature. "I'll read it out."

He did so. It was very kind and pleasant, made no allusion to their wrong doing, but congratulated them on the return of the day, begged their acceptance of the accompanying gifts, stating from whom each came, the largest a joint present from themselves. It closed with an invitation to spend the day at Ion.

"Oh, I'm more ashamed than ever, aren't you, Wal?" Dick said, his face flushing hotly as he laid the note down.

"Yes, never felt so mean in my life. To think of that little Eddie sending us these splendid whips, and the little girls these pretty books. I 'most wish they hadn't."

"But where's 'the larger gift' they say is 'a joint present from themselves'?"

"Oh, that must be what Pomp called the rest left downstairs. Come, let's hurry and get down there to see what it is."

Dressing was attended to in hot haste and in a wonderfully short time the two were on the front veranda in eager quest of the mysterious present.

Each boyish heart gave a wild bound of delight as their eyes fell upon a group in the avenue, just before the entrance—two beautiful ponies, ready saddled and bridled, in charge of an Ion servant. Old Mr. Dinsmore, Calhoun, and Arthur were standing near examining and commenting upon them with evident admiration.

"Oh, what beauties!" cried Dick, bounding into the midst of the group. "Whose are they, Uncle Joe?"

"Well, sah," answered the old Negro, pulling off his hat and bowing first to one, then to the other, "dey's sent heyah by Massa Travilla and Miss Elsie, for two boys 'bout de size o' you, dat don' neber mean to frighten young chillen no mo'."

The lads hung their heads in silence, the blush of shame on their cheeks.

"Do you answer to that description?" asked Calhoun, a touch of scorn in his tones.

"Yes, for we'll never do it again," said Walter. "But it's too much; they're too kind!" and he fairly broke down and turned away his head to hide the tears that would come into his eyes.

"That's a fact!" assented Dick, nearly as much moved as his cousin.

"You don't deserve it," said their grandfather, severely, and I'm much inclined to send them back, with a request that if they're offered you again it shall not be till a year of good conduct on your part has atoned for the past."

"Oh, grandpa, you couldn't be so hard, so very hard!" cried Dick imploringly, stroking and patting the pony nearest him. "They're such beauties."

"I should think you'd be ashamed to accept such gifts after the way you behaved," said Arthur.

"So we are; but wouldn't it be worse to send 'em back? Awful rude, I should say." Dick turned a half-saucy, half-beseeching look upon his grandfather.

The old gentleman smiled in spite of himself and consented, in consideration of the boys' penitence for the past and fair promises for the future, to allow them to accept the generous gifts.

Uncle Joe explained which was for Dick and which for Walter, and springing into their saddles they were off like a shot, their grandfather calling after them to be back in ten minutes if they wanted any breakfast.

CHAPTER ELEVENTH

If thine enemy hunger, feed him;
if he thirsts give him drink;
for in so doing thou shalt heap
coals of fire on his head.
Be not overcome of evil,
but overcome evil with good.

—*R*OMANS *12:20&21*

"OH, HOW SPLENDID!" cried Dick, wheeling about toward home, now half a mile away, "but we must hurry back or grandpa will be mad. I say, Wal, what *do* you s'pose makes Travilla and Cousin Elsie so different from us? I mean all of us at Roselands."

"I don't know" returned Walter reflectively. "Maybe because they're Christians. You know it says in the Bible we're to return good for evil."

"Yes, and so heap coals of fire on our enemies' heads. And, Wal, I feel 'em burn now. I'd give anything not to have coaxed and teased Ed into shooting that time and not to have scared him and the others with those frightful disguises."

"So would I. And we'll never do the like again, Dick, never. Will we?"

"I reckon not. And we must ride over to Ion after breakfast and tell 'em so and thank 'em for these beauties and the other things."

"Yes, didn't the note from the Travillas invite us to spend the day there?"

"Why, so it did! But I'd forgotten—the sight of these ponies knocked it all out of my head."

So great was the delight of the lads in their new acquisitions, that not even the repeated assertions of their mothers and other members of the family—seconded by the reproaches of their own consciences—that they did not deserve it, could materially dampen their joy.

An ungracious permission to accept the invitation to Ion was granted them with the remark that Calhoun and Arthur, who were included in it, would be there to keep them in order and also to report upon their conduct.

Calhoun, troubled and mortified by the suspicions which he imagined must have been entertained against him at both the Oaks and Ion since the escapade of Dick and Walter, had kept him closely at home during the past week. He had studiously avoided meeting either his uncle or Travilla, but this invitation, as the holding out of the olive branch of peace, was joyfully accepted.

The four rode over to Ion together directly after breakfast and found themselves greeted with the greatest kindness and cordiality by Mr. Travilla, Elsie, and the children, all gathered on the veranda awaiting their coming.

The two culprits, shame-faced in view of their ill-deserts, yet overflowing with delight in their ponies, poured out mingled thanks and apologies and promises for the future.

"Never mind, my lads, we'll say nothing more about it," Mr. Travilla said in his kind, cheery way, Elsie adding, "You are very welcome and we are sure you do not intend ever again to try to alarm our darlings or tempt them to do wrong."

She led the way to her beautiful summer parlor—a large, lofty apartment with frescoed walls and ceiling. The floor was a mosaic of various colored marbles with a bubbling fountain in the center with gold and silver fish swimming in its basin. The windows were draped with vines and at the farther end there was a lovely grotto where a second fountain threw showers of spray over moss-grown rocks and pieces of exquisite statuary.

Here they were presently joined by their Cousin Horace. Ices and fruits were served and the morning passed in a most agreeable manner, enlivened by music, conversation, and a variety of quiet games—Mr. and Mrs. Travilla laying themselves out for the entertainment of their guests.

Their children had been excused from lessons in honor of the day and with their sweet prattle and merry, pretty ways, contributed not a little to the enjoyment of their elders.

Mr. Dinsmore came to dinner. Calhoun fancied his manner rather cool toward him, while Dick and Walter were left in no doubt of his stern disapproval of them, until their Cousin Elsie said a few words to him in a quiet aside, after which there was a decided change for the better.

Calhoun watched his cousin furtively, as he had of late formed a habit of doing. And as he studied her character, his respect, admiration, and affection grew apace. He found her utterly unselfish and sincere, so patient and forbearing, yet firm for the right, so unaffectedly cheerful and happy.

Something of this he remarked to her when for a few moments they chanced to be alone together.

"Ah," she said smiling and blushing, "it is not, my cousin, love alone that is blind; you have been looking at me through rose-colored spectacles, as so many of my relatives and friends do."

"But are you not really happy, cousin?"

"Happy? Ah, yes, indeed! Have I not everything to make me so? I have the best of husbands and fathers, five darling children. I have comparative youth, health, and wealth that enables me to prove in my own sweet experience the truth of those words of the Lord Jesus, 'It is more blessed to give than to receive.' And best of all," she added low and reverently, the soft eyes shining through glad tears, "I have His love and tender care surrounding me, His strong arm to lean upon, His blood to wash away my sins, and His perfect righteousness put upon me. These, cousin, are more than all the rest, and you and everyone may have them if you will for His own words are 'Ask and ye shall receive; seek and ye shall find.' 'Him that cometh unto me, I will in no wise cast out.'"

"You give me a new view of religion," he said after a moment's surprised, thoughtful silence. "I have been accustomed to look upon it as something suitable, perhaps desirable, for old age, and certainly very necessary for a death bed, but too great a restraint upon youthful pleasures."

"Sinful pleasures must indeed be given up by those who would follow Christ; but they are like apples of Sodom—beautiful in appearance, but bitter and nauseous to the taste, while the joys that He gives are pure, sweet, abundant and satisfying. 'Godliness is profitable unto all things, having promise of the life that now is, and of that which is to come.' 'They shall be abundantly satisfied with the fatness of thy house, and thou shalt make them drink of the river of thy pleasures.' Ah, Cal, if one might safely die without the Christian's faith and hope, I should still want them to sweeten life's journey."

Another thoughtful pause, then the young man said frankly, "Cousin Elsie, I'm afraid I'm very stupid, but it's a fact that I never have been able to understand exactly what it is to be a Christian, or how to become one."

She considered a moment, her heart going up in silent prayer for help to make the matter plain to him, and for a blessing on her words, for well she knew that without the influence of the Holy Spirit they would avail nothing.

"To be a Christian," she said, "is to believe in the Lord Jesus Christ, receiving and resting upon Him alone for salvation. 'He hath made Him to be sin for us, who knew no sin; that we might be made the righteousness of God in Him.' 'God so loved the world, that He gave His only begotten Son, that whosoever believeth in Him should not perish, but have everlasting life.' Do not these verses answer both your queries? We have broken God's holy law, but Jesus, the God-man, has borne the penalty in our stead. 'All our righteousnesses are as filthy rags.' We dare not appear before the King clothed in them, but Jesus offers to each of us the pure and spotless robe of righteousness, and we have only to accept it as a free gift; we can have it on no other terms. It is believe and be saved; look and live."

"But there is something else for us to do, surely? We must live right."

"Yes, true faith will bring forth the fruits of holy living; but good works are the proofs and effects of our faith, not the ground of the true Christian's hope—having nothing whatever in themselves to do with our justification."

The entrance of Arthur and young Horace put an end to the conversation.

Horace was not less devoted to his elder sister now than in childhood days. Arthur, distant and reserved with most people, had of late learned to be very frank and open with her, sure of an attentive hearing, of sympathy, and that his confidence would never be betrayed.

She never sneered, never laughed in contempt, nor ever seemed to think herself better or wiser than others. Her advice, when asked, was given with sweet simplicity and humility, as of one not qualified, in her own estimation, to teach, or desirous to usurp authority over others. Yet, she had a clear intellect and sound judgment. She opened her mouth with wisdom and in her tongue was the law of kindness. There seemed a sort of magnetism about her, the attraction of a loving, sympathetic nature, that always drew to her the young of both sexes, and the large majority of older people also.

The three young men gathered round her, hanging upon her sweet looks, her words, her smiles, as ardent lovers do upon those of their mistress.

Somehow the conversation presently turned upon love and marriage, and she lectured them, half-playfully, half-seriously, upon the duties and responsibilities of husbands.

She bade them be careful in their choice, remembering that it was for life, and looking for worth rather than beauty or wealth. Then, after marriage not to be afraid of spoiling the wife with too much care and thoughtfulness for her comfort and happiness or the keeping up of the little attentions so pleasant to give and receive and so lavishly bestowed in the days of courtship.

"Ah, Elsie, you are thinking of your own husband, and holding him up as the perfect model to us," said Horace laughingly.

"Yes," she answered with a blush and smile, a tender light shining in the soft hazel eyes, "that is true. Ah, the world would be full of happy wives if all husbands would copy his example! He is as much a lover now as the day he asked me to be his wife; more indeed, for we grow dearer and dearer to each other as the years roll on. Never a day passes that he does not tell me of his love by word and deed, and the story is as sweet to me now as when first I heard it."

"Ah, good wives make good husbands," said Mr. Travilla, who had entered unobserved, just in time to hear the eulogy upon him. "Boys, let each of you get a wife like mine, and you simply can not fail to be good husbands."

"Good husbands make good wives," she retorted, looking up into his face with a fond smile as he came to her side.

"The trouble is to find such," remarked Horace, regarding his sister with tender admiration.

"True enough," said Travilla, "I know not of her like in all the length and breadth of the land."

Catching sight of Mr. Dinsmore pacing the veranda alone, Calhoun slipped quietly away from the rest and joined him.

"Uncle," he said coloring and dropping his eyes, "It is with great fear and dread that I begin to think you doubt me."

"Have I not reason, Calhoun?" Mr. Dinsmore asked, looking searchingly into the lad's face.

"Yes, sir, I own that appearances are strongly against me, and I can not disprove the tale they tell; but — oh, if you could trust me still, uncle!"

He lifted his head and gazed fearlessly into the keen, dark eyes still bent searchingly upon him.

Mr. Dinsmore held out his hand and cordially grasped the one Calhoun placed in it.

"Well, my boy, I will try; it is far pleasanter than to doubt you. But there is someone at Roselands who is disposed to aid and abet the Ku Klux in their lawless proceedings."

"I cannot deny that," said the nephew, "yet it would ill become me to say who it is. I think, sir, since grandpa has set down his foot so decidedly in opposition, there will be no more of it. Travilla and Cousin Elsie have given me their confidence again, and I assure you, sir, I am deeply grateful to you all."

CHAPTER TWELFTH

*If thou neglect'st, or do'st unwillingly
What I command, I'll rack thee with old cramps,
Fill all thy bones with aches; make thee roar,
That beasts shall tremble at they din.*

—SHAKESPEARE'S TEMPEST

THE ION FAMILY WAS SPENDING the day at the Oaks. It was now early in the fall of 1868 and political excitement ran high over the coming presidential election. There had been as yet no effectual check given to the lawless proceedings of the Ku Klux, and their frequent raids and numerous deeds of violence had inaugurated a reign of terror that was a shame and reproach to a boasted civilization and free institutions.

Many of the poorer class, both blacks and whites, dared not pass the night in their houses, but when darkness fell, fled for safety to the shelter of the nearest woods, carrying their beds with them and sleeping in the open air.

That the Ku Klux Klan was a political organization working in the interests of the Democratic Party, their words to their victims left no doubt. The latter were told that they were punished for belonging to the Union League or for favoring the Republican Party or using their influence in its behalf, and threatened with severe treatment if they dared to vote its ticket or persuade others to do so.

The outrages were highly disapproved by all Republicans and by most of the better class in the opposite party. But many were afraid to express their opinions of the doings of the Klan, lest they should be visited with its terrors, while for the same reason, many of its victims preferred to suffer in silence rather than institute proceedings or testify against their foes.

It was a state of things greatly deplored by those of the Oaks and Ion, and Messrs. Dinsmore and Travilla, who were not of the timid sort, had been making efforts to bring some of the guilty ones to justice—though, thus far, with very little success.

Such an errand had taken them to the town on this particular day.

They were returning late in the afternoon and were several miles from home. Passing through a bit of woods, a sudden turn of the road brought them face to face with a band of mounted men, some thirty or forty in number, not disguised, but rough and ruffianly in appearance and armed with clubs, pistols, and bowie knives.

The encounter was evidently a surprise to both parties, and reining in their steed, they regarded each other for a moment in grim silence.

Then the leader of the band, a profane, drunken wretch who had been a surgeon in the Confederate Army, scowling fiercely upon the friends and laying his hand on a pistol in his belt, growled out, "A couple of scalawags! Mean, dirty rascals, what mischief have you been at now, eh?"

Disdaining a reply to his insolence, the gentlemen drew their revolvers, cocked them ready for instant use, and whirling their horses half way round and backing them out of the road so that they faced it while leaving room for the others to pass, politely requested them to do so.

"Not so fast!" returned the leader, pouring out a torrent of oaths and curses. "We've a little account to settle with you two, and no time's like the present."

"Yes, shoot 'em down!" cried a loud voice from the crowd.

"Hang 'em! Hang 'em!" yelled another, "the — — rascals!"

"Yes," roared a third, "pull 'em from their horses and string 'em up to the limb o' that big ol' oak tree over yonder."

Messrs. Dinsmore and Travilla faced them with a dauntless air.

"You will do neither," said Mr. Dinsmore in a firm, quiet tone. "We are well armed and shall defend ourselves to the last extremity."

Travilla threw his riding whip into the road a foot or two in front of his horse's head, saying, as he looked steadily into the leader's eyes, "The first one who passes that to come nearer to us is that instant a dead man."

The two were well known in the community as men of undoubted courage and determination — also as excellent marksmen.

A whisper ran along the lines of their opponents. "He's a dead shot; and so's Dinsmore; and they're not afraid o' the devil himself. Better let 'em go for this time."

The leader gave the word, "Forward!" and with hisses, groans, and a variety of hideous noises, they swept along the road and passed out of sight, leaving the friends masters of the field.

"Cruelty and cowardice go hand in hand," observed Mr. Travilla, as they resumed their homeward way.

"Yes, those brave fellows prefer waging war upon sleeping, unarmed men, and helpless women and children, to risking life and limb in fair and open fight with such as you and I," returned his companion.

"They are Ku Klux, you think?"

"I am morally certain of it, though sadly, I could not bring proof to convict even that rascally Dr. Savage."

They agreed not to mention the occurrence in presence of their wives; also that it would be best for Travilla to take his family home early, Mr. Dinsmore and Horace, Jr. accompanying them as an escort.

This they could readily do without arousing the fears of the ladies, as both were constantly coming and going between the two places.

The sun was nearing the horizon when they reached the Oaks.

Rose and Elsie were on the veranda awaiting their coming with some anxiety.

"Oh," they cried, "we are so rejoiced to see you, so thankful that you are safe. We feared you had met some of those dreadful Ku Klux."

"Yes, my own little wife, we are safe, thanks to the protecting care which is over us all in every place, " Mr. Travilla said embracing her as though they had been long parted.

"Ah, yes," she sighed, "how I have been forgetful today the lessons of faith and trust I have tried to impress upon Mrs. Leland. It is far easier to preach them than to practice."

Little feet came running in from the grounds, little voices shouted, "Papa has come! Papa and grandpa, too," and a merry scene ensued — hugging, kissing, romping — presently interrupted by the call to tea.

There was nothing unusual in the manner of either gentleman and the wives had no suspicion that they had been in peril of their lives.

"I think it would be well to return home early tonight," Mr. Travilla remarked to Elsie.

"Yes," she said, "on account of the children."

So the carriage was ordered at once and shortly after leaving the table they were on their way — Elsie, children and nurses in the carriage, with Mr. Travilla, Mr. Dinsmore and son, all well-armed, as their mounted escort.

Horace had been taken aside by his father and told of the afternoon's adventure and in his indignation was almost eager for "a brush with the insolent ruffians."

None appeared, however; Ion was reached in safety. They tarried there an hour or more, then returned without perceiving any traces of the foe.

The hush of midnight had fallen upon the Oaks, Ion, Fairview, and all the surrounding region. The blinking stars and young moon, hanging a golden crescent just above the horizon, looked down upon a sleeping world. Yet, not all were asleep, for far down the road, skirting yonder wood, a strange and sinister procession approached — goblin-like figures, hideous with enormous horns, glaring eyeballs and lolling red tongues and mounted upon weird-looking steeds, were moving silently onward.

They reached a small house hard by the roadside, paused before it, and with a heavy riding whip the leader thundered at the door.

The frightened occupants, startled from their seep, cried out in alarm and a man's voice asked, "Who's there?"

"Open the door," commanded the leader in a strange, sepulchral voice.

"I must know who is there and what is wanted," returned the other, hurrying on his clothes.

A shot was fired, and penetrating the door, struck the opposite wall.

"Open instantly, or we'll break in, and it'll be the worse for you," thundered the leader; and with trembling hands amid the cries of wife and children, the man removed the bars, drew back the bolts, and looked out, repeating his question, "What's wanted?"

"Nothing, this time, Jim White, but to warn you that if you vote the Republican ticket, we'll call again, take you to the woods, and flog you within an inch of our life—beware! Forward, men!" and the troops swept onward, while White closed and barred the door again, and crept back to bed.

"Ku Klux!" said the wife shuddering. "Jim, we'll have to hide o' nights now, like the rest. Nothing'll hurt ye. Jim, ye'll mind?"

"Yes, yes, Betsy, though it galls to be ordered round like a n—, me with as white a skin as any o' them Klu Klux."

Onward, still onward swept the goblin train, and again and again the same scene was enacted, the victim now a poor white, and now a freedman.

At length they reached Fairview; they paused before the gate, two dismount, making off into the woods and presently reappeared bearing on their shoulders a long dark object — a little square of white visible on the top.

They passed through the gate, up the avenue, and silently deposited their burden at the door, returning to their companions, and with them repaired to the Negro quarter.

Dismounting, they tied their horses to the fence, and leaving them in the charge of one of their number, took themselves to the nearest cabin. They surrounded it, broke open the door, dragged out the man, carried him a little distance, and with clubs and leather straps, gave him a terrible beating.

Leaving him half-dead with pain and fright, they returned to his cabin, threatened his wife and children, and robbed him of his gun. They passed on to repeat their lawless deeds — menacing some, beating and shooting others, not always sparing women or children, the latter perhaps being hurt accidentally in the melee.

From the quarter at Fairview, they passed on to that of Ion, continuing there the same threats and acts of violence. They finish up their terror by setting fire to the schoolhouse and burning it right to the ground.

The bright light shone in at the open window of her room, and awoke the little Elsie. She sprang from her bed and ran to the window. She could see the flames bursting from every aperture in the walls of the small building and here and there through the roof, curling about the rafters, sending volumes of smoke and showers of sparks. In their light, she could see the demon-like forms of the mischief doers, some seated on their horses, looking quietly on, others flitting to and fro in the lurid glare. And she could distinctly hear the roar and crackling of the flames, and the sound of the falling timbers.

At the sight, a panic of terror seized the child. She flew into the room where her parents lay sleeping, but with habitual thoughtfulness for others, refrained from screaming out in her fright, lest she should rouse the little ones.

She went to her father's side, put her lips to his ear and said in low tremulous tones, "Papa, papa, please wake up! I'm so frightened. There's a fire and the Ku Klux are there. Oh, papa, I'm afraid they'll come here and kill you!" and she ended with a burst of almost hysterical weeping, rousing both father and mother.

"What is it, darling?" asked Mr. Travilla, starting up into a sitting posture and throwing an arm about the child. "What has alarmed my love?" he asked while the mother, exclaiming, "Vi! Is she gone again?" sprang out upon the floor and hastily threw on a dressing gown.

"No, no, no, mamma. Vi's safe in bed, but look at that red light on the wall! It's fire and the Ku Klux!"

In another moment all three were at the window overlooking the scene.

"The schoolhouse!" exclaimed Mr. Travilla. "I am not surprised, for the Klan is greatly opposed to education of the Negro and has burned down buildings used for that purpose in other places. Do you see them, wife? Those frightful horned animals?"

"Yes," she said with a shudder, followed by a deep sigh, "and, oh, Edward, what may they not be doing to our poor people? Can we do anything to save them?"

He shook his head sadly.

"No, they are out in considerable force, and I could do nothing single-handed against twenty or thirty armed men."

"Oh, papa, mamma, I am so frightened!" cried little Elsie, clinging to them both. "Will they come here and hurt us?"

"I think not, daughter," her father said soothingly. "Their raids have hitherto been almost entirely confined to the blacks and poor whites, with now and then one of those from the North whom they style and label 'carpetbaggers.'"

"Be calm, dearest, and put your trust in the Lord," the mother said, folding the trembling, sobbing child to herself. "'The beloved of the Lord shall dwell in safety by Him and the Lord shall cover him all the day long.' 'Not an hair of your head shall fall to the ground without your Father.'"

"Yes, sweet words," said Mr. Travilla, "and remember what the Lord Jesus said to Pilate, 'Thou couldst have no power at all against me, except it were given thee from above.'"

A short pause in which all three gazed intently at the scene of conflagration, then, "Do you see how the walls are tottering?" said Mr. Travilla. And even as he spoke they tumbled together into one burning mass and flames shot up higher than before, burning with a fierce heat and roar, while by their lurid light the Ku Klux could be seen taking up their line of march again.

The two Elsies watched in an almost breathless suspense until they saw them turn in a direction to take them farther from Ion.

"Thank God they are not coming here!" cried Mrs. Travilla, in low, reverent, grateful tones.

"Hark! Mamma, papa, I hear cries and screams!" exclaimed little Elsie. "Oh, it must be some of the poor women and children coming from the quarter!"

As the child spoke, there came a quick, sharp tap that seemed to tell of fright and excitement at the outer door of the suite of apartments. And an old servant, hardly waiting for the permission to enter, thrust in his head, saying in tremulous tones, "Mars Ed'ard, de people's comin' up from de quarter, an' knockin' an' cryin' to get in. Dere's been awful times down dere—de Ku Klu—."

"Yes, yes, Jack, I know; but be quiet or you'll wake the children. Open the hall door and let the poor things in, of course," said Mr. Travilla, "and I'll be down in a moment."

"Plenty room on de back veranda, Mars Ed'ard, an' 'tween dat an' de kitchen."

"Very well, they'll be safe there, but if they don't feel so, let them into the hall."

"Yes, sah."

The head was withdrawn, the door closed, and Jack's shuffling feet could be heard descending the stairs.

Mr. and Mrs. Travilla, having each hastily dressed, were about to go down; but little Elsie clung to her mother.

"Mamma, mamma, please don't go and leave me! Please, let me go, too."

"My darling, you would be quite safe here; and it is much earlier than your usual hour for rising."

"But day is breaking, mamma, and I could not sleep anymore. Besides, maybe I could help to comfort them."

"I think she could," said her father and mamma, giving consent at once.

They found the back veranda, the kitchen, and the space between, filled with an excited crowd of blacks, old and young, talking, gesticulating, crying, moaning, and groaning.

"De Ku Klux, de Ku Klux!" was on every tongue.

"Tell ye what," one was saying, "dey's debbils! Why two ob dem stop befo' my doah an' say 'You black rascal, give us some watah! Quick, now, fo' we shoot you tru de head. Den I hand up a gourd full—'bout a quart, min' yo',—an' de fust snatch it an' pour it right down his troat, an' hand de gourd back quick's a flash. Den he turn roun' an' ride off, while I fill de gourd for de udder, an' he do jes de same. Tell ye what, dey's debbils! Did yo' see de horns, an' de big red tongues waggin'?"

There was a murmur of assent and a shudder ran through the throng. But Mr. Travilla's voice was heard in cheerful, reassuring tones.

"No, boys, they are men, though they do the work of devils. I have seen their disguise and under that long red tongue, which is made of flannel and moved by the wearer's real tongue, there is a leather bag inside of the disguise. Into it they pour the water, not down their throats."

"Dat so, Mars Ed'ard?" cried several, drawing a long breath of relief.

"Yes, that is so, boys. And they've been threatening and abusing you tonight?"

"Yes, sah, dat dey hab!" cried a score of voices and one after another showed his wounds and told a piteous tale.

Elsie and her namesake daughter wept over their losses and suffering. The medicine closet was unlocked and its stores liberally drawn upon for materials to dress their wounds. Both master and mistress attended to them with their own hands, at the same time speaking soothing, comforting words and promising help to repair the damage to their property and make good their losses — also to bring their enemies to justice if that might be possible.

It was broad daylight ere the work was finished.

The veranda was nearly empty now, the people slowly returning to their homes — Mr. Travilla having assured them the danger was past for the present — when Elsie caught sight of a woman who she had not observed till that moment.

The poor creature had dropped down upon a bench at the kitchen door. Her right arm hung useless at her side. With the left she held the bloody corpse of a puny infant to her heart. The eyes she lifted to the face of her mistress were full of a mute, tearless agony.

Elsie's overflowed at the piteous sight. "Oh, my poor Minerva," she said, "what is this they have done to you and poor little Ben?"

"Oh, oh, oh, Miss Elsie! De Ku Kluxes de shot tru de doah, an' de balls flyin' all roun', an' — an' — one hit me on de arm an' killed my baby! she sobbed. "Oh, oh, oh, oh! De doctah mend de arm, but de baby, he — he — done gone foreber," and the sobs burst forth with renewed violence, while she hugged the still form closer and rocked herself to and fro in her grief.

"Gone to heaven, my poor Minerva, to be forever safe and happy with the dear Lord Jesus," her mistress said in quivering tones, the tears rolling fast down her own cheeks.

"An' he neber hab no mo' miseries, honey," said Aunt Dicey, drawing near. "No Ku Klux come into de garden ob de Lord to scare him or hurt him. Bress his little heart!"

"Wish we all dere, safe an' happy like he! Let me wash off de blood an' dress him clean for de grave," said Aunt Sally, the nurse of the quarter, taking the child. Meanwhile Mr. Travilla and Elsie bound up the wounded arm, speaking soothingly to the sufferer and promising the doctor's aid as soon as it could be procured.

Aunt Sally sat near attending to the last offices for the tiny corpse, little Elsie looking on with big tears coursing down her cheeks. Presently going to her mother's side, she whispered a few words in her ear.

"Yes, dear, you may go to the bureau drawer and choose it yourself," was the prompt reply, and the child ran into the house, returning directly with a baby's slip of fine white muslin, quite delicately embroidered.

"Put this on him, Aunt Sally," she said. "Mamma gave me leave to get it."

Then, going to the bereaved mother and clasping the dusky, toil-worn hand with her soft, white fingers, "Don't cry, Minerva," she said, "you know poor little Ben was always sick and now he is well and happy. And if you love Jesus, you will go to be with him again some day."

Evidently much gratified by the honor done her dead babe, Minerva sobbed out her thanks for that and the dressing of her wounded arm, and dropping a curtsey, followed Aunt Sally as she bore the corpse into Aunt Dicey's cabin close by.

The scanty furniture of Minerva's own had been completely demolished by the desperadoes and her husband had been terribly beaten as well.

He and one or two others had not come up with the crowd, presumably from inability to do so, and Mr. Travilla now mounted his horse and went in search of them.

They had been left by their assailants in the woods where one — "Uncle Mose" — dreadfully crippled by rheumatism, still lay on the ground half-dead with bruises, cuts, and pistol-shot wounds.

Another had crawled to his cabin and fainted upon its threshold, while a third lay weltering in his gore some yards distant from his.

Mr. Travilla had them carried into their houses and made as comfortable as circumstances would permit, and a message was dispatched in all haste for Dr. Barton.

The family at Fairview had slept through the night undisturbed by the vicinity or acts of the raiders. Mr. Leland's first intimation of their visit was received as he opened the front door at his usual early hour for beginning his morning round of the plantation.

He almost started back at the sight of a rude pine coffin directly before him, but recovering himself instantly, stooped to read a label affixed to the lid.

"Beware, odious carpetbagger! This is your third and final warning. Leave the country within ten day or your carcass fills this."

He read it deliberately through, carefully weighing each word, not a muscle of his face moving, not a tremor agitating his nerves.

Turning to his overseer, who at that moment appeared before him. "Bring me a hatchet," he said in stern, calm tones, "and be quick, Park. I would not have your mistress see this on any account."

Stepping upon the lid as he spoke, he broke it in with a crash, finishing his work when the hatchet came by quickly chopping and splitting the coffin up into kindling wood.

"There!" he said, bidding the man gather up the fragments and carry them to the kitchen. "They'll not put me into that, at all events. What mischief have they been at in the quarter, I wonder?" he added, springing into the saddle.

"Dreffle bad work, sah; mos' killed two ob de boys. Scared de rest to deff," said Park, hastily obeying the order to gather up the bits of wood. "Jes' gwine tell ye, sah, when you tole me go fer de hatchet."

"Indeed! Hellish work! Follow me, Park, as quickly as you can. And mind, not a word of this," pointing to the demolished coffin, "to anyone," and putting spurs to his horse, he galloped off in the direction of the quarter.

But presently catching sight of the still smoking embers of the Ion schoolhouse, he drew rein for an instant with a sudden exclamation of surprise and regret. "The wretches, what will they do next? Burn our houses about our ears?" and sighing, he pursued his way.

Indignant anger and tender pity and compassion filled him by turns on reaching the quarter and discovering the state of things there—worse even than Park's report had made it.

He rode from cabin to cabin inquiring into the condition of the inmates and speaking words of pity and hope.

Finding several badly bruised and cut and others suffering from gunshot wounds, he sent to the house for lint, salve, and bandages and directed a lad to run to the stables, saddle a horse, and go immediately for Dr. Barton.

"De doctah ober to Ion now, sah," returned the boy. "Debbils dere las' night, too, sah."

"Run over to Ion, then, and ask the doctor to come here when he is finished with his work there," said Mr. Leland.

Mr. Travilla came with the doctor and the two planters compared notes, in regard to damages, Mr. Leland also telling the story of the coffin laid at his door.

"What do you intend to do?" asked Mr. Travilla.

"Inclination says, 'Stay and brave it out,' but I have not fully decided. I have invested all my means in this enterprise and have a wife and family of helpless little ones to support."

"That makes it hard indeed, yet I fear your life is in great danger. But, come what may, Leland, I stand your friend. If you should be attacked, fly to Ion. You will find an open door, a hearty welcome, and such protection as I am able to give. I think we could conceal you so that it would be a matter of difficulty for your foes to find you."

"A thousand thanks! God bless you for your kindness, sir!" exclaimed Leland with emotion, warmly grasping the hand held out to him. The two parted, each wending his homeward way.

CHAPTER THIRTEENTH

Humble love,
And not proud reason,
Keeps the door of heaven;
Love finds admission,
Where proud science fails.

—*Young*

ELSIE WAS ALONE ON THE veranda looking for her husband's return to breakfast, for it was already past the usual hour.

"All alone, little wife?" he asked as he dismounted and came up the steps.

"Not now," she answered, putting her arms about his neck and looking up at him with her own fond, beautiful smile. "But your face is sad, my husband! What news?"

"Sad enough, my little friend. Poor old Uncle Mose has been so barbarously handled that he will not live through the day, Dr. Barton says. And two of the others are suffering very much.

"Yes, I told him, as tenderly as I could, and asked if he was ready to go. 'Yes, Mars Ed'ard,' he said with a triumphant smile, 'I is, for I'se got fast hold ob Jesus.'"

Elsie's head was laid on her husband's shoulder; the bright drops were coming fast down her cheeks.

"I have sent word to Mr. Wood," he went on. "The poor fellow is anxious to see him, and you also, my dear."

"Yes, yes, I will go down directly after prayers," she said.

Then he told her of the coffin laid at the door of Fairview, and the threatening words on its lid.

She heard it with a shudder and a sigh. "Oh, poor Mr. Leland! Edward, don't you think it would be wise of him to leave for the present?"

"Perhaps so. I fear they will really attempt his life if he stays, but all his means being invested in Fairview makes it very hard. Where are our children?"

"They went to deck the corpse of Baby Ben with flowers. Ah, here they come, the darlings!" as little feet came pattering through the hall.

They hastened to their father for their usual morning kiss and hung about him with loving caresses. But their manner was subdued and Vi and Harold told with a sort of wondering awe of the poor little dead baby so still and cold.

"Are you going out, mamma?" asked little Elsie an hour later as Mrs. Travilla appeared, dressed in walking costume, in the midst of the group of children and nurses gathered under a tree on the shady side of the house.

"Yes, daughter, I am going down to the quarter to see poor old Uncle Mose who is very ill, and I want you to be mother to the little ones while I am away."

"Oh, mamma, mayn't we go with you?" cried Eddie and Vi in a breath, Harold chiming in, "and me, too, mamma, me, too!"

"No, dears, not today, but some other time you shall," the mother answered, giving each a sweet, good-bye kiss.

"Mamma, stay wis us. I'se 'f'aid de Kluxes get 'oo!" said Harold coaxingly, clinging about her neck with his chubby arms while the big tears gathered in his great dark eyes.

"No, dear, they don't come in the daytime. And God will take care of me. Papa is down at the quarter, too, and Uncle Joe and mammy will go with me." And with another tender caress, she gently released herself from his hold and turned away.

The children gazed wistfully after her graceful figure as it disappeared among the trees, Uncle Joe holding a big umbrella over her to shield her from the sun, while mammy and Aunt Sally followed, each with a basket on her arm.

Uncle Mose was rapidly nearing that realm whence no traveler returns. As his mistress laid her soft white hand on his, she felt that the chill of death was there.

"You are almost home, Uncle Mose," she said, bending over him, her sweet face full of the most tender sympathy.

"Yes, my dear young Missus, I'se in de valley," he answered, speaking slowly and with difficulty, "but bress de Lord, it's not dark!"

"Jesus is with you?"

"Yes, Missus, He is my strength and my song. De riber's deep, but He'll neber let me sink. De pain in dis ole body's dreffle, but I'll neber hab no mo', bress de Lord!"

"Do your good works give you this assurance that you are going to heaven, Uncle Mose?"

"Bress yo' heart, honey, I ain't neber done none, but de bressed Lord Jesus covers me all ober wid His goodness, and God de Fader 'cepts me for His sake."

"Yes, that is it. 'He hath made Him to be sin for us, who knew no sin; that we might be made the righteousness of God in Him.' 'There in none other name under heaven given among men whereby we must be saved,' and 'he that believeth on Him shall not be confounded.'"

"Yes, honey, dose de words ob de good book. Now will you please sing de twenty-third Psalm, an' den ask de Lord Jesus keep fas' hold dis ole man, till Jordan am past, an' de gate into de city."

The request was granted. The sweet voice that had thrilled the ears of many of the rich and noble of earth, freely poured forth its richest strains to soothe the dying throes of agony of a poor, old Negro man.

Then, kneeling by the humble couch, in a few simple, touching words she commended the departing spirit to the almighty love and care of Him who had shed His blood to redeem it. She was earnestly pleading that the dying one might be enabled to cast himself wholly on Jesus and in doing so be granted a speedy and abundant entrance into His kingdom and glory.

The fervent "Amen!" of Uncle Mose joined in with hers, then low and feebly he added, "De good — Lord — bress — you — and — keep — you — my — dear — young — Missus."

A shadow had fallen on Elsie, and as she rose from her knees, she turned her head to find her father standing at her side.

He drew her to him and pressed his lips tenderly to her forehead. "You must go now. The heat of the sun is already too great for you to be out with safety."

The low quiet tone was the one of authority as of days of old.

He only waited for her good-bye to Uncle Mose, and to speak a few kindly words of farewell himself, then led her out and placed her in his carriage which stood at the door.

Mr. Travilla rode up at that instant. "That is right," he said. "Little wife, I am loath to have you exposed to the heat of the sultry day."

"And you, Edward? Can you not come home now?" she asked.

"Not yet, wife, there are several matters I must attend to first, and I want to speak to Mr. Wood, who, I see, is just coming."

He kissed his hand to her with the gallantry of the days of their courtship and cantered off, while the carriage rolled on its way toward the mansion.

"Daughter, if you must visit the quarter during this sultry weather, can you not choose an earlier hour?" asked Mr. Dinsmore.

"I think I can after this, papa," and she went on to explain how her time had been taken up before breakfast that morning. "Do you know about Mr. Leland?" she asked in conclusion.

"Yes, their next outrage will, I fear, be an attack upon him."

"Then upon you and Edward!" she said, her cheek growing very pale and her eyes filling. "Papa I am becoming very anxious."

"I would have you, dear, without carefulness," he answered taking her hand in his. "They can have no power at all against us except it be given them from above. My Child, God reigns, and if God be for us, who can be against us?"

"Yes, dear papa, and with David let us say, 'In the shadow of Thy wings will I make my refuge, until these calamities be overpast.'"

Mr. Dinsmore was still with his daughter when Mr. Travilla returned with the news that Uncle Mose's sufferings were over, and it had been arranged that he and Baby Ben should be buried that evening at dusk.

The children begged to be permitted to attend the double funeral, but their parents judged it best to deny them, fearing an onslaught by the Ku Klux— of which there was certainly a possibility.

"I have been talking to Leland," Mr. Travilla remarked aside to his friend, "and he proposes that we accompany the procession as a mounted guard.

"Good!" said Mr. Dinsmore, "Horace and I will join you, and let us all go armed to the teeth."

"Certainly, and I accept your offer with thanks. Some of the boys themselves are pretty fair marksmen but they were all robbed of their arms last night."

"Let us supply them again, Edward," exclaimed Elsie with great energy, "and have them practice shooting at a mark."

Her husband assented with a smile. "You are growing warlike in your feelings," he said.

"Yes, I believe in the privilege and the duty of self-defense against evil."

Toward evening Mr. Dinsmore rode back to the Oaks, returning to Ion with his son, shortly before the appointed hour for the funeral.

Elsie saw them and her husband ride away in the direction of the quarter—not without some fluttering of the heart and with a silent prayer for their safety. She retired with her children to the observatory at the top of the house, from whence they had a full view of the whole route from the cabin of Uncle Mose to the somewhat distant place of burial. The spot was chosen for that purpose in accommodation to the superstitious feelings of the blacks which led them to prefer to lay their dead at a distance from their own habitations.

The children watched with deep interest as the procession formed, each man carrying a blazing pine knot. They passed down the one street of the quarter and wound their slow way along the road that skirted two sides of the plantation, then half way up a little hill, where they gathered in a circle about the open grave.

Twilight was past; thick clouds hid the moon and the torches shone out like stars in the darkness.

"Mamma, what dey doin' now?" asked Harold.

"Listen! Perhaps you may hear something," she answered. And as they almost held their breath, they heard a wild, sweet Negro melody come floating upon the still night air.

"They're singing," whispered Vi, "singing Canaan, 'cause Uncle Mose and little Baby Ben have got safe there."

No one spoke again till the strains had ceased with the ending of the hymn.

"Now Mr. Wood is talking, I suppose," remarked Eddie in a subdued tone, "telling them we must all die, and which is the way to get to heaven."

"Or else he's praying," said Vi.

"Mamma, what is die?" asked Harold leaning on her lap.

"If we love Jesus, darling, it is going home to be with Him, and oh, so happy."

"But Baby Ben die and me saw him in Aunt Dicey's house."

"That was only his body, son; the soul—the part that thinks and feels and loves—has gone away to heaven, and after a while God will take the body there, too."

For obvious reasons the services at the grave were made very short, and in another moment they could see the line of torches drawing rapidly nearer, till it reached the quarter and broke into fragments.

"We will go down now," Elsie said, rising and taking Harold's hand. "Papa, grandpa, and Uncle Horace will be here in a moment."

"Mamma," whispered her namesake daughter, "how good God was to keep them safe from the Ku Klux tonight!"

"Yes, dearest, let us thank Him with all our hearts for their continued safety."

CHAPTER
FOURTEENTH

The more the bold, the bustling, and the bad,
Press to usurp the reins of power, the more
Behooves it virtue, with indignant zeal,
To check their combination.

—*T*HOMSON

THE SPIRIT OF RESISTANCE was now fully aroused within these friends of Ion and the Oaks. Mr. Travilla's was a type of the American character—he would bear long with his injuries, vexations, encroachments upon his rights, but when once the end of his forbearance was reached, woe to the aggressor. He would find himself opposed by a man of great resources, unconquerable determination, and undaunted courage.

His measures were taken quietly, but with promptness and energy. He had been seeking proofs of the identity of the raiders. He found them in the case of one of the party whose gait had been recognized by several, and his voice by one or two. And the mark of his bloody hand laid upon clothing of one of the women as he roughly pushed her out of the way seemed to furnish the strongest circumstantial evidence against him.

George Boyd's right hand had been maimed in a peculiar manner during the war and this bloody mark on the woman's nightdress was an exact imprint.

Already Mr. Travilla had procured his arrest and had him imprisoned for trial in the county jail.

Yet, this was but a small part of the day's work. Lumber had to be ordered and men engaged for the rebuilding of the schoolhouse. Merchandise also had to be ordered to replace the furniture and clothing destroyed, and arms for every man at the quarter capable of using them.

All this Elsie knew and approved, as did her father and brother. For Mrs. Carrington's sake, they deeply regretted that Boyd was implicated in the outrage, but all agreed that justice must have its course.

The question had been mooted in both families whether any or all of them should leave the South until the restoration of law and order should render it a safe abiding place for honest, peaceable folk, but unanimously decided in the negative.

The gentlemen scorned to fly from the desperadoes and resign to their despotic rule their poor dependents and the land of their love. Nay, they would stay and defend both to the utmost of their power, and the wives upheld their husbands in their determination and refused to leave them to meet the peril alone.

Returning from the burial of Uncle Mose, Mr. Dinsmore and Horace spent an hour at Ion before riding back to the Oaks.

The three gentlemen were in the library earnestly discussing the state of affairs when Elsie, coming down from seeing her little ones settled for the night, heard the sound of wheels in the avenue, and stepping to the door saw the Ashlands carriage just drawing up in front of it.

The vehicle had scarcely come to a standstill ere its door was thrown hastily open and the elder Mrs. Carrington alighted.

Elsie sprang to meet her with outstretched arms and exclamation, "My dear old friend!" though her heart beat quickly, her cheek crimsoned, and tears filled her eyes.

The old lady, speechless with grief, fell upon her neck and wept there silently for a moment. Then low and gaspingly, in a voice broken with sobs, "I—have—come to—ask about—George," she said. "Can it, oh can it be that he has done this dreadful thing?" and shuddering she hid her face on Elsie's shoulder, her slight frame shaken with the sobs she vainly strove to suppress.

"Dear Mrs. Carrington, I am sorry, so *very* sorry to think it," Elsie said, in a voice full of tears. "My heart aches, for you love him so. You have been so sorely afflicted. May the Lord give you strength to bear up under this new trial."

"He will! He does! My sister's son! Oh, 'tis sad, 'tis heart breaking! But the proofs—what are they?"

Elsie named them—first drawing her friend to a seat where she supported her with her arm.

"Yes, yes, his voice, his gait are both peculiar, and—his hand. Let me see that—that garment."

Leading her into a private room and seating her comfortably there, Elsie had it brought and laid before her.

Mrs. Carrington gave it one glance and motioning it away with a look and gesture of horror, dropped her face into her hands and groaned aloud.

Elsie kneeling by her side, clasped her arms about her and wept with her.

"A slayer of the weak and helpless — a murderer — a midnight assassin!" groaned the half-distracted and greatly grieved aunt.

"May there not possibly be some mistake? Let us give him the benefit of the doubt," whispered Elsie.

"Alas, there seems scarcely room for doubt!" sighed Mrs. Carrington, then, with a determined effort to recover her composure, "But don't think, dear Elsie, that I blame you or your husband. Can I see him? And your father if he is here?"

"Yes, they are both here and will rejoice if they can be of any comfort or service to you. Ah, I hear papa's voice in the hall asking for me!" and stepping to the door, she called to him and her husband saying, "Please come in here. Mrs. Carrington wishes to see you both."

"You here and alone at this late hour, my dear madam!" Mr. Dinsmore exclaimed, taking the old lady's hand in a cordial grasp. "Your courage surprises me."

"Ah, my good friend, they who have little to lose need not have much to do with fear," she answered. "That was what I told Sophy, who would have had me defer my call till tomorrow."

"My dear madam, you are surely right in thinking that no one would molest you — a lady whom all classes unite in loving and honoring," Mr. Travilla said, greeting her with an almost filial respect and affection.

She bowed in acknowledgment. "Do not think for a moment that I have come to upbraid you, gentlemen. Justice demands that those who break the laws suffer the penalty, and I have nothing to say against it—though the criminal be my own flesh and blood. I want to hear all about this sad affair."

They told her briefly all they knew, she listening with calm though sad demeanor.

"Thank you," she said when they had finished. "That George is guilty, I dare hardly doubt, and I am far from upholding him in this wickedness. As you all know, I was strong for secession, and am no Republican now, but I say perish the cause that can be upheld only by such measures as these. I would have every member of this wicked, dreadful conspiracy brought to punishment. They are ruining their country, but their deeds are not chargeable upon the secessionists of the war time as a class."

"That is certainly true, madam."

"We are so fully convinced of that, Mrs. Carrington," the gentlemen replied.

She rose to take leave. Mr. Travilla requested her to delay a little till his horse could be brought to the door and he would see her home.

"No, no, Travilla," said Mr. Dinsmore, "Horace and I will do that, if Mrs. Carrington will accept our offer of escort."

"Many thanks to you both, gentlemen," she said, "but I assure you I am not in the least afraid, and it would be putting you to unnecessary trouble."

"On the contrary, my dear madam, it would be a pleasure. And as our horses are already at the door, we need not delay you a moment," said Mr. Dinsmore. "It will not take us so far out of our way, either. And I should like to have a word with Sophy."

Upon that Mrs. Carrington gratefully accepted his offer and the three went away together.

Convinced of his guilt, Mrs. Carrington made no effort to obtain the release of her nephew, but several of his confederates, having perjured themselves to prove an alibi in his favor, he was soon at large again.

He showed his face no more at the Oaks or Ion, and upon occasion of an accidental meeting with Travilla or either of the Dinsmores, regarded him with dark, scowling looks, sometimes adding a muttered word or two of anger and defiance.

In the meantime, damages had been repaired in the quarters at Fairview and Ion, and the men at the latter, secretly supplied with arms; and the rebuilding of the schoolhouse was moving rapidly forward.

A threatening notice was presently served upon Mr. Travilla, ordering him to desist from the attempt, as the teaching of blacks would not be allowed by the Ku Klux.

He, however, paid no attention to the insolent demand, and the work went on as before.

Mr. Leland had succeeded in keeping the affair of the coffin from his wife, thus saving her much anxiety and distress.

To leave at this time would be a great pecuniary loss, and he had decided to remain; but had laid his plans carefully for either resistance or escape in case of an attack.

A couple of large, powerful, and very fine watch dogs were added to his establishment, and a brace of loaded pistols and a bowie knife were always within reach of his hand.

One night the family was aroused by the furious barking of the dogs. Instantly Mr. Leland was out upon the floor hastily throwing on his clothes, while his wife with the frightened cry, "The Ku Klux!" ran to the window.

"Yes, it is! They are surrounding the house! Oh, Robert, fly for your life!" she cried in the wildest terror. "Oh, God, save my poor husband from these cruel foes!" she added, dropping upon her knees and lifting hands and eyes to heaven.

"He will, Mary, never fear, wife," Mr. Leland said almost cheerfully, snatching up his weapons as he spoke. "Pray on, it's the best thing you can do to help me."

"You must fly!" she said, "you can't fight twenty men and I think there are at least that many."

"I'll slip out at the back door then and make for the woods," he answered, rushing from the room.

Both children and servants were screaming with affright, the ruffians thundering at the front door, calling loudly upon Mr. Leland to come out, and threatening to break it down if he did not immediately appear.

"Leland! Tell him to come out here at once or it will be the worse for him," cried the leader, in a feigned, unnatural voice.

"He is not here," she said.

"He'd better show himself at once," returned the ruffian. "He'll not escape by refusing to do so; we'll search every corner till we find him."

"That will be as God pleases," she said in a calm, firm tone, her courage rising with the emergency.

She was answered with a yell of rage, and a repeated order to come down and open the door.

"I shall do no such thing," she said. "And what is more, I shall shoot down the first man that sets foot on the stairs."

It was a sudden resolution that had come to her. Encouraged by Mrs. Travilla's precept and example, she had been, for months past, industriously training herself in the use of firearms, and kept her loaded revolver at hand. And now she would create a diversion in her husband's favor, keeping the raiders at bay at the front of the building while he escaped at the back. They believed him to be in the upper story. If she could prevent it, they should not learn their mistake till he had had time to gain the woods and distance in the pursuit.

The door could not much longer withstand the heavy blows dealt it. Already there were sounds as if it were about to give way.

"Archie," she said, turning to her son and speaking very rapidly, "those men are here to kill your father. You must help me to prevent them from coming up to hunt him. The rest of you children stop that loud crying, which won't do any good. Kneel down and pray, pray, *pray* to God to help your father to get away from them. Archie, throw this black cloak round you. Here are two loaded pistols. I will take one, you the other. We will station ourselves on the landing at the head of the first flight of stairs. It is darker in the house than out of doors, and they will not be able to see us, but as the door falls and they rush in we can see them in their white gowns and against the light. Come!"

They hurried to the landing.

"Now we must not be in too great haste," she whispered in his ear. "Keep cool, take sure aim, and fire low."

The words had scarcely left her lips when the door fell with a crash, and with a yell like an Indian war hoop several disguised men rushed into the hall and hastily advanced toward the stairway. But the instant the foremost set foot upon it, two shots were fired from above, evidently not without effect. For with an oath the figure staggered back and fell into the arms of his comrades.

He was borne away by two of them, while the others returned the fire at random, for they could not see their adversaries.

The balls whistled past Mrs. Leland and her son, but they stood their ground bravely, and as two of the assailants attempted to ascend the stairs, fired again and again driving them back for a moment.

At the same time, sound of a conflict came from the rear of the dwelling—an exchange of shots, whoops and yells, the hurried tramp of many feet, and the yelping, barking, and howling of the dogs. And instantly the hall was cleared, every man there hastening to join in this new struggle, apparently satisfied that their intended victim was endeavoring to make his escape in that direction.

Seeing this, Mrs. Leland and her son ran to a window overlooking the new scene of the contest, their hearts beating between hope and fear.

Mr. Leland had slipped cautiously out of the back door and, revolver in hand, stepped into the yard, but only to find himself surrounded by his foes.

They attempted to seize him, but eluding their grasp, he fired right and left, several shots in succession, the others returning his fire, and following in hot pursuit.

There was no moon that night, and the darkness and a simple black suit were favorable to Leland, while the long white gowns of the Ku Klux not only hampered their movements, but rendered each an easy target for his shot. They could take but uncertain aim at him, and on gaining the woods, he was soon lost to their view in the deepened gloom of its recesses.

However, the balls had been falling about him like hailstones, and as the sounds of pursuit grew fainter, he found himself bleeding profusely from a wound in the leg. He dropped behind a fallen tree and partially stanched the wound with some leaves that he bound on with a handkerchief, fortunately left in his coat pocket on retiring that night.

This was scarcely accomplished when sounds of approaching footsteps and voices told him the danger was not yet over.

He crouched close in his hiding place, and hardly dared breathe as they passed and repassed, some almost stepping on him. But he remained undiscovered, and at length they abandoned the search, and returning to the vicinity of the house, gathered up their wounded and went away.

Yet Leland felt that it was not safe for him to venture back to his home, as they might return at any moment. But, to remain where he was with his wound undressed was almost certain death.

He resolved to accept Mr. Edward Travilla's offered hospitality, if his strength would carry him so far. He was rising to the attempt, when the cracking of a dead branch told him that some living thing was near, and he fell back again, listening intently for the coming footsteps.

"Robert! Robert!" called a low tremulous voice.

"Oh, Mary, is it you?" he responded, in low but joyous accents, and the next moment his wife's arms were about his neck, her tears warm upon his cheek, while Archie stood sobbing beside them.

"Thank God, thank God that you are alive!" she said. "But are you unhurt?"

"No, I am bleeding fast from a wound in my leg," Leland answered faintly.

"I've brought lint and bandages," she said, "let me bind it up as well as I can in the dark."

"Daren't we strike a light?" asked Archie.

"No, my son, it might bring them on us again, and we must speak low, too."

"Yes, father, but, oh, what will we do? You can't come back home again?"

"No, I must go to Ion at once, while I can do so under cover of the darkness. Travilla has offered to hide me there. Archie, my brave boy, I can trust you with this secret."

"Father, they shall kill me before I'll tell it."

"I trust you will not be tried so far," Leland said with emotion. "I would not save my life at the sacrifice of yours. I leave your mother in your care, my boy. Be dutiful and affectionate to her, and kind to your little brother and sisters. Mary, dear, you and Archie will have to manage the plantation in my absence," and he went on to give some directions.

"I will do my best," she said tearfully, "and as we have been for months past frequent visitors at Ion, I can surely go to see you there occasionally without exciting suspicion."

"Yes, I think so."

"Father," said Archie, "you can never walk to Ion. Let me bring my pony and help you to mount him. Then I will lead him to Ion and bring you to Ion and bring my pony back again."

"What a bright thought. We will do so, if you can saddle him in the dark and bring him very quietly."

"I'll try, father," and the boy hastened away in the direction of the stables.

He returned sooner than they dared hope, with the pony saddled and bridled. Husband and wife bade a mournful adieu. Mr. Leland mounted with his son's assistance, and silently they threaded their way through the woods to Ion.

"Hoo! Hoo! Hoo!" the cry came in loud and clear through the open windows of the bedroom of the master and mistress of Ion, and startled them both from their slumbers.

"Hoo! Hoo! Hoo!" it came again and with a light laugh Elsie said, "Ah, it is only an owl, but to my sleeping ear it seemed like a human cry of distress. But Edward—"

He had sprung from the bed and was hurrying on his clothes. "I doubt if it is not, little wife," he said. "It is the signal of distress Leland and I had agreed upon and he may be in sore need of aid."

"Let me go with you!" she cried tremulously, hastening to don dressing gown and slippers. "Shall I strike a light?"

"No, not till we go down below where the shutters are closed. There is no knowing what foe may be lurking near."

Seizing his revolvers, he left the room as he spoke, she following close behind, a pistol in one hand, a lamp and matchbox in the other.

Silently they groped their way over the stairs, through the halls and corridors, till they reached a side door that Mr. Travilla cautiously unbarred.

"Who is there?" he cautiously asked scarcely above his breath.

"I, sir," and Mr. Leland stepped in and fell fainting to the floor.

Elsie had set her lamp upon a table and laid her pistol beside it, and while her husband carefully secured the door again, she struck a light and brought it near.

Together they stooped over the prostrate form.

"He is not dead?" she asked with a shudder.

"No, no, only a faint, but, see, he is wounded! Your keys, wife!"

"Here," she said, taking them from her pocket, where, with rare presence of mind, she had thrust them ere leaving her room.

They hastened to apply restoratives and bind up the wound more thoroughly than Mrs. Leland had been able to do.

Restored to consciousness, Leland gave a brief account of the affair, refreshed himself with food and drink set before him by Elsie's fair hands, and then was conducted by Mr. Travilla to an upper room in a wing of the building dating back to the old days of Indian warfare. It was distant from the apartments in use by the family and had a large closet entered by a concealed door in the wainscoting.

"Here I think you will be safe," remarked his host. "No one but my wife and myself yet knows of your coming and it shall be kept secret from all but Aunt Chloe and Uncle Joe, two tried and faithful servants. Except Dr. Barton—he is safe and will be needed to extract the ball."

"Yes, and my wife and boy and the Dinsmores," added Leland with a faint smile. "Travilla, my friend, I can never thank you enough for this kindness."

"Tut, man! 'Tis nothing! Are we not told to lay down our lives for the brethren? Let me help you to bed; I fear that leg will keep you there for some days to come."

"I fear so indeed, but am sincerely thankful to have gotten off so well," replied Leland, accepting the offered assistance.

"A most comfortable, nay a most luxurious prison cell," he remarked cheerily, glancing about upon the elegant and tasteful furniture. "Truly, the lines have fallen to me in pleasant places."

Mr. Travilla smiled. "We will do what we can to make amends for the loss of liberty. It cannot be far from daybreak now. I will remove the light, throw open the shutters and leave you to rest. You must, of course, be anxious about your family. I will ride over to Fairview and bring you news of them within the hour."

CHAPTER FIFTEENTH

It gives me wonder, great is my content,
To see you here before me.

—SHAKESPEARE'S OTHELLO

Sir, you are very welcome to our house.

—SHAKESPEARE

DAY HAD FULLY DAWNED when Mr. Travilla reentered his sleeping apartment to find Elsie in bed again, but lying there with wide-open eyes.

"How very quietly you came in, careful not to disturb me I suppose, my good, kind husband," she said greeting him with a loving look and smile, as he drew near her couch.

"Yes," he answered, bending over her and fondly stroking her hair. "I hoped you were taking a nap."

"No, I feel as if I should never be sleepy again. I'm thinking of poor Mrs. Leland. How troubled, anxious, and distressed she must feel!"

"Yes, I shall ride over there directly."

"Good, if you'd like to go. You will do her more good than I."

"I doubt it, but perhaps both together may be better than either one alone. Didn't she act bravely?"

"Yes, she's a noble woman."

They spent some moments in consulting together how to make their guest comfortable and at the same time effectually conceal his presence in the house.

They rejoiced together in the fact that no one but themselves—his own son excepted—had been cognizant of his arrival. Elsie agreed with her husband that it should be kept secret from the children—and servants also save Aunt Chloe and Uncle Joe, whose services would be needed and who could be trusted not to divulge the matter.

"Mammy will manage about his meals, I know," said Elsie, "and Dr. Barton's visits may be supposed to be paid to Violet. The darling! How glad and thankful I am that she seems to be losing her inclination to sleep walking."

"And I," said her husband, "thankful to God for His blessing on the means used and to Barton, who is certainly an excellent physician."

Their talk ended, husband and wife separated to their different dressing rooms.

Elsie rang for her maid and Aunt Chloe appeared in answer to the summons.

Aunt Chloe was no longer young, or even elderly, but had attained to a healthy and vigorous old age and still so delighted in her old pleasant task of busying herself about the person of her young mistress that she would only occasionally resign it to other hands. She was a household dignitary, head attire-woman and head nurse, and much looked up to by the younger servants.

She came in quietly and dropping a curtsey said, "Good mornin', Miss Elsie, I hope you's well, honey, but you's up so mighty early."

"Ah, mammy, I'm glad it is you, for I have some news to tell you. Yes, I'm quite well, thank you," Elsie answered, then while getting dressed quickly, went on to relate the occurrences of the last few hours, winding up by putting the wounded guest in the charge of Aunt Chloe and her husband.

The faithful old creature accepted the trust with evident pride in the confidence reposed in her.

"Dis chile an' Uncle Joe'll take care ob him, honey, neber fear," she said, carefully adjusting the folds of her mistress's riding habit. "I'll nuss him to de best ob my disability, an' de good Lord'll soon make um well, I hope."

"And you and Uncle Joe will be careful not to let any of the other servants know that he's here?"

"Dat we will, darlin', for shuah."

The sun was just peeping above the horizon as Mr. and Mrs. Travilla drew rein before the main entrance to the Fairview mansion.

Mrs. Leland came out to welcome them. She was looking pale and worn, yet met them with a smile and words of grateful appreciation of all their kindness, then, with the quick tears springing to her eyes, asked anxiously after her husband's welfare.

"I think he is safe and will do well," Mr. Travilla said. "It seems to be only a flesh wound, and will soon heal with proper treatment and good nursing. I shall go from here to Dr. Barton's, calling for my wife on my return. But first, what can I do for you? Ah, I see your door is quite demolished. We must have it replaced with a new and stronger one before night."

"Yes, that is the most pressing need just now," said Mrs. Leland. "Come in and look. There is really no other damage except a few bullet holes in the walls, and these blood stains on the matting," she said with a slight shudder. "And I am truly thankful to have escaped so well."

They stepped into the hall—their talk so far had been on the veranda—and gazed with interest upon the marks of the night's conflict, Mrs. Leland meanwhile giving a graphic account of it.

A servant was diligently at work cleaning the matting, and had nearly obliterated the stains left by the wounded Ku Klux.

"And you shot him, my dear Mrs. Leland?" Elsie said inquiringly.

"Archie or I, or perhaps both of us," Mrs. Leland answered, leading the way to the parlor.

They sat there a few moments, conversing still upon the same theme.

"You will hardly dare stay here at night now?" Elsie remarked.

"Yes, where else? I should feel very little safer from the Ku Klux in the woods, and the malaria might rob us all of health and even life."

"Come to Ion," said both her visitors in a breath, "you will be most welcome."

"A thousand thanks," she answered with great emotion. "I do not doubt my welcome, yet fear to give a clue to my husband's hiding place."

"There might be danger of that," Mr. Travilla said thoughtfully, "but what better, my dear madam, can you do?"

"Stay here and put my trust in the Lord. He will take care of my helpless little ones and me. I have been thinking of one of our noble pioneer women of the West whose husband was killed by the Indians, leaving her alone in the wilderness with six small children, no white person within several miles. Her friends urged her to leave the dangerous spot, but she said, 'No, this farm is all I have for my own and my children's support, and I must stay here. God will protect and help us.' And He did. The Indians, though they knew she was alone, never attacked her. She lay sometimes all night with a broadax in her hands, ready to defend her babes. But, though she could see the savages come into her yard and light their pipes at her brushwood fire, they never approached the house."

Elsie's eyes kindled with enthusiastic admiration, then filled with tears. "Dear, brave Christian woman! And you will emulate both her courage and her faith."

"I shall try. The hearts of the Ku Klux of today are no less in His hands than those of the Indians of that day or this."

"That is certainly true and He never fails those who put their trust in Him," Mr. Travilla said, rising. "Now, wife, I leave you here while I go for Barton."

"Oh, stay a moment, Edward," she exclaimed. "A thought has struck me. It is not usual for you to go for the doctor yourself. Might it not excite undue suspicion? And can you not trust Uncle Joe as your messenger on this errand?"

"Your plan is best," he said with a pleased smile. "Let us then hasten home and dispatch him on the errand at once."

Dr. Barton found the wound not dangerous, extracted the ball with little difficulty, and left the patient doing well.

The attack on Fairview and the disappearance of its owner caused considerable excitement in the neighborhood. There was a good deal of speculation as to what had become of him. Some thought it probable that he had hidden in the woods and died there of his wounds, others that he had gone North to stay until the reign of terror should be over.

No one, perhaps, suspected the truth, yet the wrath of the Ku Klux was excited against the Travillas and the Dinsmores of the Oaks by the kindness they showed to Leland's wife and children. Threatening notices were sent ordering them to desist from giving aid and comfort to "the carpetbagger's family."

They, however, paid no heed to the insolent demand, but exerted themselves to discover who were the men wounded in the raid, for that more than one had been hurt was evidenced by the bloody tracks in and around the house at Fairview.

In this they were not successful — doubtless because the men were from some distance. It was the custom for the organization so to arrange matters that thus they might the more readily escape recognition in their communities.

The Ion children were at play on the front veranda one morning shortly after breakfast when a strange gentleman came riding leisurely up the avenue.

Harold was the first to notice his approach. "Mammy, mammy! See who's tumin! Dat one de Kluxes?" he asked, running in affright to Aunt Chloe, who sat in their midst with the babe on her lap.

"'Spect not, honey. Don't be 'fraid," she said to him soothingly, putting her arm firmly about the little trembler.

The little girls were dressing their dolls, Eddie and Bruno racing back and forth, in and out, having a grand romp. But at Harold's question Eddie suddenly stood still with an imperative, "Down, Bruno! Down, sir! Be quiet now!" and turned to look at the stranger.

The gentleman, now close at hand, reined in his horse, lifted his hat, and with a winning smile, said,

"Good morning, my little lads and lasses. Is your mother in?"

"No, sir, she and papa have gone out riding," replied Eddie, returning the bow and smile.

Elsie laid aside her doll and stepping forward said with a graceful little curtsey, "Good morning, sir; will you dismount and come in? Papa and mamma will probably be here in a few minutes."

"Ah ha! Um h'm, ah ha! Yes, my little lady, I will do so, thank you," returned the gentleman, giving his horse into the care of a servant summoned by young Eddie.

"And will you walk into the drawing room, sir?" Elsie asked.

"No, thank you," he replied seating himself among them and sending a glance of keen interest from one to another.

One look into the pleasant, genial face banished Harold's fears and when the stranger held out his hand saying, "I am your mamma's cousin; won't you come and sit on my knee?" the child went to him at once, while the others gathered eagerly about him.

"Mamma's cousin! Then she will be very glad to see you," said Elsie.

"But she never told us anything at all about you," observed Eddie.

"Ah ha, ah ha! Um h'm! Ah ha! But did she ever tell you about her mother's kin?"

"No, sir," said Elsie, "I asked her once, and she said she didn't know anything about them. She wished she did."

"Ah ha! Ah ha, um h'm! Ah ha! Well, she soon will. Child, you look very like a picture of your great-grandmother that hangs in my house in

Edinburgh. A bonny lassie she must have been when it was painted."

"Yes, sir, and she's the picture of mamma," remarked Eddie. "Everybody says so."

"Ah ha, ah ha! Uh h'm, ah ha!"

"Has you dot any 'ittle boys and dirls at your house?" asked Harold.

"Yes, my man, a quiver full of them."

"Are they good? Do they love Jesus?" asked Vi. "Please tell us about them."

"If you like to, sir," said Eddie, with a sweet and gentle gravity. "Vi, dear, you know we mustn't tease him."

"No, I didn't mean to tease," Vi answered, blushing. "Please excuse me, sir, and please don't tell it 'less you want to."

"No, no, it will give me pleasure, my dear. I enjoy talking of my darlings, especially now when they are so far away."

He seemed about to begin, when Elsie, blushing deeply, said, "Excuse me, sir, I have been very remiss in my hospitalities. It is early, and perhaps you have not breakfasted."

"Yes, thank you, my dear, I took breakfast at the village hotel, where I arrived last night."

"But you, sir, will take a cup of coffee and some fruit—"

Her sentence was broken off, for at that instant a lady and a gentleman came galloping up the avenue and the little ones hailed them with a joyous shout, "Papa and mamma!"

Another moment and Edward had dismounted, gallantly assisted his wife to do the same and together they stepped onto the veranda. Both bowed politely to the stranger and the children running to them cried, "Mamma, mamma, it is your cousin from Scotland."

She turned inquiringly to him, a flush of pleasure on her face.

He had risen from his seat and was coming toward her with outstretched hand and earnest, admiring gaze. "My name is Richard Lilburn. Your maternal grandmother and mine were sisters," he said. "Your grandmother's marriage was displeasing to her father and all exchange between her and the rest of the family was broken off in obedience to his stern command. And thus they lost sight of each other. I have brought proofs of—"

But Elsie's hand was already laid in his, while glad tears sprang to her eyes.

"You shall show us them at another time if you will, but I could never doubt such a face as yours and cannot tell you how glad I am to have at last found a relative on my mother's side of the house. Cousin, you are welcome, welcome to Ion!" And she turned to her husband.

"Yes," he said, offering his hand with the greatest cordiality, "welcome indeed, and not more so to my little wife than to myself."

"Thanks to you both," he said with a bow and smile. "Cousin," with an earnest look at his hostess, "you are *very* like a picture I have of your grandmother. But," with a glance at the wide-eyed little ones, looking on and listening in wonder and surprise, "can it be that you are the mother of these? Yourself scarce more than a bairn in appearance."

Elsie laughed lightly. "Ah, cousin, you have not examined me closely yet. I have not been a bairn for many years. How glad papa will be, Edward, to see a relative of my mother's!"

"No doubt of it, wife, and we must send him word immediately."

Mr. Lilburn had no reason to complain of his reception. He was treated with the utmost hospitality and his coming made the occasion of general rejoicing in the household. Refreshments were promptly set before him, a handsome suite of apartments appropriated to his use, and a manservant directed to attend upon his person.

A note was sent to the Oaks inviting the whole family to Ion. The children were given a holiday, and Elsie, her husband, and father spent the morning in conversation with their guest, and in examining family records, miniatures, and photographs which he had brought with him.

The day passed most agreeably for all, and the newfound relatives were mutually pleased and interested in each other.

Mr. Lilburn was evidently a gentleman of polish, intelligence, and refinement—seemed to be an earnest Christian, too, and in easy circumstances.

The little folk made friends with him at once, and as children are apt to be quick at reading character, the older ones felt this to be a confirmation of the good opinion he had already won from them.

CHAPTER SIXTEENTH

*I know that there are angry spirits
And turbulent mutterers of stifled treason,
Who lurk in narrow places, and walk out
Muffled to whisper curses to the night.
Disbanded soldiers, discontented ruffians
And desperate libertines who lurk in taverns.*

—*B*YRON

IT WAS A BRIGHT AND A WARM day some hours after sunrise. A man of rather gentlemanly appearance, well, though not handsomely dressed, was riding leisurely along the public highway. He wore a broad-brimmed straw hat as a protection from the sun and a linen duster somewhat soiled by the dust of travel. He had a shrewd though not unkindly face and a keen, gray eye whose quick glances seemed to take in everything within its range of vision.

It was a lonely bit of road he was traveling and he moved with caution, evidently on the alert for any appearance of danger.

Presently he perceived another solitary horseman approaching from the opposite direction and at the sight laid his hand on the pistols in his belt concealed by the duster, to make sure that they were ready for instant use—but at the same time kept steadily on his way.

The newcomer was a slender boy of eighteen or twenty, not at all dangerous looking.

As the two neared each other each lifted his hat with a courteous, "Good morning, sir," the lad at the same time carelessly sliding his right hand down the left lapel of his coat.

The lad then ran his fingers lightly through his hair; the other imitated his action. The lad opened his coat and seemed to be searching for a pin. The man opened his, took out a pin, and handed it to him with a polite bow.

"Thanks! All right, sir. I perceive you are one of us," said the boy, drawing a paper from his pocket and presenting it to the man. "Miller's Woods!" and touching his hat he galloped away.

There was a twinkle in the gray eyes as they shot one swift glance after him; then the paper was opened and examined with minute care.

On it was a half moon with several dates written in different places about it, and that was all. Yet, its new possessor regarded it with great satisfaction, and after a careful scrutiny bestowed it safely in his breast pocket.

"I'll be on hand without fail," he said in a low, confidential tone, perhaps addressing his horse, as there was no one else within hearing. "Tonight! They're late serving my notice, but better late than never. For me, though perhaps not for themselves," he added with a grim smile. "Well, my preparations won't take long — dress suit's all ready."

He kept on his way at the old, leisurely pace, presently came in sight of Fairview, passed it, then Ion, diligently using his eyes as he went, made a circuit of several miles and returned to the town which he had left some hours previously.

Dismounting at the village tavern, he gave his horse into the care of the hostler, and joined a group of idlers about the barroom door. They were talking politics and one appealed to him for his opinion.

"Don't ask me," he said with quite a deprecatory gesture. "I'm no party man and never meddle with any politics."

"On the fence, hey? Just the place for a coward and a sneak," returned his interlocutor contemptuously.

The other half-drew his bowie knife, then thrusting it back again, said good-humoredly, "I'll let that pass, Green; you've taken a drop too much and are not quite sober just now."

"Be quiet, will you, Green," spoke up one of his companions. "You know well enough Snell's no coward. Why, didn't he risk his life the other day to save your boy from drowning?"

"Yes, I'd forgot. I take that back, Snell. Will you have a glass?"

"Thank you, no, it's too hot, and your wife and babies need the money, Green."

The words were half-drowned in the clang of the dinner bell. The group scattered; Snell and most of the others hurried into the dining room in answer to the welcome call.

After dinner Snell sauntered out in the direction of the stable, passed with a seemingly careless glance in at the door and strolled onward; but in the momentary glimpse had noted the exact position of his horse.

About ten o'clock that night he stole quietly out again. He made his way unobserved to the stable, saddled and bridled his steed — all in the dark. Then he mounted and rode away, passing through the village streets at a very moderate pace, but breaking into a round trot as soon as he had fairly reached the open country.

He pressed on for several miles but slackened his speed only as he neared the forest known as Miller's Woods.

For the last mile or more he had heard, both in front and rear, the thumping of horses' hoofs and occasionally a word or two spoken in an undertone by gruff voices.

He was anxious to avoid an encounter with their owners, and on reaching the outskirts of the wood, suddenly left the road, and springing to the ground, took his horse by the bridle, and led him along for some yards under the trees. Then, fastening him securely, opened a bundle he had brought with him and speedily arrayed himself in the hideous Ku Klux disguise.

He stood a moment intently listening. The same sounds were still coming from the road, evidently many men were traveling it that night. Snell reflected with grave concern, though without a shadow of fear, that if seen and recognized by any one of them, his life would speedily pay the forfeit for his temerity—for in spite of his acquaintance with their secret signs, he was not a member of the order.

He was, in fact, a detective in pursuit of evidence to convict the perpetrators of the outrages which had been so frequent of late in that vicinity.

Making sure that his arms were in readiness for instant use, he hastened on his way, threading the mazes of the wood with firm, quick, but light step.

He had proceeded but a short distance, when he came upon a sentinel who halted him. Snell slapped his hands together twice, quick and loud.

The sentinel answered in the same manner and permitted him to pass. The same thing was repeated twice, and then a few steps brought him into the midst of the assembled Klan, for it was a general meeting of all the camps in the county which together composed a Klan.

Snell glided silently and unquestioned, to a place among the others, the disguise and the fact of his having passed the sentinels, lulling all suspicion.

Most of those present were in disguise, but some were not and several of these the officer recognized as men who he knew by name and by sight, among them Green and George Boyd.

A good deal of business was transacted. Several raids were decided upon, the victims named, the punishment to be meted out to each prescribed, and the men to execute each order appointed.

One member after another would mention the name of some individual who had become obnoxious to him personally or to the Klan, saying that he ought to be punished, and the matter would be at once taken up and arrangements made to carry out his suggestion.

Boyd mentioned the name "Edward Travilla, owner of Ion," cursing him bitterly as a scalawag, a friend of carpetbaggers, and of the education and elevation of the Negroes.

"Right! His case shall receive prompt attention!" said the chief.

"Let it be a severe whipping for him administered tomorrow night, between the hours of twelve and two," proposed Green, and the motion was put to a vote and carried without a dissenting voice.

"And let me have a hand in it!" cried Boyd fiercely.

"You belong to the neighborhood and might be recognized," objected the chief.

"I'll risk it. I owe him a sound flogging or even something worse," returned Boyd.

"We all do, for he'd have every mother's son of us sent to jail or hanged, if he could," growled another voice on Snell's right. While from a mask on the left there came in sepulchral tones the words, "It had better be hands off with you then, man," the speaker pointing significantly to Boyd's maimed member.

"It shall!" cried he, "but I flatter myself this right hand, mutilated though it be, can lay on the lash as vigorously as yours, sir."

After a little more discussion, Boyd's wish was granted, his fellow raiders were named, and presently the meeting closed, and the members began to disperse.

Snell thought he had escaped suspicion thus far, but his heart leaped into his mouth as a man whom he had heard addressed as Jim Blake suddenly clapped his hand on his shoulder, exclaiming, "Ah, ha, I know you, old chap!"

"You do? Who am I then?" queried the spy in a feigned, unnatural voice, steady and cool, spite of the terrible danger that menaced him.

"Who? Hal Williams, no disguise could hide you from me."

Snell drew a breath of relief. "Ha! Jim, I didn't think you were so clever," he returned in his feigned voice and glided away, presently disappearing, as others were doing, in the deeper shadows of the wood.

He thought it not prudent to go directly to the spot where he had left his horse, but reached it by a circuitous route, doffing his disguise and rolling in into a bundle again as he went.

He paused a moment to recover breath and listen. All was darkness and silence—the conspirators had left the vicinity.

Satisfied of this, he led his horse into the road, mounted, and road back to the town.

There everyone seemed to be asleep except in a drinking saloon, whence came sounds of drunken revelry, and the barroom of the tavern where he put up. A light was burning there, but he avoided it, attended to his horse himself, returning it to the precise spot where he had found it, then slipped stealthily up to his room. And, without undressing, threw himself upon the bed and almost immediately fell into a profound slumber.

CHAPTER
SEVENTEENTH

Abate the edge of traitors, gracious lord,
That would reduce these bloody days again,
And make poor England weep
in streams of blood.

—*S*HAKESPEARE

THE SUN HAD JUST RISEN above the treetops as Solon led Beppo, ready saddled and bridled for his master's use, from the stables to the front of the mansion.

A moment later Mr. Travilla came out, gave some orders to the servant, and was about to mount, when his attention was attracted by the approach of a man on horseback who came cantering briskly up the avenue.

"Good morning," he said as the stranger drew near. "Solon, you may hitch Beppo and go ahead to your work."

"Good morning, Mr. Travilla, sir," returned the horseman, lifting his hat and bowing respectfully, as Solon obeyed the order in regard to Beppo, and with a backward glance of curiosity disappeared around the corner of the building.

"You bring news, Martin?" said Mr. Travilla, stepping nearer to the stranger and looking earnestly into his face.

"Yes, sir, and very bad, I'm sorry to say, unless," and he bent low over his saddle bow and spoke in an undertone, "unless you can defend yourself against a band of thirty-five or forty ruffians."

"Fasten your horse to that post yonder and come with me to my private room," said Travilla, in calm, quiet tones.

Martin, alias Snell, immediately complied with the request, and as soon as he found himself closeted with Mr. Travilla, proceeded to give a full account of his last night's adventure.

"I assure you, sir," he concluded, "I look upon it as a piece of rare good fortune that I came upon that lad yesterday and that he mistook me for one of the Klan, as otherwise you'd have had no warning."

"It is a kind providence, Martin," returned Mr. Travilla, with grave earnestness. "'If God be for us who can be against us?'"

"Nobody, sir, and that's the most Christian way of looking at the thing, no doubt. But, if I may ask, what will you do? Fight or fly?"

"How do you know that I shall do either?" Mr. Travilla asked with a slight twinkle in his eye.

"Because you're not the man to tamely submit to such an outrage."

"No, as my wife says, 'I believe in the duty and privilege of self-defense,' and for her sake and my children's, even more than my own, I shall attempt it. I am extremely obliged to you, Martin."

"Not at all, sir; it was all in the way of business, and in the interest of humanity, law, and order. No, no, sir, thank you, I'm not to be paid for doing my duty!" he added, hastily putting back a check that his host had filled out and now handed him.

"I think you may take it without scruple," said Mr. Travilla. "It is not a bribe, but simply a slight expression of my appreciation of an invaluable service you have already rendered me."

"Still I'd rather not, sir, thank you," returned the detective, rising to go. "Good morning. I shall hope to hear tomorrow that the raiders have got the worst of it."

Left alone, Mr. Travilla sat for a moment in deep thought; then, hearing Mr. Lilburn's voice in the hall, stepped out and exchanged with him the usual morning salutations.

"So you are not off yet?" remarked the guest.

"No, but am about to ride over to the Oaks. Will you give me the pleasure of your company?"

"With all my heart."

Elsie was descending the stairs.

"Wife," Mr. Travilla said, turning to her, "your cousin and I are going to ride over to the Oaks immediately. Will you go with us?"

"Yes, thank you," she answered brightly, as she stepped to the floor. Then, catching sight of her husband's face, and seeing something unusual there, "What is it, Edward?" she asked gliding swiftly to his side and laying her hand upon his arm, while the soft eyes met his with a loving, anxious look.

He could scarce refrain from touching the sweet lips with his own.

"My little friend, my brave, true wife," he said with a tender sadness in his tone, "I will conceal nothing from you. I have just learned through a detective that the Ku Klux will make a raid upon Ion tonight between twelve and two. My errand to the Oaks is to consult with your father about the best means of defense—unless your voice is for instant flight for ourselves, our children, and guests."

Her cheek paled, but her eye did not quail and her tones were calm and firm as she answered, "It is a question for you and papa to decide. I am ready for whatever you think best."

"Bravo!" cried her cousin, who had listened in surprise to Mr. Travilla's communication. "There's no coward blood in my kinswoman's veins. She is worthy of her descent from the old Whigs of Scotland, eh, Travilla?"

"Worthy of anything and everything good and great," returned her husband with a proud, fond glance at the sweet face and graceful form close by his side.

"Ah ha! Um h'm! So I think. And they are really about to attack you—those cowardly ruffians? Well, sir, my voice is for war. I'd like to help you give them their deserts."

"It would seem cowardly to run away and leave our wounded friend and helpless dependents at their mercy," Elsie exclaimed, her eye kindling and her cheek flushing, while she drew up her slender figure to its full height. "Our beautiful land, too, given up to anarchy and ruin—this dear sunny South that I love so well."

Her voice trembled with the last words and tears gathered in her eyes.

"Yes, that is it," said her husband. "We must stay and battle for her liberties and the rights guaranteed by her law to all her citizens."

Horses were ordered, Elsie returned to her apartments to don a riding habit, and in a few minutes the three were on their way to the Oaks.

The vote there also was unanimous in favor of the policy of resistance. Mr. Dinsmore and Horace, Jr. at once offered their services and Arthur Conly, who happened to be spending a few days at his uncle's just at that time, did the same.

"I was certainly brought up a secessionist and my sympathies are still with the Democratic Party," he said. "But these Ku Klux outrages I cannot tolerate, especially," he added, looking at Elsie with an affectionate smile, "when they are directed against the home and husband, if not the person, of my sweet cousin."

"You are to me 'a kinsman born, a clansman true,' Art," she said, thanking him with one of her sweetest smiles.

"That's right, old fellow!" cried Horace clapping his cousin on the shoulder. "We shall muster pretty strong—papa, Brother Edward, Mr. Lilburn, you and I—six able-bodied men within the fortress, with plenty of the best small arms and ammunition. All of us are fair shots, too; some excellent marksmen—we ought to do considerable execution among our assailants."

"And God being on our side," said Mr. Lilburn reverently, "we may have strong hope of being able to beat them back."

"Yes, 'the race is not always to the swift, nor the battle to the strong,'" remarked Mr. Dinsmore. "'Some trust in chariots, and some in horses; but we will remember the name of the Lord our God.'"

"And if we do so truly, fully, He will take hold of shield and buckler and stand up for our help," added Mr. Travilla.

The plan of defense was next discussed, but not fully decided upon. It was agreed that that could be done most readily upon the spot, and that accordingly, Mr. Dinsmore and the two young men should ride over to Ion shortly after breakfast to view the ground and consult again with the other two.

"Why not return with us and breakfast at Ion?" asked Elsie.

"Why not stay and breakfast with us?" said Rose.

"Certainly," said her husband.

"Take off your hat, daughter, and sit down to your father's table as of old."

"Ah, my little ones! I know they are watching for mamma and wondering at her long delay."

"Then I shall not detain, but rather speed you on your way," he said, leading her out and assisting her to mount her horse.

The children had thought mamma's ride a long one that morning and much they wondered at papa's unusual silence and abstraction. He quite forgot to romp with them, but indeed there was scarcely time, as he did not come in from the fields till the breakfast bell had begun to ring.

Grace had just been said. Everyone was sitting silent, quietly waiting to be helped—the children were all at the table for "Cousin Ronald," who had been with them for a week, was now considered quite one of the family. Mr. Travilla took up the carving knife and fork with the intent to use them upon a chicken that lay in a dish before him. But the instant he touched it with the fork, a loud squawk made everybody start, and Harold nearly tumbled from his chair.

"Why, dey fordot to kill it!" he cried breathlessly.

"But its head's off!" said Eddie, gazing into the dish in wide-eyed astonishment.

"Ah ha, um h'm! Is that the way your American fowls behave at the table?" asked Cousin Ronald, gravely, but with a slight twinkle in his eye. He pushed back his chair a little while keeping his eyes steadily fixed upon the ill-mannered bird, as if fearful that it's next escapade might be to fly in his face. "A singular breed they must be."

Elsie and her husband began to recover from their momentary surprise and bewilderment and exchanged laughing glances, while the latter, turning his head to his guest, said, "Capitally done, cousin! You wouldn't have disgraced Signor Blitz himself or any of his guild. But I had no suspicion that ventriloquism was one of your many accomplishments. What part shall I help you to?"

"The leg, if you please; who knows but I may have use for more than two tonight."

A gleam of intelligence lighted up little Elsie's face. "Oh! I understand it now," she said with a low silvery laugh. "Cousin is a ventriloquist."

"What's that?" asked Vi.

"Oh, I know!" cried Eddie. "Cousin Ronald, don't you have a great deal of fun doing it?"

"Well, my boy, perhaps rather more than I ought, seeing it's very apt to be at other folks' expense."

Their guest, mamma, and Elsie having been helped, it was now Vi's turn to claim her papa's undivided attention.

"What shall I send you, daughter?" he asked.

"Oh, nothing, papa, please! No, no, I can't eat live things," she said half shuddering.

"It is not alive my child."

Violet looked utterly bewildered. She had never known her father to say anything that was not perfectly true, yet how could she disbelieve the evidence of her own senses?

"Papa, could it holler so loud when it was dead?" she asked deprecatingly.

"It did not, my little darling; 'twas I," said Cousin Ronald, preventing papa's reply. "The chick seemed to make the noise, but it was really I."

Papa and mamma both confirmed this statement and the puzzled child consented to partake of the mysterious fowl.

Minna, standing with her basket of keys at the back of her mistress' chair, Tom and Prilla, waiting on the table, had been as much startled and mystified by the chicken's sudden outcry as Vi herself, and seized with superstitious fears, turned almost pale with terror.

Mr. Lilburn's assertion and the concurrent assurance of their master and mistress relieved their fright, but they were still full of astonishment and gazed at the guest with wonder and awe.

Of course, the story was told in the kitchen and created much curiosity and excitement there.

This excitement was, however, soon lost in a greater when the news of the expected attack from the Ku Klux circulated among them an hour or two later.

It could not be kept from the children, but they were calmed and soothed by their mamma's assurance, "God will take care of us, my dears, and help papa, grandpa, and the rest to drive the bad men away."

"Mamma," said Vi, "we little ones can't fight, but if we pray a good deal to God, will that help?"

"Yes, daughter, for the Bible tells us God is the hearer and answerer of prayer."

Elsie herself seemed entirely free from agitation and alarm, full of hope and courage. She inspired those about her with the same feelings. The domestic machinery moved on in its usual quiet and regular fashion.

The kitchen department, it is true, was the scene of much earnest talk, but the words were spoken with bated breath and many an anxious glance from door and window, as if the speakers feared the vicinity of some lurking foe.

Aunt Dicey was overseeing the making of a huge kettle of soft soap.

"'Pears like dis yer's a long time a comin'" she said, giving the liquid a vigorous stir, then lifting her paddle and holding it over the kettle to see if it dripped off in the desired ropy condition. "But dere, dis ole sinnah no business growlin' 'bout dat, yah, yah!" and dropping the paddle, she put her hands on her hips, rolled up her eyes and fairly shook with half-suppressed laughter.

"What you larfin' at, Aunt Dicey? 'Pears you's mighty tickled 'bout suffin'," remarked the cook, looking up in wonder and curiosity from the eggs she was beating.

"What's de fun, Aunt Dicey?" asked Uncle Joe, who sat in the doorway busily engaged in cleaning a gun.

"Why, don't you see? De soap ain't gwine to come till 'bout de time de Kluxes roun' heyah. Den dis chile gib 'em a berry warm deception, yah! yah! yah—a berry warm 'un!"

"A powerful hot one," observed the cook, joining in the laugh, "but dey won't min' it. Dey's cobered up, you know."

"'Tain't no diffence," remarked Uncle Joe. "De gowns an' masks, dey nuffin but cotton cloth, an' de hot soap'll permeate right tru, an' scald de rascal's skins!"

"Dat's so, an' take de skin off, too."

Uncle Joe stopped work and mused a moment, scratching his head and gazing into vacancy.

"'Clar to goodness dat's a splendid idea, Aunt Dicey!" he burst out at length. "An' let's hab a kettle ob boilin' lye to tote upstairs in de house, 'bout de time we see de Kluxes comin' up de road. Den Aunt Chloe an' Prilla can expense it out ob de windows, a dippah full at a time. Kin you git um ready fo' den?"

"Dat I kin," she replied with energy. "Dis consecrated lye don't take no time to fix. I'll hab it ready, sho' as you lib."

Meanwhile the party from the Oaks had arrived according to appointment, and with Mr. Travilla and his guest, were busy with their arrangements for the coming conflict, when quite unexpectedly old Mr. Dinsmore and Calhoun Conly appeared upon the scene.

"We have broken in upon a conference, I think," remarked the old gentleman, glancing from one to another and noticing that the entrance of himself and grandson seemed to have thrown a slight constraint over them.

"Rest assured, that you are both most welcomed in my home," replied Mr. Travilla. "We were conferring together on a matter of importance, but one which I am satisfied need not be concealed from you or Cal. I have had certain information that the Ku Klux—"

"Stay!" cried Calhoun, springing to his feet, a burning flush rising to his hair. "Don't, I beg you, cousin, say another word in my presence. I—I know I'm liable to be misunderstood—a wrong construction put upon my conduct," he continued glancing in an agony of shame and entreaty from one astonished face to another. "But I beg you will judge me leniently and never, *never* doubt my loyalty to you all," and bowing courteously to the company he hastily left the room and hurrying out of the house, mounted his horse and galloped swiftly down the avenue.

For a moment those left behind looked at each other in dumb surprise; then, old Mr. Dinsmore broke the silence by a muttered exclamation, "Has the boy gone daft?"

"I think I understand it, sir," said his son. "Poor Cal has been deceived and cajoled into joining that organization under a misunderstanding of its deeds and aims. But having learned how base, cruel, and insurrectionary they are, has ceased to act with them—or rather never has acted with them—yet is bound by oath to keep their secrets and do nothing against them."

"He would be periling his life by taking part against them," added Mr. Travilla. "I think he has done the very best thing he could do under these trying circumstances."

He then went on with his communication to the old gentleman who received it with a storm of wrath and indignation.

"It is time indeed to put them down when it has come to this!" he exclaimed. "The idea of their daring to attack a man of your standing, an old family like this — of the best blood in the country! I say it's downright insolence and I'll come over myself and help chastise them for their temerity."

"Then you counsel resistance, sir?" queried the son to the father.

"Counsel it? Of course I do! Nobody but a coward would think of anything else. But what are your plans, Travilla?"

"To barricade the verandas with bags of sand and bales of cotton, leaving loopholes here and there, post ourselves behind these defenses and do what execution we can upon the assailants."

"Good! Who's your captain?"

"Your son, sir."

"Very good. He has had little or no experience in actual warfare, but I think his maiden effort will prove a success."

"If, on seeing our preparations, they depart peaceably, well and good," remarked Travilla. "But if they insist on forcing an entrance, we shall feel no scruples about firing upon them."

"Humph! I should think not, indeed!" grunted the old gentleman. "Indeed, 'self defense is the first law of nature.'"

"And we are told by our Lord, 'all they that take the sword, shall perish with the sword,'" observed his son.

The arrangements completed, the Dinsmores returned to their homes for the rest of the day.

About dusk the work of barricading was begun, all the able bodied men on the plantation, both house servants and field hands, being set to work at it. The materials had been brought up to the near vicinity of the house during the day. The men's hearts were in the undertaking—not one of them but would have risked his own life freely in the defense of their loved master and mistress—and many hands made light and speedy work.

While this was in progress, old Mr. Dinsmore and the whole family from the Oaks arrived, Rose and her daughter preferring to be there rather than left at home without their natural protectors.

Elsie welcomed them joyfully and at once engaged them in loading for the gentlemen.

The little ones were already in bed and sleeping sweetly, secure in the love and protecting care of their earthly and their heavenly Father. Little Elsie, now ten years old, was no longer required to retire quite so early, but when her regular hour came she went without a murmur.

She was quite ready for bed, had just risen from her knees, when her mother came softly in and clasped her in a tender embrace.

"Mamma, dear, dear mamma, how I love you! And papa, too!" whispered the child, twining her arms about her mother's neck. "Don't let us be afraid of those wicked men, mamma. I am sure God will not let them get papa, because we have all prayed so much for His help—all of us together in worship this morning and this evening, and we children up here. And Jesus said, 'If two of you shall agree on earth as touching anything that they shall ask, it shall be done for them of my Father which is in heaven.'"

"Yes, darling, and He will fulfill His word. He will not suffer anything to befall but what shall be for His glory and our good. Now, dear daughter, lie down and take that promise for a pillow to sleep upon, and if waked by sounds of conflict, lift up your heart to God for your dear father, and mine, and all of us."

"I will, mamma, I will."

Leaving a loving kiss on the sweet, young lips, and another on the brow of her sleeping Violet, the mother glided noiselessly from the room.

"What is it, mammy?" she asked on finding her faithful old nurse waiting to speak with her in the outer room.

"Miss Elsie, honey, is you willin' to let us scald dem Kluxes wid boilin' soap an' lye?"

"Scald them, mammy?" she exclaimed with a slight shudder. "I can hardly bear the thought of treating a dog so cruelly!"

"But dey's worse dan dogs, Miss Elsie. Dogs neber come and detack folks dat's sleeping quietly in dere beds, does dey now?"

"No, and these men would take my husband's life. You may all fight them with any weapon you can lay hands on."

Aunt Chloe returned her thanks and proceeded to give an account of the plan concocted by Aunt Dicey and Uncle Joe.

Elsie, returning to the dining room, repeated the plan there.

"Excellent!" exclaimed her brother. "Come, Art, let's hang a bell in the kitchen and attach a string to it, taking the other end up to the observatory."

The suggestion was immediately carried out. It had been previously arranged that the two young men should repair to the observatory, and there watch for the coming of the foe. On their first appearance, probably a mile or more distant, give the alarm to those below, by pulling a wire attached to that from which the front door bell was suspended. Thus, they would be setting it to ringing loudly. Now they were prepared to sound alarm in the kitchen, also, thus giving time for the removal of the boiling lye from the fire there to the second story of the mansion, where it was to be used according to Uncle Joe's plan.

The detective had reported the assailing party as numbering from thirty-five to forty. But the Ion force, though much inferior in point of numbers — even with the addition of eight or ten Negro men belonging to the Oaks and Ion who were tolerably proficient in the use of firearms — certainly had the advantage of position and of being on the side of right and justice.

The gentlemen seemed full of a cheerful courage, the ladies calm and hopeful. Yet they refused to retire, though strongly urged to do so, insisting that to sleep would be simply impossible.

It was but ten o'clock when all was ready, yet the young men deemed it most prudent to betake themselves at once to their lookout, since there might possibly have been some change in the plans of the enemy.

The others gathered in one of the lower rooms to while away the tedious time of waiting as best they could. Conversation flagged. They tried music, but it had lost its charm for the time being. They turned away from the piano and harp and sank into silence. The house seemed strangely silent, and the pattering of Bruno's feet as he passed slowly down the whole length of the corridor without, came to their ears with almost startling distinctness.

Then he appeared in the doorway, where he stood turning his eyes from one to another with a wistful, questioning gaze. Then, words seemed to come from his lips in tones of wonder and inquiry.

"What are you all doing here at this time o' night, when honest folk should be abed?"

"Just what I've been asking myself for the last hour," gravely remarked a statue in a niche in the opposite wall.

The effect was startling even to those who already understood the trick, but more so to the others. Rosie screamed and ran to her father for protection.

"Why, why, why!" cried old Mr. Dinsmore, in momentary perplexity and astonishment.

"Don't be afraid, Miss Rosie. I'm a faithful friend, and the woman over there couldn't hurt you if she would," said Bruno, going up to the young girl, wagging his tail and touching his cold nose to her hand.

She drew it away with another scream.

"Dear child," said her sister, "it is only a trick of ventriloquism."

"Meant to amuse, not alarm," added Mr. Lilburn.

Rosie, nestling in her father's arms, drew a long sigh of relief, and half-laughing, half-crying, looked up saucily into Mr. Lilburn's face.

"And it was you, sir? Oh, how you scared me!"

"I beg your pardon, my bonnie lassie," he said. "I thought to relieve, somewhat, the tediousness of the hour."

"For which accept our thanks," said Mr. Dinsmore. "But I perceive it is not the first time that Travilla and Elsie have been witnesses of your skill."

"No," said Elsie laughing. "My dear, you are good at a story. Tell them all what happened at breakfast this morning."

Mr. Travilla complied with the request. He was an excellent storyteller and made his narrative very entertaining to ease the watchers.

But in the midst of their mirth a sudden awe struck silence fell upon them. There was a sound as of the rattling of stiffly starched robes, then a gruff voice from the hall exclaimed, "There he is, the old scalawag! Dinsmore, too. Now take good aim, Bill, and let's make sure work."

Rosie was near screaming again, but catching sight of Mr. Lilburn's face, laughed instead—a little hysterical nervous laugh.

"Oh, it's you again, sir!" she cried. "Please, don't frighten me any more."

"Ah, no, I will not, I'm sorry," he said and at that moment a toy man and woman on the table began a vastly amusing conversation about their own private affairs.

In the kitchen and the domiciles of the house servants there was the same tedious waiting and watching—old and young, all up and wide awake, gathered in groups and talked in undertones of the doings of the Ku Klux, and of the reception they hoped to give them that night. Aunt Dicey glorying in the prospect of doing good service in the defense of "her family" as she proudly termed her master, mistress and their children, kept her kettles of soap and lye at boiling heat and two stalwart fellows close at hand to obey her orders.

Aunt Chloe and Dinah were not with the others, but in the nursery watching over the slumber of "de chillens." Uncle Joe was with Mr. Leland, who was not yet able to use the wounded limb and was to be assisted to his hiding place upon the first note of alarm.

In the observatory the two young men kept a vigilant eye upon every avenue of approach to the plantation. There was no moon that night, but the clear bright starlight made it possible to discern moving white objects at a considerable distance. Horace was full of excitement and almost eager for the fray. Arthur was calm and quiet.

"This waiting is intolerable!" exclaimed the former when they had been nearly an hour at their post. "How do you stand it, Art?"

"I find it tedious, and there is in all probability at least an hour of it yet before us. But my impatience is quelled by the thought that it may be to me the last hour of life."

"True, and to me also. A solemn thought, Art, and yet might not the same be said of any day or hour of our lives?"

From that they fell into a very serious conversation in which each learned more of the other's inner life than he had ever known before. Both were trusting in Christ and seeking to know and do His will, and from that hour their hearts were knit together as the hearts of David and Jonathan.

Gradually their talk ceased till but a word or two was dropped now and then. The vigilance of their watch was redoubled, for the hour of midnight had struck—the silver chimes of a clock in the hall below coming distinctly to their ears—and any moment might bring the raiders into view.

Below stairs too a solemn hush had fallen upon each with the first stroke of the clock, and hearts were going up in silent prayer to God.

Horace was gazing intently in the direction of Fairview but at a point somewhat beyond.

"Look, Art!" he cried in an excited whisper. "Do my eyes deceive me? Or are there really some white objects creeping slowly along yonder road?"

"I—I think—yes, yes it is they!" returned Arthur, giving a vigorous pull to the string attached to the bell in the kitchen while Horace did the same by the wire connected with the other. Then, springing to the stairway, they descended with all haste.

Loudly the alarm pealed out in both places, bringing all to their feet and paling the cheeks of the ladies present.

Mr. Dinsmore's orders were given promptly in calm, firm tones, and each repaired to his post.

Aunt Dicey, assuming command in the kitchen, delivered her orders with an equal promptness and decision.

"Yo' Ben an' Jack, tote dis yer pot ob lye up stairs quick as lightnin', an' set it whar Aunt Chloe tells yo'. An' yo' Venus, stan' by de pot ob soap wid a dippah in yo' han' an' fire away at de fust Klux dat shows his debbil horns an' tongue at de do'. Min' now, yo' take um in de eye, an' he neber come roun' heyah no mo' tryin' to kill Marse Ed'ard."

Mr. Leland had fallen asleep in the early part of the evening, but woke with the ringing of the alarm bells.

"Ah, they must be in sight, Uncle Joe," he said. "Help me to my hiding place and leave me there. You will be needed below."

"Yes, Massa Leland, dey's comin'," said the old man, instantly complying with his request. "An' dis un's to demand de boilin' lye compartment ob dis army ob defense."

A narrow couch had been spread in the little concealed apartment, and in a trice Mr. Leland found himself stretched upon it.

"There, I'm quite comfortable, Uncle Joe," he said. "Lay my pistols here, close to my hand, then close the panel with all care. And when you leave the room, lock the door behind you and hide the key in the usual place."

"Yes, sah, an' please, sah, as yo's got nuffin' else for to do, keep askin' de Lord ob armies to help de right and jus'."

"That I will," answered Leland heartily.

Uncle Joe, moving with almost youthful alacrity, obeyed the orders given, and hastened to join his wife and Dinah. He found them on the upper veranda in front of the nursery widows, standing ladle in hand, one by the kettle of lye, the other leaning over the railing watching for the coming of the foe.

The old man, arming himself also with a ladle of large capacity, took his station beside the latter.

"Aunt Chloe," he said, "yo' bettah go back to de chillens, fear dey might wake up an' be powerful scared o' all dis."

"Yes, 'spect I bettah. Dere ole mammy de best to be wid de darlins," she replied, resigning her ladle to Prilla, who joined them at that moment. She hurried back to her charges.

She found her mistress bending over the crib of the sleeping babe. "I am so thankful they were not roused by the noise, mammy," she said softly, glancing at the bed where the older two lay in profound slumber, "but don't leave them alone even for a moment."

"'Deed I won't, darlin'. De bressed little lambs! Dere ole mammy'd fight de Kluxes to her last breff, fo' dey should hurt a hair ob deir heads. But don't ye fret, Miss Elsie, honey. Dey'll not come yere. De good Lord'll not let dem get into de house," she added, big tears filling her old eyes while she clasp her idolized mistress in her arms as if she were still the little girl she had so loved to caress and cuddle years ago.

Elsie returned the embrace, gave a few whispered directions, and glided into the next room. There she lingered a moment by the couch of her little girls, who were also sleeping sweetly, then hastened to rejoin Mrs. Dinsmore and Rosie in one of the rooms opening upon the lower front veranda.

They sat at a table covered with both arms and ammunition. Rose was a little pale, but calm and composed, as was Elsie also. Rosie, making a great effort to be brave, could not still the loud beating of her heart as she sat listening intently for sounds from without.

Elsie, placing herself beside her young sister and taking her hand, pressed it tenderly, whispering with a glad smile, "'They that trust in the Lord shall be as Mount Zion, which can not be removed, but abideth forever.'"

Rosie nodded a half-tearful assent.

Horace looked in. "They are just entering the avenue. Mother and sisters, be brave and help us with your prayers," he said, low and earnestly and was gone.

The ladies exchanged one swift glance, then bent forward in a listening attitude and for the next few moments every other sense seemed lost in that of listening and hearing.

The night raiders, as was their usual custom, had dismounted at the gate, and leaving their horses in the care of two of their number, approached the house on foot. They came on three abreast, but as they neared the dwelling one line branched off and passed around it in the direction of the kitchen.

In an instant more the double column, headed by the leader of the troop, had reached the steps of the veranda, where it came to a sudden halt. A sort of half-smothered grunt of astonishment came from the captain as he hastily ran his eye along the barricade, which till that moment had been concealed from himself and his comrades by the semi-darkness and a profusion of flowering vines.

The darkness and silence of death seemed to reign within. Yet, each one of the little garrison was at his post, looking out through a loophole and covering one or another of the foe with his revolver, while with his finger upon the trigger, he only awaited the word of command to send the bullet to its mark.

Young Horace found it hard to restrain his impatience. What a splendid opportunity his father was letting slip! Why did he hesitate to give the signal? For, perhaps, the first time in his life, the young man thought his father unwise.

But Mr. Dinsmore knew what he was about. Blood should not be shed till the absolute necessity was placed beyond question.

A moment of suspense, of apparent hesitation on the part of the raiders, then in stentorian tones the leader, stepping back a little bit, called out, "Edward Travilla!"

There was no answer.

An instant of dead silence reigned, then the call was repeated.

Elsie shuddered and hid her face, faltering out a prayer for her husband's safety.

Still no reply, and the third time the man called, adding, with a volley of oaths and curses, "We want you, sir; come out at once or it'll be the worse for you."

Then, Mr. Dinsmore answered in calm, firm tones, "Your purpose is known. Your demand is unreasonable and lawless, and will not be complied with. Withdraw your men at once or it will be the worse for you."

"Boys!" cried the leader, turning to his men, "Up with your axes and clubs; we've got to batter down this breastwork, and it must be done!"

With a yell of fury the hideous forms rushed forward to attack.

"Fire!" rang out Mr. Dinsmore's voice in clarion tones, and instantly the crack of half a dozen revolvers was heard, a light blaze ran along the line of loopholes and at the same instant a sudden, scalding shower fell upon the assailants from the veranda above.

Several of them dropped upon the ground and as many more threw away their axes and clubs and ran screaming and swearing down the avenue.

But the others rallied and came on again yelling with redoubled fury, while simultaneously similar sounds came from the sides and rear of the dwelling.

The scalding shower was descending there, also. Uncle Joe and his command were busy and bullets were flying and doing some execution, though sent with less certain aim than from the front.

Aunt Dicey, too, and her satellites were winning the laurels they coveted.

As she had expected, several of the assailants came thundering to her door, loudly demanding admittance, at the same time that the attack was made in front.

"Who dar? What you want?" she called.

"We want in! Open the door instantly!"

"No, sah! Dis chile don' do no sich ting! Dis Marse Ed'ard's kitchen, an' Miss Elsie's."

Then in an undertone, "Now Venus an' Lize, fill yo' dippahs quick! An when dis un says fire, slam de contentions—dat's de bilin' soap, min'—right into dar ugly faces.

"An' Sally Ann, yo' creep up dem stairs, quick as lightnin' an' hide under the bed. It's yo' dey's after. Somebody mus' a tole 'em yo' sleeps yere sense de night dat bloody hand ben laid on yo' shouldah."

These orders were scarcely issued and obeyed when the door fell in with a loud crash. A hideous horned head appeared in the opening, only to receive three ladles-full of the boiling soap full in its face and fall back with a terrible, unearthly yell of agony and rage, into the arms of its companions, who quickly bore it shrieking away.

"Tank de Lord, dat shot tole!" exclaimed Aunt Dicey. "Now stan' ready for de nex'."

The party in the front were received with the same galling fire as before. At the same moment a sound, coming apparently from the road beyond the avenue, a sound as of the steady tramp, tramp of infantry, and the heavy rumbling and rolling of artillery, smote upon their ears.

There had been a report that Federal troops were on the march to suppress the outrages and protect the helpless victims. Seized with terror, the raiders gathered up their dead and wounded and fled.

CHAPTER
EIGHTEENTH

*Thus far our fortune keeps an onward course
And we are grac'd with wreaths of victory.*

"VICTORY!" SHOUTED HORACE, JR., waving his handkerchief about his head. "Victory and an end to the reign of terror! Hurrah for the brave troops of Uncle Sam that came so opportunely to the rescue! Come, let us sally forth to meet them. Elsie, unlock your stores and furnish the refreshments they have so well earned."

"They draw nearer!" cried Arthur, who had been listening intently. "Haste! They must be entering the avenue. They will meet the raiders. Travilla, uncle, shall we make an opening here in our breast-works?"

"Yes," answered both in a breath, than as if struck by a sudden thought, "No, no, let us reconnoiter first!" cried Mr. Dinsmore. "Horace, run up to the observatory, take a careful survey, and report as promptly as possible."

Horace bounded away, hardly waiting to hear the conclusion of the sentence.

"I counsel delay," said old Mr. Dinsmore, who was peering through a loophole. "The troops have not entered the avenue, the Ku Klux may return though I do not expect it after the severe repulse we have twice given them. But 'discretion is the better part of valor.'"

"Right, sir," said Mr. Lilburn. "Let us give them no chance for a more successful onslaught."

"Oh, yes, do be careful!" cried the ladies, joining them. "Don't tear down the least part of our defenses yet."

"Have they really fled? Are you all unhurt?" asked Rose in trembling tones.

"Edward! Papa!" faltered Elsie.

"Safe and sound," they both answered.

"Thank God!" she cried as her husband folded her in his arms. Her father took her hand in his, while with the other arm he embraced Rose.

"We have indeed cause for thankfulness," said Arthur, returning from a hurried circuit of the verandas. "Not one on our side has received a scratch. But I have ordered the men to remain at their posts for the present."

Horace came rushing back. "I can not understand it! I see no sign of troops, though—"

"The darkness," suggested his mother.

"Hark! Hark! The bugle call. They are charging on the Ku Klux!" exclaimed Arthur, as a silvery sound came floating on the night breeze.

"Oh, they have come! They have come!" cried Rosie, clapping her hands and dancing up and down with delight. "Now our troubles are over and there will be no more of these dreadful raids." And in the exuberance of her joy she embraced first her mother, then her sister, and lastly threw herself into her father's arms.

"Ah, I wish it were so," he said caressing her, "but I begin to fear that the sounds we have heard with so much relief and pleasure, were as unreal as Bruno's talking a while ago."

"Oh, was it you, Mr. Lilburn?" she cried in a tone of sore disappointment.

"Ah, well, my bonnie lassie, the Ku Klux are gone at all events. Indeed, let us be thankful for that," he answered.

"What does it all mean?" asked the two young men in a breath. "What strange deception has been practiced upon us?"

"My cousin is a ventriloquist," replied Elsie, "and has done us good service in using his talent to help in driving away the Ku Klux."

He instantly received a unanimous vote of thanks, and the young people began pouring out eager questions and remarks.

"Another time—my work is but half done! I must pursue!" he cried, hastily leaving them to seek an exit from the house.

Elsie hurried away to see if her little ones still slept. All did but little Elsie and she was full of joy and thankfulness that her dear papa's cruel foes had been driven away.

"Ah, mamma, God heard our prayers and helped us out of this great trouble!" she said, receiving and returning a tender embrace.

"Indeed he has, daughter, let us thank Him for His goodness, and ever put our trust in Him. Have you been long awake?"

"It was their dreadful screams that awakened me, mamma. I couldn't help crying for one man. It seemed as if he must be in such an agony of pain.

Uncle Joe says Aunt Dicey and the others threw boiling soap into his eyes, and all over his face and head. Mamma, aren't you sorry for him?"

"Yes, indeed!" and the child felt a great tear fall on her head, resting on her mother's shoulder. "Poor, poor fellow! He finds the way of the transgressors hard, as the Bible says it is. Now, darling, lie down again and try to sleep. I think the danger is over for tonight."

Returning, she met her husband in the hall. "I have been to tell Leland the good news!" he said. "He is very happy over it. And now, dear wife, go to bed and sleep, if you can. You are looking very weary and I think need fear no further disturbance. Your grandfather, Mrs. Dinsmore, and Rosie have yielded to our persuasions and retired."

"And you and papa?"

"Can easily stand the loss of one night's sleep, but may perhaps get an hour or so of repose upon the sofas. But we will keep a constant watch till sunrise. Arthur and Horace are going up to the observatory again, while the rest of us will pace the verandas by turns."

Morning found the Ion mansion wearing much the appearance of a recently besieged fortress. How many of the Klan had lost their lives it was impossible to tell, but probably only a small number, as the aim of the party of defense had been, by mutual agreement, to disable and not to slay. But it was thought the assailants had suffered a sufficiently severe punishment to deter them from a renewal of the attack. Also, Mr. Lilburn's pursuit keeping up the delusion that troops were at hand had greatly demoralized them. So the barricades were presently taken down, and gradually the dwelling and its surroundings resumed their usual aspect of neatness, order, and elegance.

All the friends remained to breakfast, but their presence did not exclude the children from the morning table.

While the guests were being helped, there was a momentary silence broken by a faint squeal that seemed to come from under Eddie's plate.

"Mousie at de table!" cried Harold. Then, "Oh me dot a bird!" as the notes of a canary came from underneath his plate.

"Pick up your plate and let us see the mouse and the bird," said their papa, smiling.

They obeyed.

"Ah, I knew there was nothing there," said Eddie, laughing and looking at Cousin Ronald, while Harold gazing at the tablecloth in disappointed surprise, cried, "Ah, it's gone! It must have flewed away."

Calhoun Conly, knowing nothing, but suspecting a great deal, and extremely full of anxiety, repaired to Ion directly after breakfast. Blood stains on the ground without and within the gate, and here and there along the avenue as he rode up to the house confirmed his surmise that his friends had been attacked by the Ku Klux the previous night. He found them all in the library talking the matter over.

"Ah, sir! Like a brave man and a true friend, you come when the fight is over," was his grandfather's sarcastic greeting.

"It was my misfortune, sir, to be unable in this instance, to follow my inclinations," returned the young man, coloring to the very roots of his hair with mortification. "But" — glancing around the circle—"heaven be thanked that I find you all unhurt," he added with a sigh that told that a great load had been taken from his heart. "May I hear the story? I see the men are tearing down a breastwork and I suppose the attacking party must have been a large one."

"Not too large, however, for us to beat back and defeat without your kind assistance," growled his irritated grandfather.

"Ah, grandpa, he would have helped if he could," said Mrs. Travilla. "Sit down, Cal, we are very glad to see you."

His uncle and Travilla joined in the assurance, but Horace and Arthur regarded him rather coolly, and "Cousin Ronald" thought he deserved some slight punishment.

As he attempted to take the offered seat, "Squeal, squeal, squeal!" came from his coat pocket, causing him to stand and redden again, with a renewed embarrassment that colored his flesh again.

"Oh, Cousin Cal! Has *you* dot a wee little piggy in your pocket? Let me see him," cried Harold, running up and trying to get a peep at it. Then, he started back with a cry of alarm at a sudden, loud barking as of an infuriated dog at Calhoun's heels.

Bruno came bounding in with an answering bark. Calhoun thrust his hand into his pocket with the purpose to summarily eject the pig, and at the same time, wheeled about to confront his canine antagonist. He looked utterly confounded at finding none there, while to add to his confusion and perplexity, a bee seemed to be circling round his head, now buzzing at one ear, now at the other.

He tried to dodge it, he put up his hand to drive it away, then wheeled about a second time, as the furious bark was renewed in his rear, but turned pale and looked absolutely frightened at the discovery that the dog was still invisible. Then, he reddened again at perceiving that everyone present was laughing.

His cousin Elsie was trying to explain, but could not make herself heard above the furious barking. She looked imploringly at Mr. Lilburn and it ceased on the instant.

Calhoun dropped into a chair and glanced inquiringly from one to another.

His uncle answered him in a single word, "Ventriloquism."

"Sold!" exclaimed the youth, joining faintly in the mirth. "Strange I did not think of that, though how could I suppose there was a ventriloquist here?"

"An excellent one, is he not? You must hear what good service he did last night," said Mr. Travilla, and went on to tell the story of the attack and the subsequent defense.

Elsie and Eddie listened to the account with keen interest. Vi, who had been devoting herself in motherly fashion to a favorite doll, laid it aside to hear what was said, but Harold was playing with Bruno, who seemed hardly yet to have recovered from his wonder at not finding the strange canine intruder who had so raised his ire.

Harold had climbed upon his back, and with his arms around his neck was talking to him in an undertone. "Now you's my horse, Bruno. Let's go ridin' like papa and Beppo."

The dog started toward the door. "With all my heart, little master. Which way shall we go?"

"Why, Bruno, you s'prise me! Can you talk?" cried the little fellow in great delight. "Why didn't you begin sooner? Mamma, oh, mamma, did you hear Bruno talk?"

Mamma smiled and said gently, "Be quiet, son, while papa and the rest are talking, or else take Bruno out to the veranda."

Cousin Ronald was amusing himself with the children. Vi's doll presently began to cry and call upon her to be taken up and she ran to it in surprised delight, till she remembered that it was "only Cousin Ronald and not dolly at all."

But Cousin Ronald had a higher object than his own or the children's amusement. He was trying to divert their thoughts from the doings of the Ku Klux, lest they should grow timid and fearful.

CHAPTER NINETEENTH

Revenge at first though sweet,
Bitter ere long, back on itself recoils.

—MILTON

GEORGE BOYD, WHO WAS OF a most vindictive temper, had laid his plans for the night of the raid upon Ion to wreak his vengeance not upon Travilla only, but also upon the woman on whose clothing he had left the impress of his bloody hand.

With this in view, he went first to the kitchen department where, as he had learned through the gossip of the servants, she now passed the night, intending afterward to have a hand in the brutal flogging to be meted out to Mr. Travilla. He headed the attacking party there and it was he who received upon his person the full broadside from Aunt Dicey's battery of soap ladles.

The pain was horrible, the scorching mass clinging to the flesh and burning deeper and deeper as he was borne shrieking away in the arms of his comrades.

"Oh, take it off! Take it off! I'm burning up, I tell you!" he yelled as they carried him swiftly down the avenue. But they hurried on, seemingly unmindful of his cries, mingled though they were with oaths and imprecations, nor paused till they had reached the shelter of the woods at some little distance on the opposite side of the road.

"Curse you!" he said between his clenched teeth, as they laid him down at the foot of a tree. "Curse you for keeping me in this agony. Help me off with these—duds. Unbutton it, quick! Quick! I'm burning up, I tell you, and my hands are nearly as bad as my face. Oh! Oh! You fiends! Do you want to murder me outright? You're bringing all the skin with it!" he roared, writhing in unendurable torture, as they dragged off the disguise. "Oh, kill me! Bill, shoot me through the head and put me out of this torment, will you?"

"No, no, I daren't. Come, come, pluck up courage and bear it like a man."

"Bear it, indeed! I only wish you had it to bear. I tell you it can't be borne! Water, water, for the love of heaven! Carry me to the river and throw me in. My eyes are put out; they burn like balls of fire."

"Stop that yelling, will you!" cried a voice from a little distance. "You'll betray us. We're whipped and there's troops coming up, too."

"Sure, Smith?"

"Yes, heard their tramp, tramp distinctly—rumble of artillery, too. Can't be more'n a mile off, if that. Hurry, boys, no time to lose! Who's this groaning at such an awful rate? What's the matter?"

"Scalded, horribly scalded."

"He ain't the only one, though maybe he's the worst. And Blake's killed outright; two or three more, I believe. There are some with pretty bad pistol shot wounds. Tell you they made warm work of us. There's been a traitor among us, betrayed our plans and put 'em on their guard."

He concluded with a torrent of oaths and fearful imprecations upon the traitor, whoever he might be.

"Hist!" cried the one Boyd had addressed as Bill, "Hist, boys! The bugle call! They're on us. Stop your noise, Boyd, can't you?" as the latter, seized and borne onward again, not too gently, yelled and roared with redoubled vigor. "Be quiet or you'll have 'em after us in no time."

"Shoot me through the head then. It's the only thing that'll help me to stop it."

Mr. Lilburn, keeping well in the shadow of the trees, had hurried after the retreating foe, and concealing himself behind a clump of bushes close to the gate, caused his bugle note to sound in their ears as if coming from a point some half a mile distant.

Convinced that a detachment of United States troops were almost upon them, those carrying the dead and wounded dashed into the woods with their burdens. While in hot haste, the others mounted and galloped away, never drawing rein until they had put several miles between them and the scene of their attempted outrage.

Meantime, those in the woods, moving as rapidly as possible under the circumstances, were plunging deeper and deeper into its recesses.

There was an occasional groan or half-suppressed shriek from others of the wounded, but Boyd's cries were incessant and heart-rending, till a handkerchief was suddenly thrust into his mouth with a muttered exclamation, "Necessity knows no law! It's to save your own life and liberty as well as ours."

At length, well nigh spent with their exertions, the bearers paused, resting their burdens for a moment upon the ground, while they listened intently for the sounds of pursuit.

"We've baffled 'em, I think," panted Bill. "I don't hear no more of that—tramp, tramp, and the bugle's stopped, too."

"That's so and I reckon we're pretty safe now," returned another voice. "But what's to be done with these fellows? Where'll we take 'em?"

"To Rood's still-house," was the answer. "It's about half a mile further on, and deep in the woods. And I say you, Tom Arnold, pull off your disguise and go after Dr. Savage as fast as you can. Tell him to come to the still-house on the fleetest horse he can get hold of, and bring along everything necessary to dress scalds and pistol-shot wounds. Say there's no time to lose or Boyd'll die on our hands. Now up with your load, boys, and on again."

The voice had a tone of command and the orders were instantly obeyed.

The still-house was an old, dilapidated frame building, whose rude accommodations differed widely from those to which, save during army life, Boyd had been accustomed from infancy.

They carried him in and laid him down upon a rough pallet of straw furnished with coarse cotton sheets and an army blanket or two, which were not overly clean.

But in his dire extremity of pain he heeded naught of this. And his blinded eyes could not see the bare rafters overhead, the filthy uncarpeted floor, the few broken chairs and rude board seats, or the little unpainted pine table with its bit of flickering, flaming tallow candle, stuck in an old bottle.

His comrades did what they could for his relief. But it was not much, and their clumsy handling was exquisite torture to the raw, quivering flesh, and his entreaties that they would put him out of his misery at once, by sending a bullet through his brain, were piteous to hear. They had taken his arms from him or he would have destroyed himself.

The room was filled with doleful sounds—the groans and sighs of men in sore pain, but his rose above the others.

Dr. Savage arrived at length, but half drunk and, an unskilled surgeon at his best, made but clumsy work with his patients on this occasion.

Yet the applications brought, in time, some slight alleviation of even Boyd's unendurable agony. His cries grew fainter and less frequent, till they ceased altogether; and like the other wounded, he relieved himself only with an occasional moan or groan.

The doctor had finished his task and lay in a drunken sleep on the floor. The uninjured raiders had followed his example, the candle had burned itself out and all was darkness and silence save the low, fitful sounds of the suffering.

To Boyd sleep was impossible, the pain of his burns was still very great, especially in his eyes, the injury to which he feared must result in total blindness. How could he bear it, he asked himself, to go groping his way through life in utter darkness? Horrible! Horrible! He would *not* endure it. They had put the means of self-destruction out of his way now, but on the first opportunity to get hold of a pistol, he would blow his own brains out and be done with this agony. The Bible was a fable, death an eternal sleep. He had been saying it for years, till he thought his belief—or more correctly unbelief—

firmly fixed; but now the early teachings of a pious mother came back to him and he trembled with the fear that they might be true.

"It is appointed unto men once to die, but after that the judgment." "Everyone of us shall give an account of himself to God." "These shall go away into everlasting punishment." "Where their worm dieth not, and the fire is not quenched." Fire, fire! Oh, how unendurable he had found it! Dare he risk its torment throughout endless ages of eternity? Self-destruction might be but a plunge into deeper depths of anguish—from which there could be no return.

For days and weeks he lay in his miserable hiding place. He was almost untended save for the doctor's visits and the bringing of his meals by one or another of his confederates, who would feed him with a rough sort of kindness, then go away again, leaving him to the solitary companionship of his own bitter thoughts.

He longed for the pleasant society and gentle ministrations of his aunt and he knew that if sent for she would come to him, and that his secret would be safe with her; but, alas, how could he bear that she should know of his crime and its punishment? She who had so earnestly besought him to forsake his evil ways and live in peace and love with all men, she who had warned him again and again that "the way of transgressors is hard," and that "though hand join in hand, the wicked shall not be unpunished." She had loved, cared for, and watched over him with almost a mother's undying, unalterable tenderness and devotion.

How ungrateful she would deem his repeated attempt against the home and husband of one whom she loved as her own child. She would not reprove him, she would not betray him, but he would know that in her secret heart she condemned him as a guilty wretch, a disgrace to her and all his relatives. And that would be worse, far worse to his proud spirit than the dreary loneliness of his present condition and the lack of the bodily comforts she would provide.

No, he would bear his bitter fate as best he might, and though he had proved the truth of her warning words, she should never know it, if he could keep it from her.

Troops had arrived in the neighborhood the day after the raid on Ion, so to Boyd's other causes of distress was added the constant fear of detection and apprehension. This was one reason why the visits of his compatriots were few and short.

The Klan was said to be disbanded and outrages had ceased, but an investigation was going on and search being made for the guilty parties. Also, United States revenue officers were known to be in quest of illicit distilleries, to which class this one of Rood's belonged.

"What's the news?" asked Boyd one morning while Savage was engaged in dressing his hurts.

"Very bad, you'll have to get out of this at once if you don't want to be nabbed. A jail might be more comfortable in some respects, eh, old boy? But I s'pose you prefer liberty.

"'Better to sit in Freedom's hall,
With a cold damp floor, and a moldering wall,
Than to bend the neck or bow the knee
In the proudest palace of Slavery.'

"Fine sentiment, eh, Boyd?"

The doctor was just drunk enough to spout poetry without knowing or caring whether it was exactly apropos or not.

"Very fine, though not quite to the point, it strikes me," answered Boyd, wincing under the not too gentle touch of the inebriate's shaking hand. "But how am I to get out of this? Blind and nearly helpless as I am?"

"Well, sir, we've planned it all out for you—never forsake a brother in distress, you know. There's a warrant out for Bill Dobbs and he has to skedaddle, too. He starts for Texas tonight and will take charge of you."

Savage went on to give the details of the plan, then left with a promise to return at nightfall. He did so, bringing Dobbs and Smith with him. Boyd's wounds were attended to again, Dobbs looking on to learn the *modus operandi.* Then the invalid, aided by Smith on one side and Dobbs on the other, was conducted to an opening in the woods where a horse and wagon stood in readiness. He was placed in it, Dobbs taking a seat by his side and supporting him with his arm, and driven a few miles along an unfrequented road to a little country station, where they took the night train going south.

The conductor asked no questions, merely exchanged glances with Dobbs, and seeing him apparently in search of a pin in the inside of his coat, opened his own and handed him one, then passed on through the car.

❦ ❦ ❦ ❦ ❦

George Boyd was missed from the breakfast table at Ashlands on the morning after the raid upon Ion. His aunt sent a servant to his room to see if he had overslept.

The man returned with the report that "Marse George" was not there and that his bed had certainly not been occupied during the night.

Still as his movements were at times uncertain, and the ladies, having no communication with the Oaks or Ion on the previous day, were in ignorance of all that had transpired there. So his absence caused them no particular anxiety or alarm. The meal went on, enlivened by cheerful chat.

"Mamma," said Herbert, "it's a lovely morning. Do give us a holiday and let's drive over to the Oaks. We haven't seen Aunt Rose and the rest for ever so long."

The other children joined in the petition, grandma put in a word of approval, and mamma finally consented—if the truth were told nothing loath to give, or to share the treat.

The carriage was ordered at once, and they set out shortly after leaving the table.

Arrived at their destination, they found Mrs. Murray on the veranda, looking out with an eager, anxious face.

"Ah!" she said, coming forward as the ladies alighted, "I didna expect—my sight is no so keen as in my younger days, and I thocht till this moment 'twas Mr. Dinsmore's carriage, bringing them home again after their dreadfu' nicht at Ion."

Both ladies turned pale and old Mrs. Carrington leaned heavily upon her daughter-in-law for support. Her lips moved but no sound came from them and she gasped for breath.

"Oh, please tell us!" cried Sophy, "what has happened at Ion?"

The children, too, were putting the same question in varying tones and words.

"The Ku Klux," faltered the housekeeper. "An' ye hadna heard aboot it, my leddies?"

"No, no, not a word," exclaimed Sophy, "but see, my mother is fainting. Help me to carry her into the house."

"No, no, I can walk. I am better now, thank you," said Mrs. Carrington, in low, faltering tone. "Just give me the support of your arm, Mrs. Murray."

They led her in between them and laid her gently on a sofa.

"That must be where George was!" she sighed, closing her eyes wearily. Then half starting up, "Tell me, oh, tell me, was—Mr. Travilla injured?"

"No, my leddy, he had been warned and was ready for them."

"Thank God! Thank God!" came faintly from the white quivering lips as she sank back upon her pillow again, and two great tears stealing from beneath the closed eyelids rolled slowly down the furrowed cheeks.

"You have heard the particulars, then?" said Sophy, addressing the housekeeper. "And my brother and sister were there?"

"Yes, ma'am, and Master Horace and Miss Rosie, too. Yes, and some of the men-servants. Mr. Dinsmore's man John was one o' them, and he's come back and from him I learned a' was richt with our friends."

"Oh, call him in and let me hear all he can tell!" entreated the old lady.

The request was immediately complied with and John gave a graphic and in the main correct account of the whole affair.

His tale was to all his listeners one of intense, thrilling, painful interest. They lost not a word and when he had finished his story the old lady cross-questioned him closely. "Did he know who had warned Mr. Travilla? Were any of the raiders recognized—any of them?"

Both of these questions John answered in the negative. "At least," he corrected himself, "he had not heard that anyone was recognized. They were all completely disguised and they had carried away their dead and wounded, both the shot and the scalded."

At that moment Mr. Dinsmore's family carriage drove up and John bowed and retired.

There were tearful embraces between the sisters and other relatives, and between Rose and the elder Mrs. Carrington.

"I feel as if you had been in terrible danger," said Sophy, wiping her eyes. "John has just been telling us all about it. What a mercy that Mr. Travilla was warned in time!"

"By whom, Horace? If not an improper question," asked the old lady, turning to Mr. Dinsmore.

"By a detective, Mrs. Carrington, who was secretly present at the meeting and heard all of the organized arrangements of the Klu Klux."

"He then knew who were the members appointed to be of the attacking party?"

Mr. Dinsmore bowed assent.

"Was—George one?"

"My dear madam, I did not see the detective, but their raids are usually made by men coming from quite a distance."

"You are evading my question. I implore you to tell me all you know. George did not come down to breakfast, had evidently not occupied his bed last night, and this seems to explain his absence. I know, too, that he has bitterly hated Travilla since — since his arrest and imprisonment. Will you not tell me? Any certainty is to be preferred to this — this horrible suspense. I would know the worst."

Thus adjured Mr. Dinsmore told her George had been appointed one of the party, but that he could not say that he was actually there. Also, he suppressed the fact that the appointment had been made by George's own request.

She received the communication in silence, but the anguish in her face told that she felt little doubt of her nephew's guilt. And as days and weeks rolled on bringing no news of him, her suspicions settled into a sad certainty, with the added sorrowful doubt whether he was living or dead.

CHAPTER TWENTIETH

Before we end our pilgrimage, 'tis fit that we
Should leave corruption, and foul sin behind us.
But with washed feet and hands,
the heathen dared not
Enter their profane temples; and for me
To hope my passage to eternity
Can be made easy, till I have shook off
The burden of my sins in free confession,
Aided with sorrow and repentance for them,
Is against reason.

—*M*ASSINGER

IT BEGAN TO BE NOTICED THAT Wilkins Foster also had disappeared. It was said that he had not been seen since the raid upon Fairview and the general supposition was that he had taken part in the outrage, received a wound in the fray and, on advent of the troops, had fled the country.

His mother and sisters led a retired life, seldom going from home except to attend church and even there they had been frequently missing of late.

Elsie had been much engaged in efforts to comfort her old friend, Mrs. Carrington, and to entertain Mr. Lilburn, who was still at Ion. Little excursions to points of interest in the vicinity and visits to the plantations of the different families of the connection, who vied with each other in doing him honor, filled up the time to the exclusion of almost everything else, except the home duties which she would never allow herself to neglect.

Baskets of fruit and game, accompanied by kind messages, had found their way now and again from Ion to the cottage home of the Fosters, but weeks had passed since the sweet face of Ion's mistress had been seen within its walls.

Elsie's tender conscience reproached her for this when, after an absence of several Sundays, Mrs. Foster again occupied her pew in the church of which both were members.

The poor lady was clad in black, seemed to be aging fast, and the pale, thin face had a weary, heart-broken expression that brought tears to Elsie's eyes.

When the service closed she took pains to intercept Mrs. Foster, who was trying to slip away unnoticed, and taking her hand in a warm clasp, kindly inquired concerning the health of herself and family.

"About as usual, Mrs. Travilla," was the reply.

"I am glad to hear it. I feared you were ill. You are looking weary, and no wonder after your long walk. You must let us take you home. There is plenty of room in the carriage, as the gentlemen came on horseback, and it will be a real pleasure to me to have your company."

The sincere, earnest, kindly tone and manner quite disarmed the pride of the fallen gentlewoman and a momentary glow of grateful pleasure lighted up her sad face.

"But it will take you fully a mile out of your way," she said, hesitating to accept the proffered kindness of a ride.

"Ah, that is no objection. It is so lovely a day for a drive," said Elsie, leading the way to the carriage.

"This seems like a return of the good old times before the war!" sighed Mrs. Foster, leaning back upon the softly cushioned seat as they went rapidly along. "Ah, Mrs. Travilla, if we could but have been content to let well enough alone! I have grown weary, inexpressibly weary of all this hate, bitterness, and contention, and the poverty—ah, well, I will not complain!" and she closed her lips tightly and resolutely.

"It was a sad mistake," Elsie answered, echoing the sigh. "And it will take many years to recover from it."

"Yes, I shall not live to see it."

"Nor I, perhaps, not here, but yonder in the better land," Elsie answered, with a smile of hope and of gladness.

Mrs. Foster nodded assent, her heart too full for utterance. Nor did she speak again till the carriage drew up before her own door.

Then repeating her thanks, "You have not been here for a long time, Mrs. Travilla," she said, "I know I have not returned your calls, but—" she paused, seemingly again overcome with emotion.

"Ah, that shall not keep me away, if you wish me to come," returned Elsie.

"We would be very glad indeed, hardly anyone else is so welcome."

"I fear I have neglected you, Mrs. Foster, but shall try to come soon. And I shall be pleased at any time to see you at Ion," Elsie answered as the carriage drove on.

A day or two afterward she fulfilled her promise and was admitted by Annie, the eldest daughter.

She, too, looked pale and careworn, and had evidently been weeping.

"Oh, Mrs. Travilla!" she exclaimed and burst into a fresh flood of tears.

Elsie, her own eyes filling with sympathetic drops, put her arm about her, whispering, "My poor, dear child, what can I do to comfort you?"

"Nothing! Nothing!" sobbed the girl, resting her head for a moment on Elsie's shoulder, "but come into the parlor, dear Mrs. Travilla, and let me call mamma."

"Ah, stay a moment," Elsie said, detaining her. "Are you sure, quite sure that I can do nothing to help you?"

Annie shook her head. "This trouble is beyond human help. Yes, yes, you can pray for us and also for him."

The last words uttered were almost inaudible from emotion, and she hurried away, leaving the guest the sole occupant of the room.

Involuntarily Elsie glanced about her and a pang went to her heart as she noticed that every article of luxury, almost of comfort, had disappeared. The pictures were gone from the walls, the pretty ornaments from mantle and center table, coarse cheap matting covered the floor in lieu of the costly carpet of other days, and rosewood and damask had given place to cottage furniture of the simplest and most inexpensive kind.

"How they must feel the change!" she thought within herself, "and yet perhaps not just now; these minor trials are probably swallowed up in a much greater one."

Mrs. Foster came in looking shabbier and more heart-broken than at their last meeting.

"My dear Mrs. Travilla, this is kind!" she said making a strong effort to speak with composure but failing utterly as she met the tender sympathizing look in the sweet soft eyes of her visitor.

Elsie put her arms about her and wept with her. "Someone is ill, I fear?" she said at length.

"Yes—my son. Oh, Mrs. Travilla, I am going to lose him!" and she was well nigh convulsed with bitter, choking sobs.

"While there is life there is hope," whispered Elsie. "Who can say what God may do for us in answer to our prayers?"

The mother shook her head in sad hopelessness.

"The doctor has given him up, says nothing more can be done."

"Dr. Barton?"

"No, no, Savage. Oh if we could but have had Barton at first the result might have been different. I have no confidence in Savage, even when sober, and he's drunk nearly all the time now."

"Oh, then things may not be so bad as he says then. Let me send over Dr. Barton at once."

"Thank you, but I must ask Wilkins first. He was wounded some weeks ago, injured internally, and has been suffering agonies of pain ever since. I wanted Dr. Barton sent for at once, but he would not hear of it. He said the risk was too great and he must trust to Savage. But now—" she paused, overcome with grief.

"But now the greater risk is in doing without him," suggested Elsie. "May I not send immediately?"

"Excuse me one moment, and I will ask," the said leaving the room.

She returned shortly to remark that Wilkins had indeed consented that Dr. Barton should be summoned immediately and accepted Mrs. Travilla's kind offer with thanks.

Elsie at once sent her servant and carriage upon the errand and meanwhile engaged in conversation with her hostess. It was principally an account by the latter of her son's illness.

His sufferings, she said, had been intense, at first borne with fierce impatience and muttered imprecations upon the hand that had inflicted the wound. He had likened himself to a caged tiger, so unbearable was the confinement to him—almost more so than the torturing pain—but of late a great change had come over him; he had grown quiet and submissive, and the bitter hate seemed to have died out of his heart.

"As it has out of mine, I hope," continued the mother, the big tears rolling down her cheeks. "I am now sensible that the feelings I have indulged against some persons—the Lelands principally— were most unchristian, and I hope the Lord has helped me to put them away. It has been hard for us to see strangers occupying our dear old home, and yet it was certainly no fault of theirs that we were compelled to give it up."

"That is all true," Elsie said, "I think that I can understand both your feelings and theirs. But they are dear good Christian people, and I assure you bear you no ill-will."

"Ah, is that so? I am told Leland has not really gone North, as was supposed, but has returned to the plantation since—since the coming of the federal troops."

"He has, and is nearly recovered from the wound."

"He was wounded, then?"

"Yes, pretty badly."

"And was in hiding somewhere, and his wife staying on alone with her children and servants? I wonder she had the courage."

"She put her trust in the Lord, as I believe both you and I do, my dear Mrs. Foster. And He has not failed her."

Mrs. Foster mused sadly for a moment. "I have felt hard to her," she murmured at length, in low, trembling tones, "and she is a Christian, whom I should love for the Master's sake, and it was quite natural for her to—defend her husband and children. I should have done the same for mine."

She had not mentioned when or where Wilkins had received his wound, but Elsie knew now that it was at Fairview and that Mrs. Leland's or Archie's hand had sped the bullet that had done such fearful work upon him.

Dr. Barton came. Mrs. Foster went with him to the sick room and Elsie lingered, anxious to hear his opinion of the case.

But Annie came hurrying in with her tear-swollen face. "Dear Mrs. Travilla, won't you come, too?" she sobbed. "Mamma will be so glad, and—and Wilkins begs you will come."

Elsie rose and put her arm about the waist of the weeping girl. "I will gladly do all I can for him, your mamma, or any of you," she whispered.

There was no want of comfort or luxury in the sick room. Mother and sisters had sacrificed every such thing to this idol of their hearts, this only son and brother. He lay propped up with pillows, his face pale as that of a corpse, and breathing with great difficulty.

Dr. Barton sat at the bedside with his finger on the patient's pulse while he asked a few brief questions, then relapsed into a thoughtful silence.

All eyes were turned upon him with intense anxiety, waiting in almost breathless suspense for his verdict, but his countenance betrayed nothing.

"Oh, doctor!" sighed the mother at length. "Have you no word of hope to speak?"

"Let us have none of false hope, doctor," gasped the sufferer. "I would know—the—worst."

"My poor lad," said the kind, old physician, in tender and fatherly tones, "I will not deceive you. Whatever preparation you have to make for your last journey, let it be made at once."

With a burst of uncontrollable anguish the mother and sisters fell upon their knees at the bedside.

"How—long—doctor?" faltered the sick man.

"You will hardly see the rising of another sun."

The low, gently spoken words pierced more than one heart as with a dagger's point.

"Was—this—wound—mortal—in—the—first place?" asked Wilkins.

"I think not if it had had prompt and proper attention. But that is a question of little importance now. You are beyond human skill. Is there anything in which I can assist you?"

"Yes—yes—pray for—my guilty soul."

It was no new thing for Dr. Barton to do—an earnest Christian, he ministered to the souls as well as the bodies of his patients. He knelt and offered a fervent prayer for the dying one, that repentance and remission of sins might be given him, that he might have a saving faith in the Lord Jesus and trusting only in His imputed righteousness, be granted an abundant entrance into His kingdom and glory.

"Thanks—doctor," gasped Wilkins. "I—I've been a bad man, a—very bad, wicked—man. Can there be any hope for—me?"

"'Whosoever will let him take the water of life freely.' 'Him that cometh unto Me I will in no wise cast out.'"

"Isn't it—too—late?" The hollow eyes gazed despairingly into the doctor's face.

"'Whosoever will,' you may come if you will, so long as death has not fixed your eternal state."

"I will! Lord, help—save me! Me, a poor—lost—vile—helpless—sinner!" he cried, lifting his eyes and clasped hands to heaven, while great tears coursed down his sunken cheeks. "I cast myself—at—Thy feet. Oh, pardon, save me or—I am—I am—lost forever."

The eyes closed, the hands dropped, and for a moment they thought he had passed away with that agonized cry for mercy and forgiveness. But a deep sigh heaved his chest, his lips moved and his mother bent over him to catch the words.

"Leland. Send—for—him."

With streaming eyes she turned to Elsie and repeated the words, adding, "Do you think he would come?"

"I am quite sure of it. I will go for him at once."

The white lips were moving again.

The mother explained, amid her choking sobs. "He says the wife, too, and—and your husband and father. Oh, will they come? Tell them my boy is dying and would desire to go at peace with all the world."

"I will, and they will come," Elsie answered, weeping and hurried away.

She drove directly to Fairview and was so fortunate as to find her husband and father there conversing with Mr. and Mrs. Leland.

Her sad story was quickly told, and listened to by all with deep commiseration for the impoverished and afflicted family.

"You will not refuse the poor dying man's request, papa? Edward?" she said in conclusion.

"Certainly not!" they answered, speaking both together. "We will set out immediately. And you, Mr. and Mrs. Leland?"

"Will gladly accompany you. I bear the poor man no malice, and would rejoice to do him any good in my power. What do you say, Mary?"

She looked at him a little anxiously. "Is it quite safe for you?"

"Quite, I think." He replied, appealing to the other gentlemen for their opinion.

They agreed with him, Mr. Dinsmore adding, "I have no doubt the man is sincere, and I have still more confidence in his mother, whom I have long looked upon as a truly Christian woman."

"Besides," remarked Mr. Travilla, "the Ku Klux would hardly dare venture an outrage now. The most desperate have fled the country, and the rest stand in wholesome awe of the troops."

"I am quite sure there is no risk in going," said Elsie earnestly, "but whatever is done must be done quickly, for Wilkins is evidently very near his end. He may, perhaps, expire before we arrive, even though we make all haste."

At that time there was a hurried movement, and in less time than it takes to tell it, they were on their way — Mrs. Leland in the carriage with Elsie and the gentlemen on horseback.

Under the influence of restoratives administered by Dr. Barton, great apparent improvement had taken place in Wilkin's condition. He was in less pain, breathed more freely, and spoke with less difficulty than before.

At sight of his visitors his pale face flushed slightly and an expression of regret and mortification swept over his features.

"Thank you all for coming," he said feebly. "Please be seated. I am at the very brink of the grave, and — and I would go in peace with all men. I — I've hated you every one. And you — Leland, I would have killed if I could. It was in the attempt to do so that I — received my own death wound at the hands of your wife."

Mrs. Leland started, trembled, and burst into tears. That part of the story Elsie had omitted and she now heard it for the first time.

"Don't be disturbed," he said. "You were doing right — in defending yourself, husband, and your own children."

"Yes, yes," she sobbed, "but oh, I would save you now if I could! Can nothing be done?"

He shook his head sadly. "Will you, can you all forgive me?" he asked in tones so faint and low that only the deathlike silence of the room made the words audible.

"With all my heart, my poor fellow, as I hope to be forgiven my infinitely greater debt to my Lord," Mr. Leland answered with emotion, taking the wasted hand and clasping it warmly in his.

Foster was deeply touched. "God bless you for the words," he whispered. "How I've been mistaken in you, sir!"

His eyes sought the faces of Dinsmore and Travilla, and drawing near the bed, each took his hand and gave the same assurance he had already received from Leland.

Then the last named said, "I ask your forgiveness, Foster, for any exasperating word I may have spoken, or anything else I have done to rouse unkind feelings toward me."

In reply the dying man pressed Leland's hand in moved silence.

Mrs. Leland rose impetuously and dropped on her knees at the bedside. "And me!" she cried, with a gush of tears. "Will you forgive me your death? I cannot bear to think it was my work, even though done in lawful self-defense, and to save my own dear ones."

"It is — all — right between us," he murmured, and relapsed into unconsciousness.

"We are too many in here," said the physician, dismissing all but the mother.

Elsie remained in the adjoining room, trying to comfort the sisters while Mrs. Leland and the gentlemen repaired to the veranda, where they found Mr. Wood, who had just arrived, having been sent for to converse and pray with the dying man.

"How does he seem?" he asked. "Can I go at once to the room?"

"Not now, he is unconscious," replied Mr. Dinsmore, and went on to describe Foster's condition — mental, moral, and physical — as evidenced in his conversation with them and the earlier one with Dr. Barton, of which Elsie had given them all a full account.

"Ah, God grant he may indeed find mercy and be enabled to lay hold upon Christ to the saving of his soul, even at this eleventh hour!" exclaimed the pastor. "A death-bed repentance is poor ground for hope. I have seen many of them in my fifty years of ministry, but of all those who recovered from what had seemed mortal illness, but one held fast to his profession of faith.

"The others all went back to their former evil ways, showing conclusively that they had been self-deceived and theirs but the hope of the hypocrite which 'shall perish, whose hope shall be cut off, and whose trust shall be a spider's web.' Yet, with our God all things are possible, and the invitation is to all who are yet on praying ground. 'Whosoever will.'"

At this moment Elsie glided into their midst and putting her hand into that of her pastor, said in low, tearful tones, "I am glad you have come! He is conscious again and asking for you."

He went with her to the bedside.

The glazing eyes grew bright for an instant. "You have—come. Oh, tell me—what I must—do—to—be saved!"

"I can only point you to 'the Lamb of God that taketh away the sin of the world,'" returned the pastor, deeply moved. "Only repeat His invitation, 'Look unto me and be ye saved all ye ends of the earth.'"

"I—am—trying—trying," came faintly from the pale lips, while the hands moved slowly, feebly from side to side as if groping in the dark, "Lord, please save—"

A deep hush filled the room, broken presently by the mother's wail as she fell on her knees at the bedside and taking the cold hand in hers covered it with kisses and tears.

With the last word the spirit had taken its flight. To him time should be no longer, for eternity had begun.

Few and evil had been his days; he was not yet thirty, and, possessed of a fine constitution and vigorous health, had every prospect of long life had he been content to live at peace with his fellow-men, but by violent dealing he had passed away in the midst of his years.

> *Bloody and deceitful men shall not live*
> *out half their days.*
> *The wages of sin is death.*

CHAPTER
TWENTY-FIRST

Kindness has resistless charms.

—ROCHESTER

THROUGH ALL THE TRYING scenes that followed, Elsie was with the Fosters, giving aid and comfort such as the tenderest sympathy and most delicate kindness could give. She and her husband and father took upon themselves all the care and trouble of the arrangements for the funeral, quietly settled the bills, and afterward sent them, receipted, to Mrs. Foster.

Wilkins had been the chief support of the family, the ladies earning a mere pittance by the use of the needle and sewing machine. Nothing had been laid by for a rainy day and the expenses of his illness had to be met by the sale of the few articles of value left from the wreck of their fortunes. And now, but for the timely aid of these kind friends, absolute want had stared them in the face.

They made neither complaint nor parade of their poverty, but it was unavoidable that Elsie should learn much of it at this time, and her heart ached for them in their accumulation of trials.

The girls were educated and accomplished but shrank with timidity and sensitive pride from exerting themselves to push their way in the world.

"I think they could teach," Mrs. Foster said to Elsie, who, calling the day after the funeral, had with delicate tact made known her desire to assist them in finding employment more lucrative and better adapted to their tastes and social position. "I think they have the necessary education and ability, and I know the will to earn an honest livelihood is not lacking, but where are pupils to be found?"

"Are you willing to leave that to Mr. Travilla and me?" asked Elsie with gentle kindliness.

"Ah, you are too good, too kind," said Mrs. Foster, weeping.

"No, no, my dear fiend," returned Elsie. "Does not the Master say, 'This is my commandment, that ye love one another, as I have loved you?' Now, tell me, please, what sort of situations they would like, and what branches they feel competent to teach."

"Annie is a good musician and draws well. She would be glad indeed to get a class of pupils in the neighborhood to whom she might give lessons, here or at their own homes, in drawing and on the piano and harp. Lucinda thinks she could teach the English branches, the higher mathematics, and French.

"But, indeed, my dear Mrs. Travilla, they will be thankful for anything, especially if it does not take them away from me."

"We will see what can be done—my husband, papa, and I," Elsie said rising to take leave. "And do not be anxious. Remember those precious words, 'Casting all your care on Him for He careth for you.'"

"Do not go yet!" entreated Mrs. Foster, taking and holding fast the hand held out to her, "if you only knew what a comfort your presence is— Ah, dear, kind friend, God has made you a daughter of consolation to His bereaved, afflicted ones!"

Elsie's eyes filled. "It is what I have prayed that He would do for me," she whispered. "But I think I must go now. My husband was to call for me, and I see him at the gate."

Elsie repeated the conversation to her husband as they rode homeward, and consulted him in regard to a plan that had occurred to her.

He approved, and instead of stopping at Ion they rode on to Roselands.

Arrived there, Mr. Travilla joined the gentlemen in the library, while Elsie sought her aunts in the pretty parlor usually occupied by them when not entertaining company.

After a little desultory chat on ordinary topics, she spoke of the Fosters, their indigent circumstances, and her desire to find employment for the girls in teaching.

"Always concerning yourself in other people's business," remarked Enna. "Why don't you do like the rest of us and leave them to mind their own affairs?"

"Because I see that they need help, and we are told, 'Look not every man on his own things but every man also on the things of others.' And again, 'As we have therefore opportunity, let us do good unto all men, especially unto them who are of the household of faith.'

"I heard you, not long ago, Aunt Louise, wishing you could afford a day governess and knew of a suitable person. Would you—would you be willing to employ one at my expense, and give the job to Lucinda Foster?"

"And let her give it out among our acquaintances that you were paying for the education of my children!" exclaimed Louise, coloring angrily. "No, thank you."

"Not at all. She need know nothing of the arrangement except that you employ her to instruct your children, and pay her for it. You and Enna, if she will accept the same from me for herself."

"Dear me," exclaimed Enna, "how you're always spending money on strangers, when your own relations could find plenty of use for it!"

Elsie smiled slightly at this peculiar view taken of her generous offer, but only added, "I would, if you would accept—"

"I'm no object of charity," interrupted Louise, rather coldly.

"Certainly not," Elsie said, coloring. "Yet why should you object to giving so near a relative the pleasure of— But in this instance 'tis I who am asking the favor of you. I want to help the Fosters and cannot do so directly without wounding their honest pride of independence."

"You will of course employ Lucinda to teach your own children?"

"No, I am not in want of a governess. Would you like to have Anna give lessons to your girls in music and drawing?"

"Is she to teach yours?" asked Enna.

"No, Mr. Reboul has them under his instruction, and as he gives entire satisfaction, I could not feel it right to turn him away."

"H'm! Teachers that are not good enough for your children are not good enough for ours."

"If I were in want of teachers, I should employ the Misses Fosters," was Elsie's quiet reply.

Nothing more was said for a moment, then rising to go, "I am then to consider my proposition declined?" she remarked, inquiringly.

"Well, no, since you put it on the ground of a favor to yourself, I should be sorry to refuse to gratify you," said Louise.

"Thank you. And you, Enna?"

"She can teach mine if she wants to, and if I could afford it, Annie should give music lessons to Molly, drawing, too; but if I can't, I can't."

"It need be no expense to you," said Elsie.

"Very well then, you can engage her and fix the terms to suit yourself."

"Thank you. I shall enjoy their pleasure in the hearing that they have so many apt pupils already secured."

Elsie's benevolent kindness did not stop here. She called on a number of families in the vicinity, and succeeded in obtaining almost as many pupils for the girls as they could well attend to.

Then another difficulty arose—the distances were too great for the young ladies to traverse on foot and they had no means of conveyance.

But this was obviated for the present by giving them the use of Prince and Princess, either with or without the phaeton, during the hours of the day that such help was needed.

The ponies were sent over to the cottage every morning after the children had had their ride, by an Ion servant, who returned for them in the afternoon.

Mrs. Leland heard of her friend's efforts, and going over to Ion, asked, "Why did you not call on me? My children need instruction."

"I hardly liked to ask it of you."

"And I feel a delicacy about proposing the thing to the Fosters, but—I would be very glad to help them; and if you can learn that they would not mind coming to Fairview for the sake of several more scholars, I authorize you to make the engagement for me."

Elsie undertook the errand and did it so well that the Fosters were deeply touched by this kindness on the part of the one who they had formerly hated and reviled, and whose husband their brother had tried to kill.

The offer was gratefully accepted; the young Lelands became the pupils of these former foes, little courtesies and kind offices were exchanged, and in the end warm friendship took the place of enmity.

CHAPTER
TWENTY-SECOND

The mother, in her office, holds the key
Of the soul; and she it is who stamps the coin
Of character, and makes the being
who would be a savage,
But for her gentle cares, a Christian man.
Then crowns her queen of the world.

—OLD PLAY

THE FAMILIES FROM THE Oaks and Ashlands had been spending the day at Ion.

It was late in the afternoon and while awaiting the call to tea, they had all gathered in the drawing room, whose windows overlooked the avenue and lawn on one side, on the other a very beautiful part of the grounds, and a range of richly wooded hills beyond.

A pause in the conversation was broken by Mr. Travilla. "Wife," he said, turning to Elsie, "Cousin Ronald should see Viamede, and our old friend here, Mrs. Carrington, needs change of scene and climate. Two good things that would not hurt any one present. Shall we not invite them all to go and spend the winter with us there?"

"Oh, yes, yes indeed! What a delightful plan!" she cried with youthful enthusiasm. "Ah, I hope you will all accept; the place is almost a paradise upon earth, and we would do all in our power to make the time pass agreeably. Cousin Ronald, don't refuse. Papa dear, don't try to hunt up objections."

"Ah ha! Um h'm! I've not the least idea of it, cousin," said the one.

"I am not," said the other, smiling fondly upon her, "but must be allowed a little time to consider."

"Oh, papa, don't say no!" cried Rosie. "Mamma, coax him quick before he has time to say it."

"I think there's no need," laughed Rose. "Can't you see that he is nearly as eager as the rest of us? And how could he do a whole winter without your sister? How could any of us, for that matter?"

"You have advanced an unanswerable argument, my dear," said Mr. Dinsmore. "And I may as well give consent at once."

"Thank you, mamma," said Elsie, "thank you both. Now if the rest of you will only be as good!" and she glanced persuasively from one to another.

"As good!" said Sophy smiling. "If to be ready to accept the kindest and most delightful of invitations be goodness, then I am not at all inclined to be bad. Mother, shall we not go?"

"Oh, grandma, you will not say no?" cried the young Carringtons, who had listened to the kind proposition with eager delight.

"No, please don't," added wee little Elsie, putting her arms coaxingly about the old lady's neck. "Mamma, papa, grandpa, and mammy all say it is so lovely there, and we want you along."

"Thanks, dear, thanks to your papa and mamma, too," said the old lady, clasping the little girl close, while tears filled her aged eyes. "Yes, yes, I'll go; we will all go. How could I reject such kindness!"

The children, from Rosie Dinsmore—who would hardly have consented to be put into that list—down to Harold Travilla, were wild with delight, and for the rest of the evening could scarce speak or think of anything else than Viamede and the pleasures they hoped to enjoy there.

"Now that all have spoken but you, brother mine," Elsie said, turning to Horace, Jr. "You surely do not intend to reject our invitation?"

"Not entirely, sister, but papa seems to have left the considering for me, and I've been at it. There should be someone to look after the plantations here, and upon whom but myself should that duty devolve?"

"We all have good overseers."

"Yes, but there should be someone to take a general supervision over them. I think I will go with you, make a short visit and return, if you all like to trust me with the care of your property."

"You're welcome to take care of Ashlands, Cousin Horace, and I'll be obliged to you, too," spoke up young Herbert Carrington, "and so will mother and grandma, I know."

"Indeed we will," said the old lady.

"And it will leave us quite free from care, you good boy," added the younger.

Mr. Travilla expressed similar sentiments in regard to Horace's offer as it concerned Ion and Mr. Dinsmore was quite as willing to leave the Oaks in his son's care.

As it was now late in the fall and no very extensive preparations were needed, it was agreed that they would start in a few days.

"We shall make a large party," remarked Sophy. "Are you sure, Elsie, that you will have room for so many?"

"Abundance—the house is very large and the more the merrier. I wish I could persuade Aunt Wealthy and May and Harry to come with their babies, too, of course. I shall write out to Lansdale this night."

"That would be a delightful addition to the party," remarked Mr. Dinsmore, "but aunt is in her eightieth year and, I fear, will think herself much too old for so long a journey.

"Ah, yes, papa, but she is more active than most women of seventy and can go nearly all the way by water—down the Ohio and the Mississippi and along the Gulf. At all events, I shall do my best to persuade her."

"And you are so great a favorite that your eloquence will not be wasted, I think," replied Mr. Travilla.

He was right. The old lady could not resist the urgent entreaties of her dearly loved grand niece, joined to the pleasant prospect of spending some months with her and the other relatives and friends, each of whom held a special place in her warm and loving heart.

An answering letter was sent from Lansdale by return mail, promising that their party would follow the other to Viamede at an early day.

May, too, was enchanted with the thought of a winter in that lovely spot and the society of her two sisters, and Elsie, who was almost as dear.

As soon as the children learned that the winter was really to be spent at Viamede and they would set off in a few days, the whole flock—leaving their elders to settle the dry details—hastened in quest of their "mammy."

They found her in the nursery, seated before a crackling wood fire, with little Herbert in her arms.

Quickly their news was told, and gathering round her, they plied her with questions about her old Louisiana home.

"Well, chillens," she said, her old eyes growing bright with joy at the thought of soon seeing it again—for, of course, she would be included in the party—"it's jes lubly, as lubly as kin be! De grand ole house, an' de gardens, an' fields, an' orchards, an' eberyting—yes, it am de lubliest place dis chile eber see."

"Horses to ride," said Eddie.

"Yes, Mars Eddie, hosses to ride, an' kerridges to drive out in—'sides a beautiful boat on de bayou, an' fish dere dat you kin ketch wid a hook an' line. Ole Uncle Joe he kotch dem mos' ebery day for de table, an' Massa Ed'ard an' Miss Elsie say dey's bery fine."

"And what else?" asked the eager voice of little Daisy Carrington.

"Oranges, ripe oranges growing out of doors on the trees!" cried her brother Harry, clapping his hands and capering about the room, smacking his lips in anticipation of the coming feast.

"Yes, chillens, orange trees on de lawn, an' a 'mense orchard wid hundreds an' millions ob dem on de branches an' on de ground. An' den de gardens full ob roses an' lubly flowers, an' vines climbin' ober de verandas an' roun' de pillahs an' de windows, an' clar up to de roof."

"Oh, how sweet!" cried the children, their eyes dancing with delight. "But, Aunt Chloe, will there be room for us all?" asked Meta Carrington, who was next to Herbert in age.

"Yes, chile, dere's rooms, an' rooms, an' rooms in dat house."

"A playroom, mammy?" asked Eddie.

"Yes, chillens, a big room whar yo' grandma used to play when she was a little chile."

Mammy's voice grew low and husky for a moment and great tears stood in her eyes. But she struggled with her emotion and went on, "Her dolls are dere yet, an' de beautiful sets ob little dishes an' a great many tings mo', for she hab lots ob toys an' neber destroyed nuffin. An' nobody eber goes dar but Aunt Phillis when she hab a clarin' up time in dat part ob de house."

"Yes," said little Elsie, who had been as silent and intent a listener as though the tale were quite new to her, "mamma has told us about those things, and that they are always to be kept very carefully because they belonged to her dear mamma.

"And we can't ever play with them!" exclaimed Vi, "but mamma will show them all to us. She said she would when she takes us to Viamede."

"Oh, I'd like to play with them!" exclaimed Meta. "Doesn't anybody ever?"

"No, chile," said mammy, shaking her head gravely, "dere ain't nobody eber 'lowed to go in dat room but Aunt Phillis, when Miss Elsie not dar. But run away now, chillens, dere's de tea bell a ringin'."

Mamma, too, on coming up at the usual hour to see her darlings safe in bed had many questions put to her on the same subject.

They were all patiently answered, some further details given, and sweet sympathy shown in their gladness over the pleasant prospect before them.

Then, with the accustomed tender goodnight kiss and with a parting injunction not to lie awake talking, she left them.

"Did anybody ever have such a dear mamma as ours!" exclaimed Vi, nestling close to her sister.

"No, I think not," replied Elsie in a tone of grave consideration. "But now we mustn't talk anymore, because she bade us not, and I've come to bed early tonight to please you—"

"Yes, you dear, good sister, you very dearest girl in all the world!" interrupted Vi, rising on her elbow for a moment to rain a perfect shower of kisses upon the sweet face by her side.

Elsie laughed low and musically and hugging her tight returned the caresses, then went on, "but I mustn't keep you awake. So now, let's lie down and not say one word more."

"No, not a single one," returned Vi, nestling down again.

"Mamma," said Eddie, coming into the school room next morning with a slight frown on his usually pleasant face, "why do you call us to lessons? Can't we have holidays now that we are going away so soon?"

"No, my son, I think it best to attend now to our regular duties. You will have a rest from study while taking the journey and for a few days after we reach Viamede. Will not that be better?" she asked with a motherly smile, as she softly smoothed back the dark clustering curls from his broad open brow.

"But I don't want to say lessons today," he answered with a pout, and resolutely refusing to meet her glance.

"My little son," she said with tender gravity, "were we sent into this world to please ourselves?"

"No, mamma."

"No, 'even Christ pleased not Himself,' and we are trying to be like Him. Whose will did He do?"

"His Father's, mamma."

"Yes, and whose will are you to do?"

"God's will, you've taught me, mamma, but—"

"Well, son?"

"Mamma, will you be angry if I say my thought?"

"I think not; let's hear it."

"Isn't it—isn't it your will this time? About the lessons, I mean. Please, mamma, don't think I want to be naughty, asking it."

She drew him closer and bending down pressed her lips to his forehead. "No, my son, you want it explained and I am glad you told me your thought. Yes, it is my will this time, but as God bids children to honor and obey their parents, is it not His will also?"

"I s'pose so, mamma. But I wish it didn't be your will to have me learn lessons today."

Elsie was forced to smile in spite of herself. With another slight caress she asked, "Do you think I love you, Eddie?"

"Oh, yes, yes, mamma, I know you do, and I love you, too—indeed I do dearly, dearly!" he burst out, throwing his arms about her neck. "And I know you just want to make me good and happy and that your way's always best. So I promise I won't be naughty anymore."

At that there was a general exclamation of delight from the other three who had been silent, but deeply interested listeners, and all crowded round mamma vying with each other in bestowing upon her tender caresses and words of love.

Each had felt more or less disinclination for the regular routine of work, but that vanished now and they went through their allotted tasks with more than usual spirit and determination.

Ah, what a sweetener of toil is love — love to a dear earthly parent, and still more love to Christ. There is no drudgery in the most menial employment where that is the motive power.

CHAPTER TWENTY-THIRD

Put a knife to thy throat,
if thou be a man given to appetite.

—*P*ROVERBS *23:2*

THE HAPPY DAY CAME, full soon to the fathers and mothers, at long, long last to the eager, expectant children.

Old Mr. Dinsmore had accepted the pressing invitation from his granddaughter and her husband to join the party, and with the addition of servants it was a large one.

As they were in no haste and the confinement of a railroad car would be very irksome to the younger children, it had been decided to make the journey by water.

It was late in the afternoon of an unusually warm, bright November day that they found themselves comfortably established on board a fine steamer bound for New Orleans.

There were no sad leave-takings to mar their pleasure. The children were in wild spirits and all seemed cheerful and happy as they sat or stood upon the deck watching the receding shore as the vessel steamed out of the harbor.

At length the land had quite disappeared; nothing could be seen but the sky overhead and a vast expanse of water all around. The passengers found leisure to turn their attention upon each other.

"There are some nice-looking people on board," remarked Mr. Travilla, in an undertone, to his wife.

"Besides ourselves," added Cousin Ronald, laughing in his usual mirthful tones.

"Yes," she answered, "that little group yonder—a young minister and his wife and child, I suppose. And what a dear little fellow—he is just about the age of our Harold, I should judge."

"Yes, mamma," chimed in the last named gentleman, "he seems a nice little boy. May I go speak to him? May I, papa?"

Permission was given and the next moment the two stood close together each gazing admiringly into the other's face.

"Papa," remarked the little stranger, looking up at his father, "I very much wish I had a face like this little boy's."

"Do you, son?" was the smiling rejoinder. "He certainly looks like a very nice little boy. Suppose you and he shake hands, Frank."

"Yes, sir," said the child, holding out a small, plump hand. "What's your name, little boy?"

"Harold Travilla, and yours is Fank?"

"Yes, Frank Daly. Don't you like this nice big boat we're on?"

"Yes, I do. Won't you come wis me and speak to my mamma and papa?"

Frank looked inquiringly at his father.

"Yes, you may go if you wish," returned the latter and the two started off hand in hand.

"Mamma, see, isn't he a dear little boy?" asked Harold, leading his new friend up before her with an air of proud ownership.

"Yes, indeed," she said, bending down to kiss Frank and stroke his hair.

"I think he's a good boy, 'cause he didn't come till his papa told him to," continued Harold.

"Indeed, a very good way to judge of a boy," said Cousin Ronald.

"His name is Fank," said Harold. "Fank, that's Cousin Ronald, and this is papa, and this is grandpa," and so on, leading him from one to another till he had introduced him to the whole party, not even omitting Baby Herbert and mammy.

Then Frank's papa came for him, saying the air was growing cool, and it was time to go in.

The friends were of the same opinion and all repaired to the ladies' salon, where, through the children, they soon made acquaintance of the Dalys.

Mr. Daly was a minister going south for the winter for the sake of his own and his wife's health.

Cousin Ronald took Frank on his knee and asked, "What are you going to do, my little fellow, when you get to be a man?"

"Preach the gospel, sir."

"Ah ha, ah ha, um h'm! And what will you say?"

"I'll tell the people we'll sing the twenty-third piece of ham. How will that sound?"

"Rather comical, I think, my man. Are ye no afraid the folk might laugh?"

"No sir, they don't laugh when papa says it."

"Ah ha, ah ha, um h'm!"

Mr. Daly smiled. "I never knew before," said he, "that my boy intended to follow my profession."

The ladies were weary and retired shortly after tea to their staterooms, but the gentlemen sought the open air again and paced the deck for some time into the evening.

"Have a cigar, sir?" asked Mr. Lilburn, addressed Mr. Daly.

"Thank you, no; I don't smoke."

"Ah ha! Um h'm! In that you seem to be of one mind with my friends here, the Dinsmores and Travilla," remarked Lilburn, lighting one for himself and placing it between his lips. "I wonder now if you know what you miss by your abstinence?"

"Well, sir, as to that, I know what some of my friends and acquaintances would have missed if they had abstained from the use of the weed. One would have missed a terrible dyspepsia that laid him in his grave in the prime of life; another cancer of the lip which did the same by him after years of terrible suffering."

"Ah ha! Um h'm! Ah, ha! But surely those were rare cases?"

"I think not very."

"You don't think the majority of those who use it feel any ill effects?"

"I do indeed, though probably comparatively few are aware that tobacco is the cause of their ailments."

"Doubtless that is the case," remarked Mr. Dinsmore. "I was a moderate smoker for years before I discovered that I was undermining my constitution by the indulgence. At length, however, I became convinced of that fact and gave it up at once—for that reason and for the sake of the example to my boy here, who has been willing to profit from his father's experience and abstain altogether."

"I have never used the weed in any way," said Horace, Jr.

"And I," remarked Travilla, "abandoned its use about the same time that Dinsmore did and for the same reason. By the way, I met with a strong article on the subject lately, which I cut out and placed in my wallet."

"Ah ha! Um h'm! Suppose you give us the benefit of it," suggested Lilburn good-naturedly. "I'm open to conviction."

"With all my heart, if you will kindly step into the gentlemen's cabin where there's light."

He led the way, the others following, and taking out a slip of paper read from it in a distinct tone, loud enough to be heard by those about him, without disturbing the other passengers.

"'One drop of nicotine—extract of tobacco—placed on the tongue of a dog will kill him in a minute. The hundredth part of a grain picked under the skin of a man's arm will produce nausea and fainting. That which blackens old tobacco pipes is empyreumatic oil, a grain of which would kill a man in a few seconds.

"'The half dozen cigars which most smokers use a day contain six or seven grains—enough, if concentrated and absorbed, to kill three men, and a pound of tobacco, according to its quality, contains from one quarter to one and a quarter ounces.

"'Is it strange, then, that smokers and chewers have a thousand ailments or that German physicians attribute one half of the deaths among the young men of that country to tobacco? Or that the French Polytechnical Institute had to prohibit its use on account of its effect on the mind? That men grow dyspeptic, hypochondriac, insane, delirious from its use?

"'One of the direct effects of tobacco is to weaken the heart. Notice the multitude of sudden deaths and see how many are smokers and chewers. In a small country town seven of these 'mysterious providences' occurred within the circuit of a mile, all directly traceable to tobacco; and any physician, on a few moments' reflection, can match this fact by his own observation.

"'And then such powerful acids produce intense irritation and thirst—thirst which water does not quench. Hence a resort to cider and beer. The more this thirst is fed, the more insatiate it becomes, and more fiery drink is needed.

"'Out of seven hundred convicts examined at the New York state prison, six hundred were confined for crimes committed under the influence of liquor, and five hundred said they had been led to drink by the use of tobacco.'" [as stated by J. E. Vose in the *Family Christian Almanac* for 1876]

"Ah ha, ah ha! Um h'm, ah ha! That's strongly put," remarked Mr. Lilburn, reflectively. "I'm afraid I'll have to give it up. What say you, sir?" turning to Mr. Daly. "Has a man a right to choice in such a matter as this? A right to injure his body—to say nothing of the mind—by a self-indulgence the pleasure of which seems to him to overbalance the possible or probable suffering it may cause?"

"No, sir. 'What! Know ye not that your body is the temple of the Holy Ghost which is in you, which ye have of God, and ye are not your own? For ye are bought with a price: therefore glorify God in your body, and in your spirit which are God's.'"

"Right, sir, I was thinking of those words of the apostle and also of these others, 'If any man defile the temple of God, him shall God destroy: for the temple of God is holy, which temple ye are.'

"We certainly have no right to injure our bodies either by neglect or self-indulgence. 'Know ye not that your bodies are the members of Christ?' and again, 'I beseech you therefore, brethren, by the mercies of God, that ye present your bodies a living sacrifice, holy, acceptable unto God, which is your reasonable service.'"

"It must require a good deal of resolution for one who has become fond of the indulgence to give it up," remarked Mr. Daly.

"No doubt, no doubt," returned Mr. Lilburn, "but, 'If thy right eye offend thee, pluck it out, and cast it from thee for it is profitable for thee that one of thy members should perish, and not that thy whole body should be cast into hell.'" There was a pause broken by young Horace, who had been watching a party of men gathering about a table at the further end of the room

"They are gambling yonder, and I'm afraid that young fellow is being badly fleeced by that man just opposite."

The eyes of the whole party were at once turned in that direction.

"I'm afraid you're right, Horace," said Mr. Travilla, recalling with an inward shudder, the scene he had witnessed in a gambling hall many years ago, in which the son of his friend Beresford so nearly lost his life. "What can be done to save him? Some effort must be made!" and he started up as if with the intent of approaching the players.

"Stay a moment, Edward," exclaimed Lilburn in an undertone, and laying a detaining hand upon Travilla's arm, but with his gaze intently fixed upon the older gamester. "Ah ha! Um h'm! That fellow is certainly cheating. I saw him slip a card from his coat sleeve."

The words had scarcely passed his lips when a voice spoke apparently close at the villain's side.

"Ah ha, I zees you vell, how you runs de goat shleeve down mit de gards and sheats dat boor poy vat ish blay mit you. Yoh, sir, you ish von pig cheat!"

"How dare you, sir? Who are you?" cried the rascal, starting up white with rage and turning to face his accuser.

"Who was it? Where is that Dutch scoundrel that dared accuse me of cheating?" he cried, sending a fierce glance about the room.

"Vat ish dat you galls me? Von Dutch scoundrel? You man mit de proken nose, I say it again; you ish von pig cheat."

This time the voice seemed to come from a state-room directly behind the gambler. Towering with rage, he rushed to the door and tried to open it. Failing in that, he demanded admittance in loud angry tones, at the same time shaking the door violently, and kicking against it with a force that seemed likely to break in the panels.

There was an answering yell, a sound as of someone bouncing out of his berth upon the floor, the key turned hastily in the lock, and the door was thrown wide open. A little Frenchman appeared on its threshold in night attire, bowie knife and pistol in hand, and black eyes flashing with indignant anger.

"Sir, Monsieur, I vil know vat for is dis disturbance of mine slumbers?"

"Sir!" said the other, stepping back, instantly cooled down at the sight of the weapons, "I beg pardon—was looking for a scoundrel of a Dutchman who has been abusing me, but I see he's not here."

"No, sir, he is not here!" and the door promptly was slammed violently to.

"Ha, ha! Man mit de proken nose, you vake up de wrong bassenger. Ha, Ha! I dells you again you ish von pig cheat!"

Now the voice came from the skylight overhead, apparently, and with a fierce imprecation the irate gamester rushed from the deck and ran hither and thither in search of his tormentor.

His victim, who had been looking on during the little scene and listening to the mysterious voice in silent wide-eyed wonder and fear, now rose hastily, his face deathly pale, with trembling hands, gathered up the money he had staked and hurrying into his stateroom, locked himself in.

The remaining passengers looked at each other.

"What does it mean?" cried one.

"A ventriloquist aboard, of course," returned another. "Let's follow and see the fun."

"I wonder which of us it is!" remarked the first, looking hard at each party.

"I don't know, but come on. That fellow Nick Ward is a noted blackleg and ruffian. He had his nose broken in a fight and is sensitive on the subject. He was cheating, of course."

They passed out, the ventriloquist's party close in their rear.

"Where's that Dutch villain?" Ward was screaming, following up his question with a volley of oaths.

"Who?" asked the mate, "I've seen none up here, though there are some in the steerage."

Down to the steerage flew the gambler without waiting for a reply. Bounding into the midst of a group of German emigrants seated there, quietly smoking their pipes, angrily demanded which of them it was who had been on the upper deck just now abusing him and calling him a cheat and a man with a broken nose.

They heard him in silence, with a cool and phlegmatic indifference most exasperating to one in his present mood.

Drawing his revolver, "Speak!" he shouted, "tell me which one it was, or I'll—I'll shoot every mother's son of you!"

His arms were suddenly pinioned from behind while a deep voice grunted, "You vill, vill you? I dinks not. You ish mine brisoner. Dere ish nopody here as did gall you names, and you vill put up dat leetle gun."

A man of giant size and Herculean strength had laid aside his pipe and slowly rising to his feet, seized the scoundrel in his powerful grasp.

"Let me go!" yelled Ward making a desperate effort to free his arms.

"Ha, ha! Man mit de proken nose, you ish vake up de wrong bassenger again," came mockingly from above. "It ish me as galls you von pig cheat, and I dells you it again."

"There, the villain's up on the deck now!" cried Ward, grinding his teeth in an impotent rage. "Let go my arms! Let go, I say, and I'll teach him a lesson."

"I dinks no. I dinks I deach you von lesson," returned his captor, not relaxing his grasp in the least bit.

But the captain's voice was heard asking in stern tones, "What's the cause of all this disturbance? What are you doing down here, Ward? I'll have no fighting aboard."

The German released his prisoner and the latter slunk away with muttered threats and imprecations upon the head of his tormentor.

Both that night and the next day there was much speculation among the passengers in regard to the occurrence. But Mr. Lilburn's party kept their own counsel, and the children, cautioned not to divulge Cousin Ronald's secret, guarded it carefully, for all had been trained to obedience, and besides being anxious not to lose the fun he made for them.

Mr. Lilburn and Mr. Daly each at a different time, sought out the young man, Ward's intended victim, and tried to influence him for good.

He thought he'd been rescued by the interposition of some supernatural agency, and solemnly declared his fixed determination never to again approach a gaming table, and throughout the voyage adhered to his resolution, in spite of every influence Ward could bring to bear upon him to break it.

Yet there was gambling again the second night, between Ward and several others of his profession.

They kept it up till after midnight. Then, Mr. Lilburn, waking from his first sleep, in a stateroom nearby, thought he would break it up once more.

A deep stillness reigned in the cabin. It would seem that everyone on board the vessel, except themselves and the watch on deck, was wrapped in profound slumber.

An intense voiceless excitement possessed each of the players, for the game was a close one, and the stakes were very heavy. They bent eagerly over the board, each watching with feverish anxiety his companion's movements, each casting, now and again, a gloating eye upon the great heap of gold and greenbacks that lay between them, and at times half stretching out his hand to clutch it.

A deep groan startled them and they sprang to their feet, pale and trembling with sudden terror, each holding his breath and straining his ear to catch a repetition of the dread sound.

But all was silent, and after a moment of anxious waiting, they sat down to their game again, trying to conceal and shake off their fears with a forced, unnatural laugh.

But scarcely had they taken the cards into their hands when a second groan—deeper, louder, and more prolonged than the first—again startled them to their feet.

"I tell you this is growing serious," whispered one in a shaking voice, his very lips white with fear.

"It came from under the game table," gasped one. "Look what's there."

"Look yourself."

"Both together then," and simultaneously they bent down and peered into the space underneath the board.

There was nothing there.

"What can it have been?" they asked each other.

"Oh, nonsense! What fools we are! Of course, somebody's ill in one of the staterooms." And they resumed their game for the second time.

But a voice full of unutterable anguish came from beneath their feet, "'Father Abraham have mercy on me, and send Lazarus, that he may dip the tip of his finger in water, and cool my tongue: for I am tormented in this flame.'" In mortal terror they sprang up, dashed down their cards and fled, not even waiting to gather up the "filthy lucre" for which they were selling their souls.

It was the last game of cards for that trip.

The captain coming in shortly after the sudden flight of the gamblers, took charge of the money, and the next day restored it to the owners.

To Elsie's observant eye it presently became evident that the Dalys were in very straitened circumstances. They made no complaint, but with her warm sympathy and delicate tact, she soon drew from the wife all the information she needed to convince her that here was a case that called for the pecuniary assistance Providence had put in her power to give.

She consulted with her husband and the result was a warm invitation to the Dalys to spend the winter at Viamede, where they would have all the benefit of the mild climate, congenial society, use of the library, and horses, and be at no expense.

"Oh, how kind, how very kind!" Mrs. Daly said with tears of joy and gratitude, "we have hardly known how we should meet the most necessary expenses for the trip, but have been trying to cast our care upon the Lord, asking Him to provide. And how wonderfully He has answered our petitions. But—it seems too much, too much for you to do for strangers."

"Strangers, my dear friend, strangers?" Elsie answered, pressing her hand most affectionately. "Are we not sisters in Christ? 'Ye are all the children of God by faith in Christ Jesus.' 'Ye are all one in Christ Jesus.'

"We feel, my husband and I, that we are only stewards of His bounty and that because He has said, 'Inasmuch as ye have done it unto one of the least of these my brethren, ye have done it unto Me,' it is the highest privilege and delight to do anything for His people."

Mr. Travilla had already expressed the same sentiments to Mr. Daly, and so the poor minister and his wife accepted the invitation with glad and thankful hearts. And Harold and Frank learned with delight that they were to live together for what to their infant minds seemed almost an interminable length of time.

The passage to New Orleans was made without accident or detention.

As the party left the vessel a voice was heard from the hold, crying in dolorous accents, and a rich Irish brogue, "Och, captin, dear, help me out, help me out! I've got fast betwane these boxes here, bad cess to 'em! An' can't hilp mesilf at all, at all!"

"Help you out, you passage thief!" roared the captain in return. "Yes, I'll help you out with a vengeance, and put you into the hands of the police straight away."

"Ah ha! Um h'm ah ha, you'll have to catch him first," remarked Mr. Lilburn with a quiet smile, stepping from the plank to the wharf as he spoke.

"Ah, my dear cousin, you are incorrigible!" said Elsie, laughingly.

CHAPTER TWENTY-FOURTH

The fields did laugh,
the flowers did freshly spring,
The trees did bud and early blossoms bear,
And all the quire of birds did sweetly sing,
And told that gardens' pleasures in their caroling.

—SPENSER'S FAIRY QUEEN

NOTHING COULD BE LOVELIER than Viamede was as they found it upon their arrival.

The children, one and all, were in an ecstasy of delight over the orange orchard with its wealth of golden fruit, glossy leaves, and delicate blossoms, the velvety lawn with its magnificent shade trees, the variety and profusion of beautiful flowers, and the spacious lordly mansion.

They ran hither and thither jumping, dancing, clapping their hands, and calling to each other with shouts of glee.

The pleasure and admiration of the older people were scarcely less, though shown after a more sober fashion. But no check was put upon the demonstrations of joy of the younger ones. They were allowed to gambol, frolic, and play, and to feast themselves upon the luscious fruit to their hearts' content.

Nor was the gladness all on the side of the new arrivals. To the old house servants, many of whom still remained, the coming of their beloved young mistress and her children had been an event looked forward to with longing for years.

They wept for joy as they gathered about her, kissed her hand and clasped her little ones in their arms, cuddling them and calling them by every endearing name known to the Negro vocabulary.

And the children, having heard a great deal, from both mamma and mammy, about these old people and their love and loyalty to the family, were neither surprised nor displeased but quite ready to receive and return the affection lavished upon them.

The party from Lansdale arrived only a few days after the others and was welcomed with great rejoicings, in which even Bruno must have a share. He jumped and gamboled about Harry and May, tried to kiss the babies, and finally put his nose into Aunt Wealthy's lap, saying, "Ye're a dear auld leddy, ma'am, and I'm glad ye've come!"

"Ah," she answered, patting his head and laughing her low, sweet, silvery laugh, "you betray your Scotch accent, my fine fellow, and I'm too old a chaff to be caught with a bird."

Mr. Mason was still chaplain at Viamede, and with his wife and children occupied a pretty and commodious cottage which had been built on the estate expressly for their use.

When he and Mr. Daly met they instantly and delightedly recognized each other as former classmates and intimate friends, and the Dalys, by urgent invitation, took up their abode for the winter in the cottage. But Mr. and Mrs. Travilla were careful that it should still be entirely at their expense.

A suite of apartments in the mansion was appropriated to each of the other families and it was unanimously agreed that each should feel at perfect liberty to withdraw into the privacy of these, having their meals served to them there if they so desired. Or, at their pleasure they could mingle with the others in the breakfast parlor, dining room, drawing rooms, or library.

The first fortnight was made a complete holiday to all, the days being filled up with games, walks, rides, drives, and excursions by land and water.

In consequence of the changes occasioned by the war, they found but little society in the neighborhood now, yet scarcely missed it, having so much within themselves.

But at length even the children began to grow somewhat weary of constant play. Harry Duncan and Horace, Jr. announced their speedy departure to attend to business, and the other adults of the party felt that it was time to take up again the ordinary duties of life.

Mr. Daly, anxious to make some return for the kindness shown him, offered to act as tutor to all the children who were old enough for school duties. But Rosie put her arms about her father's neck and looking beseechingly into his eyes said she preferred her old tutor—at which he smiled, and stroking her hair, said she should keep him, for he was quite as loath to give up his pupil. And Elsie's children, clinging about her, entreated that their lessons might still be said to mamma.

"So they shall, my darlings,' she answered, "for mamma loves to teach you."

The young Carringtons, too, and their mother, preferred the old way.

So Mr. Daly's kind offer was declined with thanks. And perhaps he was not sorry—being weak and languid and in no danger of suffering from ennui with horses to ride and plenty of books at hand.

A schoolroom was prepared, but only the Travillas occupied it. Sophy preferred to use her dressing room, and Rose studied in her own room and recited to her papa in his or the library.

Elsie expected her children to find it a little hard to go back to the old routine, but it was not so. They came to her with bright, happy faces, were quiet and diligent, and when the recitations were over, gathered about her for a little chat before returning to their play.

"Mamma," said Eddie, "we've had a nice long holiday and it's really pleasant to get back to lessons again."

"So it is!" said Vi. "Don't you think so, Elsie?"

"Yes, indeed! It's nice to get back to our books, but we've had lessons almost every day. Grandpa and papa and mamma have been teaching us so much about the birds, insects, and all sorts of living things, and the flowers and plants, trees, stones, and oh, I don't know how many things that are different here from what we have at home."

"At home! Why, this is home , isn't it, mamma?" exclaimed Eddie.

"Yes, my son, one of our homes."

"Yes, and so beautiful," said Vi, "but Ion 'pears the homiest to me."

"Does it, darling?" asked mamma, giving her a smile and a kiss.

"Yes, mamma, and I love Ion dearly—Viamede 'most as well, though, because you were born here, and your dear mamma."

"And because that dear grandma is buried here," remarked her sister, "and because of all those dear graves. Mamma, I do like those lessons I was speaking of, and so do Eddie and Vi. But Herbert and Meta and Harry don't. They say they think them very stupid and dull."

"I am glad, my children, that you so love knowledge," their mother said, "because it is useful. The more knowledge we have the more good we can do if we will.

"And then it is a lasting pleasure. God's works are so wonderful that we can never learn all about them while we live in this world, and I suppose throughout the endless ages of eternity we shall be ever learning, yet always finding still more to learn."

"Mamma, how pleasant that will be," said Elsie thoughtfully.

"And oh, mamma," cried Vi, "that reminds me that we've been out of doors 'most all the daytimes, and haven't seen grandma's playroom and things yet. Won't you show them to us?"

"Yes, we will go now."

"Me, too, mamma?" asked Harold.

"Yes, all of you come. I want you all to see everything that I have that once belonged to my own dear mother."

"Aunt Rosie wants to see them, too," said Vi.

"And Herbert and Meta and the others," added wee Elsie.

"They shall see them afterward. I want no one but my own little children now," replied mamma, taking Harold's hand and leading the way.

She led them to the room, a large and very pleasant one, light and airy, where flowers were blooming and birds singing. Vines were trailing over and about the windows, lovely pictures on the walls, cozy chairs and couches, work tables, well supplied with all the implements of sewing, others suited for dráwing, writing, or cutting out, standing here and there, quantities of books, games, and toys. Nothing seemed to have been forgotten that could give pleasant employment for their leisure hours, or minister to their amusement.

There was a burst of united exclamations of wondering delight from the children, as the door was thrown open and they entered. Now they understood why mamma had put them off when several times they had asked to be brought to this room. She was having it fitted up in a way to give them a joyful surprise.

"Do you like it, my darlings?" she asked with a pleased smile.

"Oh, yes, yes! Yes, indeed!" they cried, jumping, dancing, and clapping their hands. "Dear, dear mamma, how good, how good you are to us!" And they nearly smothered her with caresses.

Releasing herself, she opened another door leading into an adjoining room which, to Eddie's increased delight, was fitted up as a workroom for boys, with every sort of tool used by carpenters and cabinet makers. He had such at Ion and was somewhat acquainted with their use.

"Oh, what nice times Herbert and Harry and I shall have!" he exclaimed. "What pretty thing's we'll make! Mamma, I don't know how to thank you and my dear father!" he added, catching her hand and pressing it to his lips with a son's passionate affection.

"Be good and obedient to us, kind and affectionate to your brothers, sisters, and playmates," she said stroking his hair. "That is the kind of thanks we want, my boy. We have no greater joy than to see our children good and happy."

"If we don't be, it's just our own fault, and we're ever so wicked and bad!" cried Vi vehemently.

Mamma smiled at her little girl's impetuosity, then in grave, tender tones said, "And is there not Someone else more deserving of love and thanks than even papa and mamma?"

"God, our kind heavenly Father," murmured little Elsie, happy, grateful tears shining in her soft, hazel eyes.

"Yes, it is from His kind hand that all of our blessings come."

"I love God," said Harold, "and so does Fank. Mamma, can Fank come up here to play wis me?"

"Yes, indeed. Frank is a dear, good little boy, and I like to have you together."

Mamma unlocked the door of a large, light closet, as she spoke, and the children, looking eagerly in, saw that its shelves were filled with beautiful toys. "Grandma's things!" they said softly.

"Yes, these are what my dear mother played with when she was a little girl like Elsie and Vi," said mamma. "You may look at them."

Inside there was a large dollhouse, beautifully furnished. There were many dolls of various sizes, and little chests and trunks full of nicely made clothes for them to wear—nightclothes, morning wrappers, bright silks and lovely white dresses, bonnets and hats, shoes and stockings, too, and ribbons and laces for the lady dolls. And for the gentlemen dolls there were coats and hats, vests, cravats, and everything that real grownup men wear. And for the baby dolls there were many suits of beautiful baby clothes; and all made so that they could be easily taken off and put on again.

There were cradles to rock the babies in and coaches for them to ride in. There were dinner and tea sets of the finest china and of solid silver; indeed, almost everything in the shape of toys that the childish heart could desire.

The lonely little girl had not lacked for any pleasure that money could procure—but she had hungered for that best earthly gift—the love of father, mother, brothers, and sisters—which can be neither bought nor sold.

The children examined all these things with intense interest and a sort of wondering awe, then begged their mother to tell them again about "dear grandma."

They had heard the story—all that mamma and mammy could tell—many times, but it never lost its charm for them.

"Yes, dears, I will. I love to think and speak of her," Elsie said, sitting down in a low chair while they gathered closely round her, the older two, one on each side, the others leaning upon her lap.

"Mamma, it is a sad story, but I love it," little Elsie said, drawing a deep sigh, as the tale came once again to an end.

"Yes, poor little girl, playing up here all alone," said Eddie.

"'Cept mammy," corrected Vi.

"Yes, mammy to love her and take care of her, but no brother or sister to play with, and no dear mamma or papa like ours."

"Yes, poor dear grandma!" sighed little Elsie. "And it was almost as hard for you, mamma, when you were a little girl. Didn't you feel very sad?"

"Ah, daughter, I had Jesus to love me, and help me in my childish griefs and troubles," the mother answered, with a glad smile, "and mammy to hug and kiss and love me just as she does you."

"But, oh, didn't you want your mamma and your papa, too?"

"Yes, sorely, sorely at times, but I think no little child could be happier than I was when at last my dear father came home, and I found that he loved me dearly. Ah, I am so glad, so thankful that my darlings have never suffered for lack of love."

"I, too, mamma."

"And I."

"And I," they exclaimed, clinging about her and loading her with caresses.

"Hark!" she said, "I hear your dear grandpa's step, and there, he is knocking at the door."

Eddie ran to open it.

"Ah, I thought I should find you here, daughter," Mr. Dinsmore said, coming in. "I, too, want to see these things. It is long since I looked at them."

She gave him a pleased look and smile, and stepping to the closet he stood for some moments silently gazing upon its treasures.

"You do well to preserve them with care as mementos of your mother," he remarked, coming back and seating himself by her side.

Oh, grandpa, you could tell us more about her, and dear mamma, too, when she was a little girl!"

said Elsie, seating herself upon his knee, twining her arms about his neck and looking coaxingly into his face.

"Ah, what a dear little girl your mamma was at your age!" he said, stroking her hair and gazing fondly first at her and then at her mother. "The very joy of my heart and delight of my eyes — though not dearer than she is now!"

Elsie returned the loving glance and smile, while her namesake daughter remarked, "Mamma just couldn't be nicer or sweeter than she is now — nobody could."

"No, no! No, indeed!" chimed in the rest of the little flock. "But grandpa, please tell the story. You never did tell it to us."

"No," he said half sighing, "but you shall have it now." Then he went on to relate how he had first met their mother's mother, then a very beautiful girl of fifteen.

An acquaintance took him to call upon a young lady friend of his to whom Elsie Grayson was paying a visit, and the two were in the drawing room together when the young men entered.

"What did you think the first minute you saw her, grandpa!" asked Eddie.

"That she had the sweetest, most beautiful face and perfect form I had ever laid eyes on, and that I would give all I was worth to have her for my own."

"Love at first sight," his daughter remarked with a smile, "and it was mutual."

"Yes, she told me afterward that she had loved me from the first; though the longer I live, the more I wonder it should have been so, for I was a wild, wayward youth. But she, poor thing, had none to love or cherish her but her mammy."

"Grandpa, I think you're very nice," put in little Vi, leaning on his knee and gazing affectionately into his face.

"I'm glad you do," he said, patting her soft, round cheek.

"But to go on with my story, I could not keep away from my charmer and for the next few weeks we saw each other daily.

"I asked her to be my own little wife and she consented. Then, early one morning we went to a church and were married, no one being present except the minister, the sexton, her friend and mine, who were engaged to each other, and her faithful mammy.

"Her guardian was away in a distant city and knew nothing about the matter. He was taken sick there and did not return for three months. During that time Elsie and I lived together in a house she owned in New Orleans.

"We thought that now that we were safely married, no one could ever separate the two of us and we were very, very happy.

"But one evening her guardian came suddenly upon us as we sat together in her boudoir, and in a great passion ordered me out of the house.

"Elsie was terribly frightened and I said, 'I will go tonight for peace sake, but Elsie is my wife and tomorrow I shall come and claim her as such, and I think you'll find I have the law on my side.' Elsie clung to me and wept bitterly, but I comforted her with the assurance that the parting was only for a few hours."

Mr. Dinsmore's voice faltered. He paused a moment, then went on in tones husky with emotion.

"We never saw each other again. When I went back in the morning the house was closed and quite deserted; not even a servant in it, and I knew not where to look for my lost wife.

"I went back to my hotel and there found my father waiting for me in my room. He was angry about my marriage, the news of which had brought him from home. He made me go back with him at once and he sent me North to college. I heard nothing of my wife for months, and then only that she was dead and had left me a little daughter."

"And that was our mamma!" cried the children, once more crowding about her to lavish caresses upon her.

They thanked their grandfather for his story, and Vi looking in at the closet door again, said in her most coaxing tones, "Mamma, I should so, so like to play a little with some of those lovely things. And I would be very careful not to spoil them."

"Not now, daughter, though perhaps I may allow it some day when you are older. But see here! Will not these do quite as well?"

And rising, Mrs. Travilla opened the door of another closet displaying to the children's delighted eyes other toys as fine and in as great profusion and variety as those she considered sacred to her mother's memory.

"Oh, yes, yes, mamma! How lovely! How kind you are! Are they all for us?" they exclaimed in joyous tones.

"Yes," she said, "I bought them for you while we were in New Orleans and you shall play with them whenever you like. And now we will lock the doors and go down to dress for dinner. The first bell is ringing."

After dinner the playroom and the contents of the two closets were shown to Mrs. Dinsmore, Rosie, and the Carringtons. Then, Mrs. Travilla locked the door of the one that held the treasured relics of her departed mother and carried away the key.

CHAPTER
TWENTY-FIFTH

She'd lift the teapot lid
To peep at what was in it,
Or tilt the kettle if you did
But turn your back a minute.

META CARRINGTON HAD MANY excellent traits of character—she was frank, generous, unselfish, and sincere; but these good qualities were offset by some very serious faults—she was prying and full of desire for whatever was forbidden.

The other children played contentedly with the toys provided for them, but Meta secretly nursed a longing for those Mrs. Travilla had chosen to withhold. She was constantly endeavoring to devise some plan by which to get possession of them.

She attempted to pick the lock with a nail, then with a knife, but failing in that, seized every opportunity of doing so unobserved, to try keys from other doors in different parts of the house, till at length she found one that would answer her purpose. Then, she watched her chance to use it in the absence of her mates.

At length such a time came. The ladies had all gone out for an airing, the little ones, too, in charge of their nurses. Vi and the boys were sporting on the lawn, and Elsie was at the piano practicing— certain, faithful little worker that she was, not to leave it till the allotted hour had expired.

Having satisfied herself of all this, Meta flew to the playroom and half trembling at her own temerity, admitted her self to the forbidden treasures.

There was no hesitancy in regard to her further proceedings. For weeks past she had had them all carefully arranged in her mind. She would have a tea party, though, unfortunately, there could be no guests present but the dolls. Yet at all events, she could have the great pleasure of handling that beautiful china and silver and seeing how a table would look set with them. A pleasure doubled by the fact that she was enjoying it in opposition to the known wishes and commands of her mother and the owner—for in Meta's esteem "stolen waters were sweet" indeed.

She selected a damask tablecloth from a pile that lay on one of the lower shelves, several napkins to match, slipping each of them into a silver ring taken from a little basket that stood alongside. And proceeded with quiet glee to deck a table with them and the sets of china and silver she most admired.

"Beautiful! Beautiful! I never saw anything so pretty!" she exclaimed half aloud, as, her task finished, she stood gazing in rapt delight at the result of her labors. "Oh, I think it's real mean of Aunt Elsie to say we sha'n't play with these and to lock them away from us. But now for the company!" and running into the closet again, she brought out several of the largest dolls.

"I'll dress them for dinner," she said, still talking to herself in an undertone. "That'll be fun. What lots of lovely things I shall find in these trunks. I'll look them over and select what I like best to have them wear. I'll have time enough. It isn't at all likely anybody will come to disturb me for an hour." And as she opened the first trunk, she glanced hastily at the clock on the mantel.

She was mistaken. Time flew away much faster than she was aware of, and scarce half an hour had passed when a pair of little feet came dancing along the hall, the door—which in her haste and preoccupation Meta had forgotten to lock—flew open and Vi stood before her.

The great blue eyes turning toward the table opened wide with astonishment. "Why, Meta!"

Meta's face flushed deeply for a moment, but thinking the best plan would be to brave it out she asked, "Isn't it pretty?" simply as unconcernedly as she could.

"Yes, oh, lovely! But—where did you—aren't they my grandma's things? Oh, Meta, how could you ever dare—"

"Pooh! I'm not going to hurt 'em. And why should you think they were hers? Can't other people have pretty things?"

"Yes, but I know they're grandma's, I rec—recog—recognize them. Oh, what shall we do? I wouldn't venture to touch 'em, even to put them back."

"What a big word that was you used just now," said Meta laughing. "It 'most choked you."

"Well, when I'm bigger it won't," returned Vi, still gazing at the table. "Oh, how lovely they are! I do wish mamma would let us play with them."

"So do I—and these dolls, too. It's just delightful to dress and undress them. Here, Vi, help me put this one's shoes on."

The temptation to handle the tiny, dainty shoes and see how well they fit the feet of the pretty doll was great, and not giving herself time to think, Violet dropped down on the carpet by Meta's side and complied with the request. "Just to slip on those lovely shoes, now that they were there right before her, was not much," so said the tempter. Then, "Now having done a little, what difference if she did a little more?"

Thoughtless and excitable, she presently forgot mamma and her commands and became as eagerly engaged as Meta herself in the fascinating employment of looking over the contents of the trunks, and trying now one and now another suit upon the dollies.

"Now this one's dressed and I'll set her up to the table," said Meta, jumping up. "Oh, my!"

Something fell with a little crash on the lid of the trunk by Vi's side and there at her feet lay one of the beautiful old china plates broken into a dozen little pieces.

The child started up perfectly aghast, the whole extent of her delinquency flashing upon her in that instant. "Oh, oh! What have I done? What a wicked, wicked girl I am! What will mamma say?" And she burst into an agony of grief and remorse.

"You didn't do it, nor I either," said Meta, stooping to gather up the fragments. "The doll kicked it off. There, Vi, don't cry so. I'll put the things back just as they were, and never, never touch one of them ever again."

"But you can't, because there's one broken. Oh dear, oh dear! I wish you had let them alone, Meta. I wish, I wish I'd been a good girl and obeyed my mamma!"

"Never mind. If she goes to whip you, I'll tell her it was 'most all my fault. But she needn't know. It won't be a story to put them back and say nothing about it. And most likely it won't be found out for years and years — maybe never. You see, I'll just put this plate between the others in the pile and it won't be noticed at all that it's broken, unless somebody takes them all down to look."

"But I must tell mamma," sobbed Violet. "I couldn't hide it. I always tell her everything, and I'd feel so wicked."

"Violet Travilla, I'd never have believed you'd be so mean as to tell tales," remarked Meta severely. "I'd never have played with you if I'd known it."

"I'll not. I didn't mean that. I'll only tell on myself, Meta."

"But you can't do that without telling on me, too, and I say it's real mean. I'll never tell a story about it, but I don't see any harm in just setting the things away and saying nothing. 'Tain't as if you were throwing the blame on somebody else," pursued Meta, gathering up the articles taken from the closet and replacing them, as nearly as possible as she had found them.

"Come, dry your eyes, Vi," she went on, "or somebody'll see you've been crying and ask what it was about."

"But I must tell mamma," reiterated the little girl, sobbing anew.

"And make her feel worried and sorry because the plate's broken, when it can't do any good, and she needn't ever know about it. I just call that real selfishness, Vi."

This, to Vi, was a new view of the situation. She stopped crying to consider it.

It certainly would grieve mamma to know that the plate was broken and perhaps even more to hear of her child's disobedience, and if not told she would be spared that pain.

But on the other hand, mamma had always taught her children that wrongdoing should never be concealed. The longer Vi pondered the question the more puzzled she grew.

Meta perceived that she wavered and immediately seized her advantage.

"Come now, Vi, I'm sure you don't want to give pain to your mamma, or to get me into trouble, now do you?"

"No, Meta, indeed I don't, but—"

"Hush! Somebody's coming," exclaimed Meta, locking the closet door, having just finished her work and hastily dropped the key into her pocket.

"Come, girls, come quick! We're sending up a balloon from the lawn!" cried Eddie throwing open the door to make his announcement, then rushing away again.

The girls ran after him in a state of much excitement, forgetting for the time the trouble they were in—for, in spite of Meta's sophistry, her conscience was by no means easy.

The ladies had returned and in dinner dress were gathered on the veranda. Mr. Travilla seemed to be managing the affair with Mr. Dinsmore's assistance, while the other gentlemen, children and servants were grouped about them on the lawn.

Meta and Violet quickly took their places with the rest and just at that moment the balloon, released from its fastenings, shot up into the air.

There was a general shout and clapping of hands, but instantly hushed by a shrill sharp cry of distress from overhead.

"Oh! Oh! Pull it down again! Pull it down! Pull it down! I only got in for fun and I'm so frightened! I shall fall out! I shall be killed! Oh! Oh! Oh!"

The voice grew fainter and fainter, till it quickly died away in the distance as the balloon rose rapidly higher and higher into the deep blue of the sky.

A wild excitement seized upon the little crowd.

"Oh, oh, oh! Which ob de chillens am up dar?" the mammies were asking, each sending a hasty glance around the throng to assure herself of the safety of her own particular charge.

"Who is it? Who is it?" asked the children, the little girls beginning to sob and cry.

"Oh, it's Fank! It's Fank!" screamed Harold. "Papa, papa, please stop it quick. Fank, don't cry anymore; papa will get you down. Won't you, papa?" And he clung to his father's arm, sobbing quite bitterly.

"Son, Frank is not there," said Mr. Travilla, taking the little weeper in his arms. "There is no one in the balloon. It is not big enough to hold even a little boy like you or Frank."

"Isn't it, papa?" returned the child, dropping his head on his father's shoulder with a sigh of relief.

"Oh, it's Cousin Ronald, it's just Cousin Ronald!" exclaimed the children, their tears changing at once to laughter.

"Ah ha, ah ha! Um h'm, um h'm! So it is, bairnies, just Cousin Ronald at his old tricks again," laughed Mr. Lilburn.

"Oh, there's nobody in it; so we needn't care how high it goes," cried Eddie, jumping and clapping his hands. "See! See! It's up in the clouds now and doesn't look as big as my cap."

"Not half so big, I should say," remarked Herbert. "And there, it's quite gone."

The dinner bell promptly rang and all repaired to the dining room.

CHAPTER
TWENTY-SIXTH

Train up a child in the way he should go;
and when he is old, he will not depart from it.

—*P*ROVERBS 22:6

AS NATURALLY AS SUNFLOWERS to the sun, did the faces of Elsie's little ones turn to her when in her loved presence. At the table, at their sports, their lessons, everywhere and however employed, it was always the same, the young eyes turning ever and anon to catch the tender, sympathetic glance of mamma's.

But at dinner today, Vi's great blue orbs met hers but once and instantly dropped upon her plate again, while a vivid blush suffused the fair face and neck.

And when the meal was ended and all gathered in the drawing room, Vi still seemed to be unlike her usual happy, sunny self, the merriest prattler of all the little crowd of children, the one whose sweet, silvery laugh rang out the most often. She stood alone at a side table turning over some engravings, but evidently with very little interest. The mother, engaged in conversation with the other ladies, watched her furtively, a little troubled and anxious, yet deeming it best to wait for a voluntary confidence on the part of her child.

Longing, yet dreading to make it, Vi was again puzzling her young brain with the question whether Meta was right in saying it would be selfish to do so. Ah, if she could only ask mamma which was the right way to go! This was the first perplexity she had not been able to carry to her mother for disentanglement.

Remembering the words of the Lord Jesus, "Sanctify them through thy truth: thy word is truth," Elsie had been careful to store her children's minds with the blessed teachings and precious promises of God's Holy Book. She had also taught them to go to God their heavenly Father with every care, sorrow, doubt and difficulty.

"I'll ask Jesus," thought Vi. "He'll help me to know, because the Bible says, 'If any of you lack wisdom, let him ask of God that giveth to all men liberally and upbraideth not; and it shall be given him.'"

She slipped into an adjoining room, where she was quite alone, and kneeling down, whispered softly, with low sobs and many tears, "Dear Father in heaven, I've been a very, very naughty girl; I disobeyed my dear mamma. Please, forgive me for Jesus' sake and make me good. Please, Lord Jesus, help me to know if I ought to tell mamma."

A verse—one of the many she had learned to recite to her mother in that precious morning half hour—came to her mind as she rose from her knees. "He that covereth his sins shall not prosper; but whoso confesseth and forsaketh them shall have mercy."

"I didn't cover them," she said to herself, "I told God—but then, God knew all about it before, He sees and knows everything. But mamma doesn't know. Perhaps it means I mustn't cover them from her. I think Jesus did tell me."

Wiping away her tears she went back into the drawing room. The gentlemen were just leaving it, her father among the rest. A sudden resolution seized her and she ran after them.

"Papa!"

He turned at the sound of her voice. "Well, my little daughter?"

"I—I just want to ask you something."

"Another time, then, dear, papa's in a bit of a hurry now."

But seeing the distress in the dear little face he came to her and laying his hand on her head in tender fatherly fashion, said, "Tell papa what it is that troubles you. I will wait to hear it now."

"Papa," she said, choking down a sob, "I—I don't know what to do."

"About what, daughter?"

"Papa, s'pose—s'pose I'd done something naughty, and—and it would grieve dear mamma to hear it. Ought I to tell her and—and make her sorry?"

"My dear little daughter," he said bending down to look with grave, tender eyes into the troubled face, "never, never conceal anything from your mother. It is not safe for you, darling. And she would far rather bear the pain of knowing. If our children knew how much, how very much we both love them, they would never want to hide anything from us."

"Papa, I don't, but—somebody says it would be selfish to hurt mamma so."

"The selfishness was in doing the naughty thing, not in confessing it. Go, my child, and tell mamma all about it."

He hastened away, and Violet crept back to the drawing room.

The other children were leaving. "Come, Vi," they said, "we're going for a walk."

"Thank you, I don't wish to go this time," she answered with gravity. "I've something to attend to right away."

"What a grown up way of talking you have, you little midget," laughed Meta. Then, putting her lips close to Vi's ear, "Violet Travilla," she whispered, "don't you tell tales, or I'll never, never play with you again as long as I live."

"My mamma says it's wicked to say that," returned Vi, "and I don't tell tales."

Then, as Meta ran away, Violet drew near to her mother's chair.

Mamma was talking, and she knew she must not interrupt, so she waited, longing to have the confession over, yet feeling her courage almost fail with the delay.

Elsie saw it all, and at length seized an opportunity while the rest were conversing among themselves to take Vi's hand and draw her to her side.

"I think my little girl has something to say to mother," she whispered softly, smoothing back the clustering curls and looking tenderly into the tiny, tear-stained face.

Violet nodded assent; her heart was so full she could not have spoken a word without bursting into tears and sobs.

Mamma understood, rose and led her from the room. She led her to her own dressing room where they could be quite secure from intrusion. Then, seating herself and taking the child on her lap, "What is wrong with my dear little daughter?" she asked tenderly.

"Oh, mamma, mamma, I'm so sorry, so sorry!" cried the child, bursting into a passion of tears and sobs, putting her arms about her mother's neck and hiding her face on her shoulder.

"Mamma is sorry, too, dear, sorry for anything that makes her Vi unhappy. What is it? What can mother do to comfort you?"

"Mamma, I don't deserve for you to be so kind, and you'll have to punish, 'stead of comforting. But I just want to tell about my own self. You know I can't tell tales, mamma."

"No, daughter, I do not ask or wish it, but tell me about yourself."

"Mamma, it will make you sorry, ever so sorry."

"Yes, dear, but I must bear it for your sake."

"Oh, mamma, I don't like to make you sorry! I wish I hadn't, hadn't been naughty, oh so naughty, mamma! I played with some of your mamma's things that you forbade us to touch, and—and one lovely plate got broken all up."

"I am very sorry to hear that," returned the mother, "yet far more grieved by my child's sin. But how did you get the door open and the plate off the shelf?"

"I didn't, mamma, they were out."

"Someone else did it?"

"Yes, mamma, but you know I can't tell tales. It wasn't any of our children, though; none of them were naughty, but just me."

"Were you playing with the plate? Did you break it, Violet?"

"No, mamma, I didn't touch the plate, but I was dressing one of the dollies. They are all locked up again now, mamma, and I don't think anybody will touch them any more."

A little tender, serious talk on the sin and danger of disobedience to parents, and the mother knelt with the child and in a few simple words asked God's forgiveness for her. Then, telling Vi she must remain alone in that room till bedtime, she left her.

Not one harsh or angry word had been spoken. And the young heart was full of passionate love to her mother that made the thought of having grieved her a far more bitter punishment than the enforced solitude, though that was at any time irksome enough to one of Vi's social, fun-loving temperament.

It cost the mother a pang to inflict the punishment and leave the daughter alone in her trouble, but Elsie was not one to weakly yield to inclination when it came in conflict with duty. Hers was not a selfish love; she would bear any present pain to secure the future welfare of her children.

She rejoined her friends in the drawing room apparently as serenely happy as her wont, but through all the afternoon and evening her heart was with her little one in her banishment and grief, yearning over her with tenderest mother love.

Little Elsie, too, missed her sister, and returning from her walk, went in search of her. She found her at last in their mamma's dressing room seated at the window, her cheek resting on her hand, the tears coursing slowly down, while her eyes gazed longingly out over the beautiful fields and lovely orange groves.

"Oh, my own Vi, my darling little sister! What's the matter?" asked Elsie, clasping her in her arms, and kissing the wet cheek.

There was a burst of bitter sobs, while the small arms clung about the sister's neck and the golden head rested for an instant on her shoulder. Then came the words, "Ah, I'd tell you, but I can't now, for you must run right away, because mamma said I must stay here all alone till bedtime."

"Then I must go, dear; but don't cry so. If you've been naughty and are sorry, Jesus and mamma, too, will forgive you and love you just the same," Elsie said, kissing her again, then releasing her, hurried from the room, crying heartily in sympathy.

On the upper veranda, whither wee Elsie went to recover her composure, before rejoining her mates, she found her mother pacing slowly to and fro.

"Is my Elsie in trouble, too?" Mrs. Travilla asked, pausing in her walk and holding out her hand.

"For my Vi, mamma," sobbed Elsie, taking the hand and pressing it to her lips.

"Yes, poor little dear! Mother's heart aches for her, too," Mrs. Travilla answered, her own eyes filling. "I am glad my little daughters love and sympathize with each other."

"Mamma, I would rather stay with Vi, than be with the others. May I?"

"No, daughter, I have told her she must spend the rest of the day alone."

"Yes, mamma, she told me so and wouldn't let me stay even one minute to hear about her trouble."

"That was right."

Time crept by very slowly to Violet. She thought that afternoon the longest she had ever known. After a while she heard a familiar step, and almost before she knew it papa had her in his arms.

With a little cry of joy she put hers around his neck and returned the kiss he had just given her.

"Oh, I'm so glad!" she said, "but, papa, you'll have to go away, because nobody must stay with me, I'm—"

"Papa may," he said, sitting down with her on his knee. "So you told mamma about the naughtiness?"

"Yes, sir."

"I am glad you did. Always tell your mamma everything. If you have disobeyed her never delay a moment to go and confess it."

"Yes, papa, but if it's you?"

"Then come to me in the same way. If you want to be a happy child, have no concealment from father or mother."

"Shall I tell you about it now, papa?"

"You may do as you like about that since your mother knows it all."

"Papa, I'm afraid you wouldn't love such a naughty girl any more."

"Mamma loves you quite as well, and so shall I, because you are our own, own little daughter. There were tears in mamma's eyes when she told me that she had had to punish our little Vi."

"Oh, I'm so sorry to have made mamma cry," sobbed the child.

"Sin always brings sorrow and suffering sooner or later, my little girl. Remember that and that it is because Jesus loves us that He would save us from our sins."

After a little more talk, in which Violet repeated to him the same story of her wrong doing that she had already told her mother, her papa left her. She was again alone till mammy came with her supper—a bowl of rich, sweet milk and bread from the coarse flour, that might have tempted the appetite of an epicure.

"Come, honey, dry dose wet eyes an' eat yo' supper," said mammy, setting it out daintily on a little table which she placed before the child and covered with a fine damask cloth fresh from the iron. "De milk's mos' all cream an' de bread good as kin be. An' you kin hab much as eber you want ob both ob dem."

"Did mamma say so, mammy?"

"Yes, chile, an' don't shed no mo' dose tears now. Ole mammy lubs you like her life."

"But I've been very naughty, mammy," sobbed the little girl.

"Yes, Miss Wi'let, honey, an' we's all been naughty, but de good Lord forgib us for Jesus' sake if we's sorry an' don't 'tend neber to do so no mo'."

"Yes, mammy. Oh, I wish you could stay with me! But you mustn't, for mamma said I must be all alone."

"Yes, darlin', an' if you wants mo' supper, jes ring dis, an' mammy'll come."

She placed a small silver bell on the table beside Vi, and with a tender, compassionate look at the tear-swollen face, went away.

The young Travillas were sometimes denied dainties because of misconduct, but always allowed to satisfy their youthful appetites with an abundance of wholesome, nourishing food.

Vi ate her supper with a keen relish and found herself greatly comforted by it. How much one's views of life are brightened by a good comfortable meal that does not overtax the digestive organs. Vi suddenly remembered with a feeling of relief that the worst of her trouble—the confession—was over, and the punishment nearly so.

It was only a little while till mamma came, took her on her lap, kissed, and forgave her.

"Mamma, I'm so, so sorry for having disobeyed and grieved you!" whispered the child, weeping afresh, "for I do love you very, very much, my own mamma."

"I know it, dearest; but I want you to be far more sorry you have disobeyed God, who loves you more, a great deal more than your parents do, and has given you every good thing you have."

"Yes, mamma, I've asked God many times to forgive me for Jesus' sake, and I think He has."

"Yes, if you asked with your heart, I am sure He has, for Jesus said, 'Verily, verily, I say unto you, Whatsoever ye shall ask the Father in my name, He will give it you.'"

There was a little pause, Vi nestling close in her mother's arms, then with a quiver in her voice, "Mamma," she sighed, "will you ever trust me again?"

"Just the same as before, my child, because I believe you are truly sorry for your sin against God and against me."

"Thank you, dear, dear mamma! Oh, I hope God will help me to keep from ever being naughty anymore."

CHAPTER
TWENTY-SEVENTH

Conscience makes cowards of us all.

META HERSELF WAS NOT IN A CHEERFUL or a companionable mood during the walk that afternoon. The stings of conscience goaded her and she was haunted by the fear that Violet, so young and innocent, so utterly unused to concealments, would betray her share in the mischief done, even without intending to do so.

"Meta, what's the matter with you?" Herbert asked at length. "You haven't spoken a pleasant word since we came out."

"I'm not ill," was the laconic reply.

"Then you must be in the sulks and ought to have stayed at home," returned the plainspoken brother.

"Oh, don't tease her," said little Elsie. "Perhaps she has a headache and I know by myself that that makes one feel dull and sometimes even cross."

"You cross! I don't believe you ever were in your life," said Herbert. "I've never seen you anything but pleasant as a May morning."

"Don't quarrel, children, but help me to gather some of these lovely flowers to scatter over the graves up on the hill," said Rosie Dinsmore.

"Our graves," said Eddie softly. "Yes, I'd like to, but Aunt Rosie, I don't believe we can get in."

"Yes, we can," she answered. "Uncle Joe's up there at work, weeding and trimming the rose bushes."

"Then I'll gather plenty of these beauties," said Eddie, stooping to pluck the lovely, many-hued blossoms that spangled the velvety grass at their feet in every direction.

"How beautiful! How beautiful they are! And some of them are so fragrant!" exclaimed Elsie, rapidly filling a pretty basket she carried in her hand. "How good God is to give us so many lovely things!"

"Yes," returned Rosie, "it seems a pity to pluck them from their stems and make them wither and die; but there is such a profusion that what we take can hardly be missed."

"And it's honoring our graves to scatter flowers over them, isn't it, Aunt Rosie?" Eddie asked.

"Why do you say our graves? Just as if you were already buried there," laughed Herbert.

"Come," said Rosie, "I think we have enough flowers now."

"Oh, Aunt Rosie, down in that little dell yonder they are still thicker than here and more beautiful, I think," exclaimed Elsie.

"But we have enough now. Your basket is full. We'll go to that dell as we come back and gather some to take home to our mammas."

"Oh, yes, that will be best," Elsie said with cheerful acquiescence.

"I shall go now and get some worthy to honor the dead," said Meta, starting off in the direction of the dell.

"Meta likes to show her independence," said Rosie, smiling. "We won't wait for her."

They climbed the hill, pushed open the gate of the little enclosure and passed in—very quietly, for their youthful spirits were subdued by the solemn stillness of the place and a feeling of awe crept over them at the thought of the dead whose dust lay sleeping there.

Silently they scattered the flowers over each lowly resting place, reserving the most beautiful for that of her who was best known to them all—the first who had borne the name of Elsie Dinsmore.

"Our own dear grandma!" whispered Elsie and Eddie, softly.

"I can't help feeling as if she were some relation to me, too," said Rosie, "because she was both my sister's mother and papa's wife."

The breeze carried the words to the ear of Uncle Joe, who was at work on the farther side of the enclosure and had not, till that moment, been aware of the vicinity of the young people.

He rose and came hobbling toward them, pulling off his hat and bowing respectfully.

"Dat's so, Miss Rosie, ef you lubs de Lord, like she did, de dear young Missus dat lays heyah; for don't de 'postle say ob de Lord's chillen dat dey's all one in Christ Jesus? All one, Miss Rosie, heirs ob God and joint heirs wid Christ."

"Yes, Uncle Joe, that is true."

"Ah, she was lubly an' lubbed de Master well," he went on, leaning upon his staff and gazing fixedly at the name engraved on the stone. "She's not dead, chillen, her soul's wid de Lord in dat land ob light an' glory, an' de body planted heyah till de mornin' ob de resurrection."

"And then she will rise more beautiful than ever," said little Elsie. "Mamma has told me about it. 'The dead in Christ shall rise first.'"

"'Then we who are alive and remain shall be caught up together with them in the clouds to meet the Lord in the air: and so shall we ever be with the Lord,'" repeated Rosie.

"Yes, Miss Rosie. Bressed hope." And Uncle Joe hobbled back to his work.

"Here, look at these!" said Meta hurrying up, heated and out of breath with running. "Aren't they simply beauties?"

She emptied her apron upon the grave as she spoke, then pulled out her handkerchief with a jerk, to wipe the perspiration from her face. Something fell against the tombstone with a ringing, metallic sound.

"A key! A door key!" cried Herbert, stooping to pick it up. "Why, Meta, what key is it? And what are you doing with it?"

"I never heard that it had a particular name," she answered tartly, snatching it from him and restoring it to her pocket while her cheeks flushed crimson.

The others exchanged surprised glances, but said nothing to Meta.

"But what door does it belong to? And what are you doing with it?" persisted Herbert.

"Talk of the curiosity of women and girls!" sneered Meta. "Men and boys have quite as much, but it's against my principles to gratify it."

"Your principles!" laughed Herbert. "You, prying, meddling Meta—talking about other people's curiosity! Well, that's a good one!"

"You insulting boy! I'll tell mamma of you," retorted Meta, beginning to cry.

"Ha! Ha! I wish you would! Tell her my remarks about the key, and she'll soon make you explain where it belongs, and how it came to be in your possession, Meta."

At that Meta, deigning no reply, put her little handkerchief to her eyes and hurried away toward the house.

"There, she's gone to tell mamma," said Harry.

"Not she," said Herbert. "She knows better. She'd only get reproved for telling tales and be forced to tell all about that key. She's been at some mischief; I haven't a doubt. She's always prying, and meddling with what she's been told not to touch. Mamma says that's her besetting sin."

"And what does she say is yours?" asked Rosie, looking him steadily in the eye.

Herbert colored and turned away.

His mother had told him more than once or twice that he was quite too much disposed to domineer over and reprove his younger brother and sisters.

"Well, I don't care!" he muttered to himself. "'Tisn't half so mean a fault as Meta's. I'm certainly the oldest, and Harry and the girls ought to be willing to let me tell them of it when they go wrong."

The key, which belonged to a closet in Mr. Lilburn's dressing room, seemed to burn in Meta's pocket. She was frightened that Herbert and the others had seen it.

"They looked as if they knew something was wrong," she said to herself, "and to be sure, what business could I have with a door key? Dear me! Why wasn't I more careful? But it's like 'murder will out,' or what the Bible says, 'Be sure your sin will find you out.'"

She was afraid to meet her mother with the key in her possession, so took so circuitous a route to reach the house, and walked so slowly that the others were there some time before her.

Her mother was on the veranda looking out for her. "Why, how late you are, Meta," she said. "Make haste to your room and have your hair and dress made neat, for the tea bell will soon ring."

"Yes, ma'am," and Meta flew into the house and up to her room, only too glad on an excuse for not stopping to be questioned.

She was down again barely in time to take her seat at the table with the others. She glanced furtively at the faces of her mother, grandmother, and Aunt Elsie, and drew a sigh of relief as she perceived that they had evidently learned nothing of her misconduct.

After tea she watched Mr. Lilburn's movements and was glad to see him step into the library, seat himself before the fire, and take up a book.

"He's safe to stay there for awhile," she thought, "so fond of reading as he is," and ran up to her room for the key, which she had left there hidden under her pillow.

She secured it unobserved and stole cautiously to the door of his dressing room. She found it slightly ajar, pushed it a little wider open, crept in, gained the closet door, and was in the act of putting the key into the lock, when a deep groan coming from within the closet, apparently, so startled her that she uttered a faint cry. Then a hollow voice said, "If you ever touch that again, I'll—"

But Meta waited to hear no more; fear seemed to lend her wings, and she flew from the room in a panic of terror.

"Ah ha! Ah ha! Um h'm! Ah ha! You were at some mischief, no doubt my lassie. 'The wicked flee when no man pursueth,' the good Book tells us," said the occupant of the room, stepping out from the shadow of the window curtain.

He had laid down his book almost immediately, remembering that he had some letters to write, and had come up to his apartments in search of one he wished to answer.

It was already dark, except for the light of a young moon, but by some oversight of the servants, the lamps had not yet been lighted here.

He was feeling about for some matches, when hearing approaching footsteps he stepped behind the curtain and waited to see who the intruder was.

He recognized Meta's form and movements and sure that no legitimate errand had brought her there at that time, resolved to give her a fright.

Tearing down the hall in her fright, Meta suddenly encountered her mother, who, coming up to her own apartments, had reached the head of the stairs just in time to witness Meta's exit from those of Mr. Lilburn.

"Oh, I'm so frightened! So frightened, mamma!" cried the child, throwing herself wholly into her mother's arms.

"As you richly deserve to be," said Mrs. Carrington, taking her by the hand and leading her into her dressing room. "What were you doing in Mr. Lilburn's apartments?"

Meta hung her head in silence.

"Speak, Meta; I will have an answer," her mother said, with determination.

"I wasn't doing any harm—only putting away something that belonged there."

"What was it?"

"A key."

"Meddling again! Prying even into the affairs of a gentleman!" groaned her mother. "Meta, what am I to do with you? This dreadful fault of yours mortifies me beyond everything. I feel like taking you back to Ashlands at once and never allowing you to go from home at all, lest you should bring a life-long disgrace upon yourself and me."

"Mother, I wasn't prying or meddling with Mr. Lilburn's affairs," said Meta, bursting into great sobs and tears.

"What were you doing there? Tell me all about it without any more ado."

Knowing that her mother was a determined woman, and seeing that there was now no escape from a full confession, Meta made it.

Mrs. Carrington was much distressed.

"Meta, you have robbed your Aunt Elsie, your Aunt Elsie who has always been so good, so kind to me and to you. And I can never make good her loss—never replace that plate."

"Just that one tiny plate couldn't be worth so very much," muttered the offender.

"Its intrinsic value was perhaps not very great," replied Mrs. Carrington, "but to my dear friend it was worth much as a memento of her dead mother. Meta, you shall not go with us tomorrow, but shall spend the day locked up in your own room at home."

An excursion had been planned for the next day, in which the whole party—adults and children—were to have a share. They were to leave at an early hour in the morning, travel several miles by boat, and spend the day picnicking on a deserted plantation—

one Meta had not yet seen, but had heard spoken of as a very lovely place.

She had set her heart on going and this decree of her mother came upon her as a great blow. She was very fond of being on the water, and of seeing new places. And she had pictured to herself the delights of roaming over the large old house, which she had heard was still standing, peeping into closets, pulling out drawers, perhaps discovering secret stairways and — of delightful thought — possibly coming upon some hidden treasure forgotten by the owners in their hasty flight.

She wept bitterly, coaxed, pleaded, and made fair promises for the future, but all in vain. Her mother was firm.

"You must stay at home, Meta," she said. "It grieves me to deprive you of so great a pleasure, but I must do what I can to help you to overcome this dreadful fault. You have chosen stolen pleasures at the expense of disobedience to me, and most ungrateful, wicked behavior toward my kind friend. As a just and necessary punishment you must be deprived of the share you were to have had in the innocent enjoyments planned for tomorrow. You shall also make a full confession to your Aunt Elsie and ask her forgiveness."

"I won't!" exclaimed Meta angrily. Then, upon catching the look of pained surprise in her mother's face, she ran to her and throwing her arms about her neck, "Oh, mamma, mamma, forgive me!" she cried. "I can't bear to see you look so grieved. I will never say that again. I will do whatever you bid me, mamma."

Mrs. Carrington kissed her child in silence, then taking her by the hand, "Come and let us have this painful business over." She said, and led the way to Mrs. Travilla's boudoir.

Elsie had no reproaches for Meta, but kindly forgave her and even requested that she might be permitted to share in the morrow's enjoyment, but Mrs. Carrington would not hear of it.

CHAPTER
TWENTY-EIGHTH

Nature I'll court in her sequester'd haunts,
By mountain, meadow, streamlet grove, or cell.

—SMOLLET

MR. DINSMORE WAS PACING the front veranda, enjoying the cool, fresh morning air, when little feet came pattering through the hall and a sweet child voice hailed him with "Good morning, my dear grandpa."

"Ah, grandpa's little Cricket, where were you last evening?" he asked, sitting down and taking her on his knee.

It was his pet name for Vi because she was so merry a little one.

The fair face flushed, but putting her arms about his neck, her lips to his ear, "I was in mama's dressing room, grandpa," she whispered. "I was 'bliged to stay there 'cause I'd been naughty and disobeyed my mamma."

"Ah, I am sorry to hear that! But I hope you don't intend to disobey anymore."

"No, indeed, grandpa."

"Are you considered good enough to go with us today, then?"

"Yes, grandpa. Mamma says I was punished yesterday, and I don't be punished twice for the same thing."

"Mamma is quite right," he said, "and grandpa is very glad she allows you to go."

"I don't think I deserve it, grandpa, but she's such a dear, kind mamma."

"So she is, dear, and I hope you will always be a dear good daughter to her," said grandpa, holding the little face close to his.

Meta was not allowed to come down to breakfast. Vi missed her from the table, and at prayers, and going up to Mrs. Carrington, asked, "Is Meta sick, Aunt Sophy?"

"No, dear, but she has been too naughty to be with us. I have said she must stay in her own room all day."

"And not go to the picnic? Oh, please let her go, dear auntie!"

The other children joined their entreaties to Vi's, but without avail; and, with streaming eyes, Meta, at her window, saw the embarkation and watched the boats glide away till lost to view in the distance.

"Too bad!" she sobbed, "it's too, too bad that I must stay here and learn long hard lessons while all the rest are having such a good time!"

Then she thought remorsefully of her mother's sad look, as she bade her good-bye and said how sorry she was to be obliged to leave her behind. As some atonement, she set to work diligently at her tasks.

The weather was very fine, the sun shone, the birds filled the air with melody, and a delicious breeze danced in the tree tops, rippled the water, and played with the brown and golden ringlets of little Elsie and Vi, and the flaxen curls of Daisy.

The combined influences of the clear, pure air, the pleasant motion as the rowers bent to their oars, and the lovely scenery meeting the eye at every turn were not to be resisted. All—old and young—were soon in merriest spirits. They sang songs, cracked jokes, told anecdotes, and were altogether a very merry company.

After a delightful row of two hours or more, the rounding of a point brought suddenly into view the place of their destination.

The boats were made fast and the party stepped ashore, followed by the men servants bearing rugs and wraps and several large, well-filled hampers of provisions.

With joyous shouts the children ran hither and thither. The boys tumbled on the grass, the girls gathered great bouquets of the beautiful flowers, twisted them into their curls and wove garlands for their hats.

"Walk up to de house, ladies an' gentlemen. Massa an' Missus not at home now, but be berry glad to see you when dey gets back," said a pleasant voice close at hand.

All but Mr. Lilburn looked about for the speaker, wondered at seeing no one, then laughed at being so often and so easily deceived.

"Suppose we accept the invitation," said Mr. Travilla, leading the way.

The two ladies preferred a seat under a wide spreading tree on the lawn. But the others accompanied him in a tour of the deserted mansion already falling rapidly to decay.

They climbed the creaking stairs, passed along the silent corridors, looking in the empty rooms, and out of the broken windows upon the flower garden, once trim and bright, now choked with weeds, and sighed over the desolations of war.

Some of the lower rooms were still in a pretty good state of preservation, and in one of these the servants were directed to build a fire and prepare tea and coffee.

Plenty of dry branches strewed the ground in a bit of woods but a few yards distant. Some of these were quickly gathered and a brightly blazing fire presently crackled upon the hearth and roared up the wide chimney.

Leaving the house, which in its loneliness and dilapidation inspired only feelings of sadness and gloom, the party wandered over the grounds, still beautiful even in their forlornly neglected state.

The domain was extensive, and the older boys—having taken an opposite direction from their parents—were presently out of their sight and hearing, the house being directly between.

Wandering on, they came to a stream of limpid water flowing between high grassy banks and spanned by a little rustic bridge.

"Let's cross over," said Herbert, "that's such a pretty bridge and it looks lovely on the other side."

"No, no, 'tain't safe, boys, don't you go for to try it," exclaimed Uncle Joe.

"Pooh! What do you know about it?" returned Herbert, who always had great confidence in his own opinion. "If it won't bear us all at once, it most certainly will one at a time. What do you say, Ed?"

"I think Uncle Joe can judge better whether it's safe than little boys like us."

"Don't you believe it. His eyes are getting old and he can't see half so well as you or I."

"I kin see dat some ob de planks is gone, Marse Herbert, an' de ole timbahs looks shaky."

"Shaky! Nonsense! They'll not shake under my weight and I'm going to cross."

"Now, Herbie, don't you do it," said his brother. "You know mamma wouldn't allow it at all if she was here."

"'Twouldn't be disobedience, though, as she isn't here and never has forbidden me to go on that bridge," persisted Herbert.

"Mamma and papa say that obedient children don't do what they know their parents would forbid if they were present," said Eddie.

"I say nobody but a coward would be afraid to venture on that bridge," said Herbert, ignoring Eddie's last remark. "Suppose it should break and let you fall? The worst would be a ducking."

"De watah's deep, Marse Herbert, and you might git drownded!" said Uncle Joe. "Or maybe some ob de timbahs fall on you an' break yo' leg or yo' back."

They were now close to the bridge.

"It's very high up above the water," said Harry, "and a good many boards are off. I'd be afraid to go on it."

"Coward!" sneered his brother. "Are you afraid too, Ed?"

"Yes, I'm afraid to disobey my father, because that's disobeying God."

"Did your father ever say a word about not going on the bridge?"

"No, but he's told me never to run into danger needlessly. That is when there's nothing to be gained by it for myself or anybody else."

"Before I'd be such a coward!" muttered Herbert, deliberately walking on to the bridge.

The other two boys watched his movements in trembling, breathless silence, while Uncle Joe began looking about for some means of rescue in case of an accident.

Herbert picked his way carefully over the rotten timbers till he had gained the middle of the bridge, then stopped, looked back at his companions and pulling off his cap, waved it around his head. "Hurrah! Here I am. Who's afraid? Who was right this time?"

Then leaning over the low railing, "Oh!" he cried, "you ought just to see the fish—splendid, big fellows! Come on, boys, and look at 'em!"

But at that instant the treacherous railing gave way with a loud crack, and with a wild scream for help, over he went, head first, falling with a sudden plunge into the water and disappearing at once below the surface.

"Oh, he'll drown! He'll drown!" shrieked Harry, wringing his hands, while Eddie echoed the cry for help.

"Run to de house, Marse Ed, an' fotch some ob de boys to git him out," said Uncle Joe, hurrying to the edge of the stream with an old fishing rod he had found lying among the weeds on its banks

But a dark object sprang past him, plunged into the stream, and as Herbert rose to the surface, seized him by the coat collar, and so holding his head above water, swam with him to the shore.

"Good Bruno! Brave fellow! Good dog!" said a voice near at hand, and turning to look for the speaker, Uncle Joe found Mr. Daly standing by his side.

Leaving his happier companions, the minister had wandered away, book in hand, to this sequestered spot. Together he and Uncle Joe assisted the dog to drag Herbert up the bank and laid him in the grass.

The fall had stunned the boy, but now consciousness returned. "I'm not hurt," he said, opening his eyes. "But don't tell mother. She'd be frightened half to death."

"We'll save her as much as we can, and I hope you've learned a lesson, young sir, and will not be so foolhardy another time," said Mr. Daly.

"P'raps he'll tink ole folks not such fools, nex' time," remarked Uncle Joe. "Bress de Lord dat he didn't get drowned!"

The men and boys came running from the house, bringing cloaks and shawls to wrap about the dripping boy. They would have carried him back with them, but he stoutly resisted, declaring himself quite as able to walk as anybody.

"Let him do so, the exercise will help to prevent his taking cold provided he is wrapped up," said Mr. Daly, throwing a cloak over the lad's shoulders and folding it carefully about him.

"Ill news flies fast," says the proverb. Mrs. Carrington met them upon the threshold, pale and trembling with affright. She clasped her boy in her arms with a heart too full for utterance.

"Never mind, mother," he said. "I've only had a ducking, that's all.

"But it may not be all. You may get your death of cold," she said. "I've no dry clothes for you here.

By this time the party had hurried to the spot.

"There's a good fire, suppose we hang him up to dry," said old Mr. Dinsmore with a grim smile.

"His clothes rather—rolling him up in cloaks and shawls in the meantime," suggested Herbert's grandmother. "Let us ladies go back to the lawn, and leave his uncle to oversee the business."

Herbert had spoiled his holiday so far as the remainder of the visit to this old estate was concerned. He could not join the others at the feast presently spread under the tree on the lawn or in the sports that followed. He had to pass the time idly on a pallet beside the fire with nothing to entertain him but his own thoughts and watching servants, until, their work done, they too wandered away in search of amusement.

Most of the afternoon was spent by the gentlemen in fishing in that same stream into which Herbert's folly and self-conceit had plunged him.

Eddie had his own little fishing rod and with it in his hand sat on a log beside his father, a little apart from the rest, patiently waiting for the fish to bite. Mr. Travilla had thrown several out upon the grass, but Eddie's bait did not seem to attract a single one.

He began to grow weary of sitting still and silent, and creeping closer to his father whispered, "Papa, I'm tired, and I want to ask you something. Do you think the fish will hear if I speak low?"

"Perhaps not. You may try it, if you like," returned Mr. Travilla, looking somewhat amused.

"Thank you, papa. Well, Herbert said nobody but a coward would be afraid to go on that bridge. Do you think he was right, papa?"

"No, my boy, but if you had gone upon it to avoid being laughed at or called a coward, I should say you showed a great lack of true courage. He is a brave man or boy who dares to do right without regard to consequences."

"But, papa, if you'd been there and said I might if I wanted to?"

"Hardly a supposable case, my son."

"Well, if I'd been a man and could do as I chose?"

"Men have no more right to do as they please than boys. They must obey God. If His will is theirs, they may do as they please, just as you may if it is your pleasure to be good and obedient.

"Papa, I don't understand. Does God say we must not go into dangerous place?"

"He says, 'Thou shalt not kill.' We have no right to kill ourselves or to run the risk of doing so merely for amusement or to be considered brave or dexterous."

"But if somebody needs us to do it to save them from being hurt or killed, papa?"

"Then it becomes quite a different matter. It is brave, generous, and right to risk our own life or limbs to save those of others."

"Then I may do it, papa?"

"Yes, my son. Jesus laid down His life to save others, and in all ways He is to be our example."

A hand was laid lightly on the shoulder of each, and a sweet voice said, "May my boy heed his father's instructions in this and in everything else."

"Wife!" Mr. Travilla said, turning to look into the fair face bent over them.

"Mamma, dear, mamma, I do mean to," said the younger Eddie.

"Is it not time to go home?" she asked. "The little ones are growing weary."

"Yes, the sun is getting low."

In only a few moments the whole party had disembarked—in less exuberant spirits than in the morning—yet, perhaps not less happy—little disposed to talk, but with hearts filled with a quiet, peaceful content.

Viamede was reached without accident, a supper awaiting them there partaken of with keen appetites, and the little ones went gladly to bed.

Returning from the nursery to the drawing room, Elsie found her namesake daughter sitting apart in a bay window, silently gazing out over the beautiful landscape sleeping in the moonlight.

She looked up with a smile as her mother took a seat by her side and passed an arm about her waist.

"Isn't it lovely, mamma? See how the waters of our lakelet shine in the moonbeams like molten silver! And look at the fields, the groves, and the hills! How charming they look in the soft light."

"Yes, darling. was that what you were thinking of, sitting here alone?"

"Yes, mamma, and of how good God is to us to give us this lovely home and a kind father and mother to take care of us. It is so sweet to come back home when I've been away. I was enjoying it all the way coming in the boat tonight. That and thinking of the glad time when we shall be gathered into the lovelier home Jesus is preparing for us."

"God grant we may!" said the mother, with emotion. "It is my heart's desire and prayer to God for all my dear ones, especially my children. 'Eye hath not seen, nor ear heard, neither have entered into the heart of man, the things which God hath prepared for them that love Him.'"

The End